Praise for *The Chinese*

"Shelley's buoyancy is frustratingly naïve, and often completely foolish if you have any understanding of how brutal living in America actually is, but you root for Shelley in part because Shelley is rooting for Shelley . . . By the end, he does indeed come out on top, even if it's in ways neither he nor the reader could have predicted."

—SCAACHI KOUL, *The New York Times Book Review*

"Through the hardships and hustle, Shelley gets to know his adopted city while discovering the inner resources he needs to fight for himself and others—and to finally find his people. His optimism and savvy are contagious."　　　　—CAROLE V. BELL, *The Atlantic*

"A charmingly narrated immigrant tale turned upside down. Kathryn Ma has written a funny, largehearted, and uniquely American story about where dreams and reality collide. I feel the Chinese groove!"

—RACHEL KHONG, author of *Goodbye, Vitamin*

"Tender in all the ways that matter, *The Chinese Groove* peels back our American absurdities and illustrates that love, more than anything, is powerful enough to sustain us through darkness and disaster. A wondrous novel where nothing, and no one, is as it seems."

—MATEO ASKARIPOUR, author of *Black Buck*

"Bighearted, funny, and tender. Kathryn Ma had me rooting for her unlikely hero every step of the way."

—BONNIE TSUI, author of *Why We Swim* and *American Chinatown*

"Terrific in every way: smart, warm, witty, keenly observed, and best of all, refreshing."　　　　—NATALIE BASZILE, author of *Queen Sugar* and *We Are Each Other's Harvest*

ALSO BY KATHRYN MA

The Year She Left Us

All That Work and Still No Boys

The Chinese Groove

A NOVEL

Kathryn Ma

Counterpoint
BERKELEY, CALIFORNIA

Copyright © 2023 by Kathryn Ma

All rights reserved under domestic and international copyright. Outside of fair use (such as quoting within a book review), no part of this publication may be reproduced, stored in a retrieval system, or transmitted in any form or by any means, electronic, mechanical, photocopying, recording, or otherwise, without the written permission of the publisher. For permissions, please contact the publisher.

First Counterpoint edition: 2023
First paperback edition: 2024

The Library of Congress has cataloged the hardcover edition as follows:
Names: Ma, Kathryn, author.
Title: The Chinese groove : a novel / Kathryn Ma.
Description: First Counterpoint edition. | Berkeley California : Counterpoint, 2023.
Identifiers: LCCN 2022023051 | ISBN 9781640095663 (hardcover) | ISBN | 9781640095670 (ebook)
Subjects: LCGFT: Novels.
Classification: LCC PS3613.A13 C48 2023 | DDC 813/.6—dc23/eng/20220516
LC record available at https://lccn.loc.gov/2022023051

Paperback ISBN: 978-1-64009-618-9

Cover design by Na Kim
Book design by Laura Berry

COUNTERPOINT
2560 Ninth Street, Suite 318
Berkeley, CA 94710
www.counterpointpress.com

Printed in the United States of America
10 9 8 7 6 5 4 3 2 1

For SK
la fiamma del focolare

The
Chinese
Groove

1.
Eastward Ho

THE RELATIVES TREATED ME RUDELY, BEATING ME and calling me names, and so on my eighteenth birthday my father buried his head in his hands and cried until the bottle was empty and his tears were spent and he was at last decided. It was time to let me go. Grubs like us didn't get many chances, and he'd promised Mother before she died that he'd send me, their son and only child, away from this unhappy life and into a brighter world. There was an uncle, he said, conveniently rich, living in San Francisco. I should leave our home in Gejiu, Yunnan Province, the most beautiful realm in all of China, and move in with Uncle and figure out from there *foot in the door* and *student visa* and *green card* and a score of other words my father called out in the weeks that followed as I cleaned our shoes and boiled our broth and swept our single room, words that made no sense to me but ladled not an ounce of care into my black-haired head. I was all for the plan. Bathed in Mother's dream for me, I'd been waiting for years to depart. I didn't want to be like my friends who were lined up to work at the Beautiful Objet d'Arts and World Crafts Tin Factory. Theirs wasn't the fate for me. My future lay outside those gates, for where in a factory could I become the man I intended to be, which was a cool guy and a poet? I told my father yes.

The relatives hated me for ancestor reasons, which you might think unfair but I well understood because I was born into the despised branch of the family. My great-grandfather, a handsome devil, was known to all as the wayward son of his father's third wife, a gambler and an opium addict—the son, not the wife, though who knows? Maybe the third wife ate the flower too. In the photo my father has of her, she's really skinny. My father knew how tough it was to be the bastard son of the bastard son of a bastard—okay, maybe not that many bastards and technically untrue. Third wives were all the rage in the Ancient Days of Yore to those with brains and money. But as far as the aunties were concerned, Father and I were lodged on the lowest rung of the family ladder, and nothing we could do would lift us from the mud. I thank my many cousins for teaching me that lesson, for it was their whirling wallops upside my youthful head and their painful pinches along my bony arms that resolved me with every blueing to move far away, earn a lot of money, and stride the earth as a man. They didn't mean to do me any favors but in fact they did, as you're about to discover. From where I stood in proud Gejiu, tin capital of China but lousy with kicking cousins, I couldn't quit soon enough. I'd hold Father in a warm embrace and promise to make him proud. Then I'd soar straight to Uncle's house, where my new family was waiting. Cousin Deng, the only one who was ever kind to me though he was five years older, swore to me that poets in the U.S. made a ton of dough, which I was glad to know since I'd promised my girl-friend, Lisbet (right before she left me), that I'd become a poet and write three splendid poems just for her. Cousin Deng told me that poets in America got fancy cars and special housing, revered as they were by their fellow citizens as keepers of the famous American freedoms. Thus my foolproof plan took shape. I'd head to Califor-nia, settle myself at Uncle's, polish up my English (already A-plus), and win Lisbet back.

Six months after my birthday, during which time Cousin Deng employed me so I could buy meat for Father along with our healthy veg, Father told me that he'd gotten the funds I needed from his boss at the bus depot and he'd written to my uncle in San Francisco who'd said okay, but for only two weeks since he was a busy guy and they didn't have an extra bedroom. Don't worry, said Father. They're going to love you so much, they'll never want you to leave. He wiped his eyes in a tremble of sadness. We agreed that Uncle was being modest about the extra bedroom because all Americans have way more space than they need, except for the chaps who live under the highways and even they have the prairie.

I chose January 3 as the perfect date to depart. Father wanted me to wait until after Lunar New Year, but in San Francisco, 2015 had already started. I didn't need to wait for the Year of the Ram to begin. Though I'm one of the friendliest fellows you're ever likely to know and one of the sincerest, circumstances permitting, I consider it my bastard-back-then birthright to buck the mooing herd. Just when every other person in the vast nation where I was born would be making their annual pilgrimage to return to the family pen, I'd be leaping sure-footedly peak to peak, a bighorn sheep, king of the craggy Rockies if the Rockies began where the Golden Gate stood.

I packed in a jiffy. I had no difficulty deciding what to take because everything I owned fit into one suitcase, a sparkly pink affair that belonged to Cousin Deng and before that, to his mother. At midnight, my father came home and threw his arm around my neck and cried fat tears, half salt, half whiskey, that I was going away and he'd never see me again. He cursed the day he'd promised my mother that I would learn English, which she believed I needed to succeed in the modern world, though that was when she was alive and I was little and given how times have changed, can we say it's true anymore? No matter. What I'm telling you is this: on the eve of my departure, Father cursed the promise, cursed the loss, cursed the grief that held him. He didn't curse my mother. She was his paragon.

I coaxed Father onto the bed and covered him with the quilted blanket I spread over him every night, talking to him the whole time about how, as soon as money started to flow into my pockets, I would send him enough for his very own laptop and ask Deng to teach him how to use it; that with his new computer, we would talk to each other day or night, for as far as I was concerned, any hour was good for a confabulation, father to son to father.

"Better yet," I said, "I'll find someone from right here in Gejiu who is traveling back home to choose a pretty wife or bury a dead parent. 'Fellow countryman,' I'll say, 'could you kindly deliver straight into my father's hands this latest Apple device with all the bells and whistles?' And wherever I roam, Father, you need only to tell it to find me and it will track me to the very pinpoint of globe where I squat. I'll appear to you so clearly on its magic screen that you'll smell my zesty breath and want to kiss me on the tip of my honking Zheng-family nose. When you show the relatives the tricks your Apple can do, they'll gnaw their knuckles in envy."

I waited. He was supposed to grin and reply, *I read you.* This was our custom, our coded handshake dating back from when I was a kid and my mother was too sick to scrub my neck or cook my supper. She lay in bed, stifling her groans so as not to scare me while my father warmed my breakfast, buttoned my jacket, cinched the strap on my backpack, amusing me the whole time by telling me how, when my mother was my age, she had speckled legs whenever it rained because she couldn't resist a good puddle, and how he never would have dared to ask her for a date until she cornered him after school and told him that if he didn't ask her out, she would tell his mother that he had cheated on the maths test. Which he had. So he did. Father and I were always in balance. I sat on his handlebars as we weaved our way to school and after we parted, me on the school step, he to the bus depot, I waved to him for a full minute, watching the gray square of his jacket glide into the stream of traffic until it merged with all the other grays, from which then would emerge at the end of the school day my father's face, smiling.

"We'll have a whole fish tonight," he would tell me, "and fresh clams and turtle."

"And Mother will sit with us at the table," I'd reply. "And the good food will make her well."

He'd nod hydraulically, drawing me up like water. *I read you*, he would say, or sometimes in joking English, *copy that*. We both knew we were telling each other tales. My mother fondly called them *your father's little stories*, not the ancient folktales and legends she knew by heart, but myths-of-the-moment that Father conjured strictly for her delight. She would beg him for one when her pain was just so.

"I'm wearing the iron shoes tonight," she would say. An iron-shoe night was a bearable night. Not a body-on-fire night, when the pain was so bad that only a pill or three would ease it. On an iron-shoe night, my mother could sit up and listen. She would lean with her head tipped back against the wall, her eyes resting on my father as he assembled a story out of the chapters of his day. He'd start with a detail, mouse-dropping small—an old lady's sour expression, which made my mother smile, or the scent of jasmine—a sigh escaped her—or the stink of the public toilets; she covered her nose and laughed. If I'd been with him all day and knew he'd not seen such an old lady, or passed by a flowering garden, or taken a piss before we returned home, I didn't correct him, wanting, as my mother did, to hear where the story would go. Soon that old grandmother transformed herself into an empress, and the scent of jasmine ushered in a beautiful maiden, and in the public toilets a boy a lot like me with a big nose and a yen for adventure stumbled over a dripping mop that flew him high above Gejiu. Every person Father described in a voice that swooped from boom to whisper seemed as real as the room we sat in, and I rushed to bring him water whenever his mouth grew dry. As long as the tale lasted, my mother stayed upright, her breaths light and quiet.

But on my last night at home, Father didn't read me. He didn't *copy that*. He was asleep and snoring, emptied of little stories, as he'd been since the day Mother died. In the morning I rose early, ready to say goodbye and deliver that long embrace, but he had tiptoed out, tucking in his sadness the exact same way that a corrupt official who's about to be paraded stops to tuck in his shirt. He fools no one, except for maybe himself.

Cousin Deng had said he would drive me to the station, but something important must have commanded his urgent attention because he didn't show up as promised. I scrambled, hair flying, to catch my bus to Kunming, Yunnan's capital, City of Eternal Spring. At the airport, a little girl in the departure lounge admired my sparkly suitcase. I sat on the floor beside her and began telling her how Cousin Deng had given it to me free and clear, though first he was obliged to use it to carry away a half dozen yowling cats who'd overrun the courtyard at the *lao jia*, the old family home. She smiled a tooth-missing smile and showed me a picture in her book of the cutest little tabby, and I would've tarried to amuse her some more but an airport attendant rushed over to gesticulate that my plane was about to fly away without me.

"Don't worry," I said to the girl. "There were plenty more kitties left over."

I decided not to mention that Cousin Deng had drowned the suitcased cats in the tin factory effluvium, a deeper and swifter waterway than the nearest river. Not every detail belongs in every story, as you and I well know.

I opened my suitcase and tapped my stash of souvenirs, choosing a genuine Gejiu tin frog with-the-coin-in-his-mouth. I'd brought ten of them, excellent for gifts as they showed off the magnificent talents of the artisans of the city of Gejiu, but the frogs were making my bag heavy, and the airline attendant had warned me that I would have to pay extra. I gave one tin frog to the little girl and one to the attendant, and I left for California, eastward ho.

THE PLANE TOOK OFF, and it was exactly as Deng had described: a thrilling roar, a mighty lift, and a vista I'd often imagined, my known life falling away and open skies above. I wished that, just once, Father would slip his bonds and send himself aloft so that he might spectate the gape-worthy view, but I knew he'd never venture beyond the confines of his woe. That lesson, too, I'd learned early. By the time I'd turned eight, I had no mother to come home to and soon I was staying out all day, walking for hours after school down crowded streets and narrow alleys and along zigzagging paths in the park to learn what I could from looking closely because poets, like spies, have to be both watchers and seers. At night when I returned, I made sure Father had eaten supper and gone to sleep in his bed. Often his dreams woke him in the early hours and then I'd go out and buy him a bun and come back to make him tea and listen to him sorrow over times long past.

I watched the clouds pass, blanket rucked at my knees. A black fish wriggled in my tummy over how I was going to tell my rich American uncle that I was staying forever, which was longer than two weeks. Now that I'd finally been freed, I couldn't face going back.

I must've looked like I needed a friendly word because a gentleman in a shiny necktie and a fine blue jacket appeared and handed me a can of Sprite. I tried to hand it back, telling him I couldn't pay, but he insisted that it was free and I should take it. This got me thinking about the Chinese groove. The drink couldn't have been free, and yet the gentleman told me it was so that I could accept it without embarrassment over the fact that I couldn't pay him. Since both of us understood that this was his true purpose, there was no need to spell it out. The groove had made things clear between us, leaving us both undisturbed.

Surely my uncle knew all about the Chinese groove. Even though, sadly, he no longer counted as a countryman, being the son of a son who had journeyed to Gold Mountain, his Chinese-ness couldn't have completely leached away after a mere two generations. No, that kind of knowledge, passed wordlessly through the ages and residing in the bones, doesn't vanish from a man's corporeal being any more than his marrow does, or his spermatozoa. His father, once a citizen of Yunnan who'd been sent at sixteen to the U.S. after the war, would've lived by the groove, same as mine did, and would've conferred upon his son the groove's awesome powers just as Father had done for me. I sipped my Sprite and my worry swam away. When he'd protested to my father that he didn't have room for me, my uncle had meant exactly the opposite. It was his duty to apologize, as every host does in advance and ever after, for the hard bed, the meager supper, the inadequate prospect of his garden view. What I was meant to understand was that when I arrived, he and his wife would greet me, arms opened wide. I drew up the blanket and fell asleep for hours until the ocean vanished and the land was rushing up. I paused in my elation to blow a last kiss to Father. Then I made myself tidy for Passport Control and hugging.

2.

Arrival

THERE HE WAS, A ZHENG IF I EVER SAW ONE. HE WAS tall and lanky with my same big nose and stalk neck and hands that looked like they'd been assigned too many knuckles. Clean-shaven, puffy under the chin. He had the smooth high forehead of an educated man, the thinking sort with a head full of troubling notions that disturb him to distraction and bother no one else. His face looked worn, his eyes a little dull. The black mole on his right earlobe resembled a feasting tick, a family trait the two of us shared with Cousin Deng and all the pinching cousins.

"Uncle!" I cried. I galloped to him, pink suitcase careening.

"Hello," he said, backing up and sticking out a hand. His teeth were so white! "How was your journey? Did you take a pleasant trip?" Up and down his eyes swiveled as he took my measure from the crown of my head to my shoes, a brand-new pair of trainers presented to me as a good-luck gift from my friend and classmate Yu, who was Cousin Deng's girlfriend. Uncle seemed surprised that I stretched as far as he did.

"I'm afraid I've just used up all the Chinese I know," he said, switching to English. "I hope your English is better than my Chinese."

"Best in show," I assured him. A snort escaped him. "Best in class," I corrected, trying to settle my nerves. In school and on my own, I'd studied English for years, my teachers a mumbling, amateur lot except for the last, Miss Chipping-Highworth, who came from a place called Sussex. Yu was her pupil too. We loved Miss Chips with her hoarfrost hair and flabby Churchillian dewlaps. She gave me the name Shelley, her favorite poet. "Shelley, sing away!" She spoke exclusively in English and demanded we do the same. *Hoarfrost*, she taught us, *dewlaps, farting. Hugger-mugger. Bric-a-brac.* We recited Shakespeare—"fear no more the heat o' the sun, nor the furious winter's rages"—and sang Christian hymns, not, Miss Chips said, because she was a believer, but because the words were so simple that any church fool could learn them. Every other Saturday, she took Yu and me for tea and cakes, the Gejiu version. When she left, she gave Yu a leather-bound diary and me her very own copy of a book of English poems, *for Shelley*, she wrote, *poet pupa.*

"How was your flight?" Uncle said. He looked confounded and I knew exactly why. My left eye wanders; it's impossible to look into both my eyes at once. The left one wants to head to the moon while its partner charts a course for the horizon, which means, to my good fortune, that I carry my comedy with me. Beady stare, murderous look, worried gaze, sarcastic squint, they all lose their way before they reach me. I wait patiently, tickled inside, while people figure out that no matter how precisely they try to aim their vector, they're not going to pin me.

"The airplane ride was very nice," I said. I was grinning like a demon and looking around for his wife, Aviva. I needed to charm that auntie posthaste if I was to stretch two weeks into many.

"Let's get you home. Are you hungry?" Uncle asked.

Always.

"I meant to take you to lunch but there isn't time. No worries. We're stopping to load up at Costco. Can I help you with that? You need something?"

I was squatting next to my suitcase, pulling out a Gejiu frog. I stood and faced him. "Thank you, Uncle, for welcoming me to San Francisco." With both hands, I offered him my grandest bullfrog, silver-colored and shiny. After a second, he took it.

"Thank you." He hefted, then hoisted. He held it at eye level and studied its winning grin. "Wow, that's really something."

"Genuine Gejiu tin. Very special. The coin in his mouth means lucky." I squatted again and rummaged. For Auntie Aviva, I had other lovely things.

"That's okay," he said quickly, "we can do that later. We better go; they're waiting."

"Auntie?" I said, jumping to my feet. I'd met her once before, on the day of my thirteenth birthday, when Uncle and Auntie and their son, Eli, had visited Kunming. A minibus of relatives had jockeyed at the airport to be the first to say hello, their arms full of gladiola stems as long as a soldier's rifle. Father would've been there too, had he been invited. I was summoned at the very last minute to tote Cousin Deng's photographic equipment, pride of the Japanese, the best that money could buy or, in Deng's case, acquire.

At my mention of Auntie Aviva, Uncle cleared his throat. "She's at home. With the others." *Ah*, I thought. *Uncle is apologizing for his wife's poor manners. He does live by the Chinese groove.*

"We're having a little party, so Aviva's got her hands full. We better get to Costco before all the good stuff is gone."

A party! For me! A warm-welcome gathering to honor my humble self. A very good reason for the skimpy airport greeting, and the way he'd said *home*, taking it for granted, made my glad heart sing.

Uncle checked his watch. "Better hurry," he said.

WE GOT IN UNCLE'S car, the crapmobile he called it, though to me it was very nice, having four wheels and two axles, and drove to a store so monumental that Gejiu's half million could've supplied themselves for a year. I realized he'd been making a dry-witted joke about all the stuff being gone, and I put myself on alert to Uncle's humors. For the next thirty minutes, I scouted the rows and sniffed the air like a hunter, tasting inside my nostrils the perfumes and garden scents of cleansers and refresheners and an elegant scalloped box of something called vaginal tablets. I ate well, too, out of little paper cups handed to me by smiling ladies. After two dozen, I was ready for a meal. Down the aisle, I saw Uncle looking relieved as he crossed off the last item on a list from Auntie Aviva written in purple ink and dotted with exclamations. He signaled me and we bushwhacked to the exit.

I admit to you now that I was feeling nervous. Uncle, being family, was bound by the rules—the Chinese groove—to play host, even to me, the renegade's weevil, but his wife might resent the fact that I'd stuck my flag on their map. I wished that I knew more about her since the mistress of the house could make things go roughly or smoothly. The real source of my worry? She wasn't Chinese—she was white. The relatives called that *American*.

"Are you sure his wife will let me stay?" I'd asked Father before I left. "What if, like the aunties, she looks down on those who are different?" They disapproved of Uncle's marriage, or, more precisely, the mix. *After his education was complete, his father should've sent him home to us. We would've found him an excellent wife.*

"The aunties, bah. What a vicious lot. Why would Uncle's wife cast you out? She married a Chinese man, didn't she?"

Chinese American. I hoped a minor distinction.

"Don't forget the sadness she bears," Father had warned me. "With her poor son dead, you'll have to tiptoe about."

He'd been killed, you see. Their son, Eli, along with Uncle's mother, a couple of months after Uncle, his wife, and Eli had visited Kunming. The news gave the aunties a transpacific thrill. A carjacking, they said, or was it a school shooting? They didn't have the details but at least they had a tragedy to hand round and round.

"That was five years ago," I said to Father. Five years seemed a long time by my barely-wound clock, the faulty timepiece of the young. Now that I'm older, Perspective and I are friends. "Why didn't they have another kid?"

"Too old. Don't bring them fresh pain. Say nothing about the boy." Tears filled his eyes; he was thinking as always of Mother. "Anyway," he said, "Uncle's wife is Jewish. She believes in family. She has to take you in."

I felt sad for Uncle and his wife. The aunties had been sad too, but only for a minute. *Maybe they'll divorce and next time around, he can marry a Chinese.* When I mentioned this to Father, he erupted.

"The aunties are wrong! Wrong about everything but especially wrong about love. If there's love, what does it matter when races bind themselves together against the family tide?" My tender-hearted father! Storyteller, weaver of dreams, the kite that Mother had flown. When she was alive, I used to hear Father murmuring to her after I'd gone to bed about his hope for a Shangri-la, a Peach Blossom Land where strangers were welcome and love drifted down like petals and everybody, high or low, clever or stupid, rickety-boned or oxlike, *everybody* got along. He sympathized with strays, outcasts, and misfits, more kin to him than family.

"Once your choice is made," Father assured me, "you never want to have to choose another."

UNCLE'S PHONE BUZZED. "That's a message from home," he said. "Aviva can't wait to see you."

A squeeze in his voice made me look for the Zheng mustache. It's a little squiggly line that shows up sideways between the nose and the lip when a Zheng man is temporizing. Yes, there it was, a crease right under his nose where a mustache would've sat if Uncle had been a pirate. It appeared at stressful moments on Father and me and half the Zheng family men, though Cousin Deng had foiled my detections by growing a real mustache which in sunlight looked coppery red, so who was really the bastard? The telltale mark on Uncle told me I was right to be worried about Auntie. Soon she'd be heaping on me the same condemnation I'd received my whole life: how I was a worthless fellow with his head in the clouds like Father, and whatever her husband had promised, I'd better not think of attaching myself like ivy. I thought sadly of my suitcase full of gifts that I was about to offer into her cold-palmed hands. Maybe I should hide them and bring them instead to strangers who would find me a straw mat and a place to lay my head. But when we pulled up in the crapmobile in front of a white house with orange trim, the door at the top of the steps opened and my Auntie Aviva flew out.

"Let me give you a hug," she said, and before I could say a word, she clasped me to her as though I were one of her own. She was short and soft and round, with rich brown hair as curly as a lamb's.

"It's wonderful to meet you," she said.

"To meet him *again*," Uncle corrected. "You met him before, on our trip to China."

"As if I could remember all those people," she said, laughing. She drew back and looked at me in appraisal. "I see the family resemblance. Ted, do you see it? No, you wouldn't. You hate looking at yourself." She linked my elbow with hers and bustled me forward.

"Straight on up the stairs," she said. "Everyone is here."

3.

The Bouncy Castle

THE PARTY, IT TURNED OUT, WAS NOT FOR ME. "HAPPY NEW YEAR" read shiny letters on a string. Balloons with cartoon faces bobbed past me, clutched in the hands of screaming kids moving too fast for me to count. Aviva's arm encircled me to propel me toward a corner.

"Dump your stuff and let's get you settled. Here. No, sorry, here. It's a madhouse, I know. We'll sort it out later. Ted!" she called. He staggered up the stairs, arms full of Costco. "What took you so long? In the kitchen! Put it all in the kitchen." He vanished through a doorway. "I'm hopeless," she said to me. "If I didn't have Ted, I'd be a bigger mess than I am. Now. This is a New Year's party. We always have one for our friends. Our New Year, not yours, of course. We do Chinese New Year too, if we remember. I don't want you thinking I've completely co-opted Ted. And Jewish New Year later. We're a full-service family. Are you hungry? Eat. There's a ton of food. I don't know why I told Ted to get more. We're awash in raisin bagels."

She sallied into the kitchen and I trotted after her, eager to do as she said. My big American adventure had started, and any party, even if not for me, where I was a guest like all the others made a very nice change indeed. At a Zheng family gathering, I'd be moving tables or mopping tiles while the relatives drew long noodles down their voluptuous gullets. I always ate last, scraping the pot bottom.

"Tell me how to say your name," Aviva said. "Zheng Xue Li? Am I close, or have I just called you something horribly offensive?"

"Call me Shelley," I said. She was being so nice to me, an aunt who knew how to love! "My English teacher called me that."

"Great, that makes things easy. We better go check on the kids." She hustled down some stairs into the backyard. I saw a large pink-and-purple structure—a castle, I later learned—its towers—its turrets—violently trembling. Inside the castle, children tossed about. I knew just how they felt, overjoyed to be turned upside down.

"What a beautiful day!" Aviva said. "The sun is shining for a change. I'll never get used to living in the Sunset District. False advertising, that's what I call it. We've got the beach and the park but no sun. Before we bought this house, we rented in a better part of the city. You'd think Ted would've warned me. About everything, in fact. Never mind. Today is gorgeous." She looked around and beamed. "We can thank the drought for that."

"Aviva," a parent called from the castle. "You think of everything. These kids are having a blast."

"I made one call! It was easy," Aviva answered. "The bouncy people do the rest." She added privately, to me, "Those people, oy. They were a total pain in the ass."

I suspected that this American auntie had her own brand of Chinese groove.

MY STOMACH GONGED; THE party trays were calling, but I had to wait while Aviva took me around to her guests. I couldn't tell if it was noon or midnight, but I wasn't a bit sleepy. Excitement kept me awake.

"This is Shelley," she said, "Ted's nephew who's just arrived from China. He's come to study English at City College." They shook my hand and said hello and I was agape—I'd never seen such combinations. Ten couples in the house and none of the partners matched. There was a husband and wife like Ted and Aviva: Chinese guy, white American woman. Three pairs were in reverse: Chinese women, white American men. Some of the couples were white and Mexican, or white and from another south-of-the-border country that supplied the U.S. with a steady stream of people who did all the honest work, *as did the Chinese in an earlier era*, Miss Chips spoke in my head. A man shook my hand—a Japanese guy with a Black American wife. The loving look between them would've sent the aunties squawking.

The youngsters were a different matter. Forget categories. Forget easy labels. That party pack of kids held every color of the rainbow if every color of the rainbow were a different shade of brown. It was hard to guess who belonged with which parents, though the shapes of their eyes and the floaty-ness of their hair scattered clues as they ran. They were one mixed-up lot laughing and bopping balloons and bouncing in the castle, and nobody seemed to care. Here in San Francisco was a utopia of the races, the best of all possible worlds, and I, the traveler, by the dint of Mother's desires, had landed in Peach Blossom Land.

"Shelley!" Aviva said. "Let me introduce you. This is Ted's friend Kate and this is her, um, Orit." *Or-Reet.*

"Kate's wife," Orit said, sticking out a hand.

"Sorry, yes," Aviva said. "They're married. And that's their son, Leo." She pointed to a little kid who was standing to one side, watching the others play.

I blushed as I shook hands. I'd never before met a woman-and-woman pair, though I'd heard that they existed, like the rare white rhinoceros or Texas armadillo. Two hours into my brand-new life, I'd been thrown for a loop-de-loop. Out of the corner of my eye, I saw Aviva watching me, waiting for my reaction. Sweat creepy-crawled down the back of my weedy neck. I was failing some test that I hadn't known I'd be taking. If I said the wrong thing, would I be sent packing? I knew no one else. I had only enough money to eat for a single day.

"Are you here for the semester?" Kate asked kindly.

I'm here for good, I tried to say but not a word emerged until I remembered what Miss Chips had taught me: *Proper manners will carry the traveler over many a bumpy road.*

"I'm delighted to meet you," I said. I wiped my sleeve across my misted forehead. A minute later, the Japanese guy brought me a heaping plate of food, excellent man that he was. It happened just as Miss Chips had promised. Even bounders like me had a use for *politesse.*

"I'D RATHER YOU call me Ted," Uncle said. "I'm not technically your uncle, you know. We're second cousins once removed. She's Aviva. We're Ted and Aviva. Our last name is C-H-E-N-G. Spelled with a *C-H* instead of a *Z*. Too bad," he added, looking at his wife. "You could've been Aviva Zheng. That has a zertain zing to it."

Cheng. Zheng. Same character. All in the family. Father had told me that Uncle's great-grandfather was my great-great-grandfather. That difference made us "removed," I guessed. *Call him Uncle,* Father had said. *He'll be offended if you don't.*

"We're pretty informal around here," Uncle said. "You'll learn that about us. Besides, I hate to think of myself as old enough to have an eighteen-year-old nephew."

"Poor sweetie," Aviva said. "Of course you are. You're twice his age. Plus."

"Aviva's brother's kids are six and eight. That's uncle enough for me."

"Eight and eleven," Aviva said. The party was over; they were sprawled at a table piled high with cups and plates. Smashed cake dotted a path down the hallway and balloons drifted above their heads. There were only two chairs, so I leaned against the doorway, half in and half out.

"That was fun," Aviva said. "Wasn't that fun, Ted? I wish they'd stayed longer. The kids were having a ball."

Father had assured me that Uncle wanted for nothing. *His family owns a big department store on the best corner in San Francisco. They never run out of customers because people who have a great amount of things buy more, more, more, like one of your video games—always get to the next level. You go to work for Uncle, you'll run the place someday.*

But looking around at the emptied house, I was more than a little worried. Where was the housekeeper? Where was the cook? Why was Auntie Aviva groaning herself to her feet to bring the soiled plates to the garbage?

I must've scratched my scalp or contracted my silky eyebrows—I have a fine-haired pair that Lisbet once stroked, which later I confirmed to myself were the softest bits on my body—because Uncle decided he'd confused me with all that ancestor talk. He fetched a pad of paper and gallantly offered to diagram the family tree. He should've realized that I knew the domain completely, the phylum and the class, the genus and the species. My whole life to that point had been confined to that kingdom, and what countryman can't recite his genealogy by heart? As the resident sponger at less than half his age, I had to let him instruct me, but the honest-to-goodness truth was that in those early days, Uncle underestimated my Gejiu sophistication. I beg you, please. Don't make the same mistake.

Aviva brought a big black sack to the table and asked me to hold it open while she tossed in the waste.

"Wasn't it wonderful to see all the kids?" she asked Uncle.

He ignored her and began drawing his chart, starting with *Ted* and *Aviva*. He put in his mother's name, *Diana*, and then his pen wavered. I held my breath—would there be a mark for his child?

"Here's where your father goes," he said to me, moving his hand across the page. "The illustrated version." He drew a picture of a grinning man who didn't look anything like Father. As a joke, he added a long beard.

"He and I are the same generation, but he's a lot older than me."

Aviva caught my eye and winked. I said I thought Father looked distinguished with a beard and while he was at it, could he draw the *lao jia*, the old family home with the courtyard? He drew an igloo and a polar bear, another sort of joke. Uncle said he'd been pleased to receive Father's letter and wanted to know how Father had learned to write such excellent English, remarkable for a man who'd been born during those bad Cultural Revolution years.

"An English lady taught me, and Father studied too." The last part was a lie, a very small one. Father had hired an agent to write the letter to Uncle and help me get admitted into the Intensive English Program at City College S.F. She'd written wonderful things about me that were only a little embellished.

"Did we meet your father in Kunming?" Aviva asked. "We must've. Like I said, every last one of Ted's relatives showed up, plus the extras who magically appeared when it came time to hand out red envelopes."

"I was there," I volunteered. "Father was working." His feelings had been hurt that he hadn't been invited. He still held out the bootless hope that one day he and I would be treated well by the rest, maybe even asked to live at the *lao jia* with the aunties and cousins who shared the place, like Cousin Deng and his mother. I'd received my red envelope from Uncle, same as the others, and brought its contents, ten U.S. dollars, to Father to help pay our rent. Later, Cousin Deng collected a fatter envelope from the restaurant where he'd made the arrangements for the banquet Uncle had hosted. *A finder's fee,* he'd called it and palmed me a couple of yuan.

"Will your dad be okay on his own?" Aviva asked. "Won't that be hard for him? You said it's just him and you."

I assured her that Father would be brilliant without me, given the busy life he led with a rewarding job and friends. If they'd known to look for it, my Zheng mustache would've given me clean away. "My cousin Deng will look after him." At least that much was true. I showed Uncle where to put Cousin Deng on the chart.

"Dutiful Deng," Aviva joked. "Every family needs someone to do the unsung work. I may not look it, but I'm a good Chinese wife. I was trained for the job by Jews."

Chinese wife, Jewish wife; I didn't care what she called herself as long as she let me stay.

"It can be hard to take care of our old parents," Aviva said. "Mine are passed, but Ted's . . ." She glanced his way, but he didn't look up from the table.

"Sometimes Father gets sad that Mother is passed," I said. "He misses her very much."

"My mother died too," Uncle chimed in abruptly. I peeked at what he was drawing: tiny leaves along a vine that grew from Diana to Ted.

"I wish she'd come with us on that trip," Aviva said. "It would've made the whole thing easier. She never got the chance to go back."

"She was born here," Ted said. "She was raised right here in San Francisco."

"You know what I mean," Aviva said. "I just wish she'd come. She'd never, ever been. She was dying to see China."

Aviva caught herself. Ted's hand stopped moving.

"She didn't want to leave the store," Ted said. "People depended on her. She was there day and night."

"She spoke Cantonese like a native," Aviva told me. "Her family was from Toisan in the Pearl River Delta, like most of the Chinese who came when her parents did."

I knew about his mother's Guangdong roots because the aunties chattered over that mismatched marriage as well. Uncle's father, like the rest of us, was born in Yunnan Province. His parents had sent him and his younger sister to the U.S. at the end of the war. The parents had planned to leave too, but they died in Yunnan shortly after. Uncle's father went to college, made his way to San Francisco, and married a local girl. *From Chinatown*, the aunties sniffed. They were offended that he'd never returned to help them or visit the bones of his parents, but still they admired him, *The One Who Got Away*.

"There's a whole interesting history of the Chinese in America," Aviva said. "You probably know all about it."

Nope. Not a chance. History and I didn't need to be better acquainted. The point of starting over was to break free of my rotten roots.

"I'm a storyteller," Aviva said proudly. "Well, I'm a children's librarian, but storytelling's my passion. I love learning about other cultures through their myths and folktales. Ted's a storyteller too."

"Used to be," said Ted, shortly.

"Oh, honey, don't give up."

"There's more than one way to tell a story," Ted said, holding up the chart.

Aviva peered. "You left out your father." She tapped a spot on the page, but Ted made no move to add him. He was taking great pains to look utterly nonchalant.

"His name is Henry. He's eighty-two," Aviva told me. "Sharp as blazes."

Henry Cheng. The One Who Got Away. I wondered if Uncle had told him about me—maybe the old man was good for a red envelope or better— but a glimpse of Ted's expression and his careful posture told me via Chinese groove not to stir the air with questions. I examined the chart. From our common ancestor, Ted had one long line running down the page, descended from a single couple. He hadn't put in great-great-grand's three wives, which meant he didn't know the crucial difference between us: that he was descended from wife number one, the eldest daughter of a rich Yunnanese merchant, and I from number three, the dissolute concubine reported to be a beauty but contemptible to the rest. I didn't correct his mistake. His ignorance was my fortune. If he didn't know my true origins, there was no one on the premises with reason to beat or pinch me. I set the chart on the table.

"I read you," I said. "You are Ted and she is Aviva."

MY EYES KEPT SNAPPING shut; I'd been up more than twenty-four hours. Aviva told me to take a nap in the "bonus room" downstairs. "Aren't we fancy? We don't live in a Sunset saltbox. We live in a saltbox *stretch*."

She led me down the steps and left me in a dark room with no bed. My suitcase had materialized beside a sagging sofa. I lay down on the scratchy surface and spread the blanket folded there. No doubt my proper bedroom was not yet fully prepared, and this room next to the garage was merely a way station. They were waiting till nightfall to make a touching fuss over showing me to my room, presenting me with my pillow. *Two* pillows, extra plump. When I awoke a while later, only Ted was in the house. Aviva was at the gym, he said, and he had to go out as well.

"Do you need help at the store?" I asked. The sooner I went with him, the quicker he'd see that I was ready to learn the family trade, an excellent way to establish myself until poet money rolled in.

"The store?" Ted said.

"I'm a jack-of-all-trades." Miss Chips had called me that. "You can depend on me day and night."

"Ah. Oh. My mother's store." His Zheng mustache did a two-step there and back. "We'll talk about it later. I'm going to meet a friend."

He rode off on a bike. Their other cars were probably out for their weekly wax and buff. After a quick refreshment of two raisin bagels and a chicken leg I found on a paper plate on the bookshelf, I inspected my new abode. It was two stories, that was good, but it was built upside down with most of the living space on the second floor to make room for the garage at ground level. In fact, every house as far as I could see down the whole length of the block was set close to the street down a short strip of driveway, little house above, big garage below. Apparently, garages were important in San Francisco. Cars needed a place to live even more than people.

Upstairs, the front room had a row of vertical windows

overhanging the garage. A squat TV occupied one corner, poor relation to the flat-screen behemoths that all my cousins owned. Weak light filtered through the windows. The view was of the street, every house identical and built inches apart.

There was a small dining area with an oval table and a desk crammed into the corner. Nothing to see there but an old laptop—as soon as I could, I'd send Father something better. I passed into the kitchen. The table was cleared of all but a dried-up plant and a bottle of chili oil. I shook a fat blob onto the back of my hand. I had to lick like a mother cow to register the barest tingle. Father and I liked our food *hot* hot. My stomach rumbled and I wondered if dinnertime was soon and if they were bringing food or if I was supposed to forage. I'd often gathered necessities plus sometimes bonus goods for Cousin Deng and his friends, but I'd expected, coming here, that I could lay those skills to rest.

I looked around the room, my expectations further sinking. I'd had big plans for this part of the house, since kitchens and bathrooms were the stuff of my Gejiu dreams, but the stove was chipped and pitted and the oven door screamed when I opened it to find no lovely chicken resting, no pork roast waiting for me to cleave off a juicy hunk, just a stack of dented pots and pans blackened inside and out. There was a small sink and a crowded countertop and a yellowed light dangling from the ceiling. Only the refrigerator buttered both sides of my mood, for it was as silvery as moonlight and making such an intelligent hum that I thought it might address me. A wedge of coconut cake, thick-frosted, called my name from the middle shelf, and naturally I answered.

Then I aimed for the bathroom, that delicious private quarter for the daily care of my top and bottom. My whole life, I'd shared a shower trough and a toilet with sixteen or more families and the occasional whelping cat. Father and I had indulged ourselves before

I departed, describing pulsating jet streams, lighted mirrors. Warm surfaces where you wanted them and cool ones where you didn't. I traveled halfway down the hallway and threw open the bathroom door.

A damp, cramped cell as ordinary as a bucket. A stained sink and a shower stall of molded plastic. Meaner than any bathroom in Cousin Deng's portion of the old family home. The rug was dun when it should've been lilac, and the floor froze my soles. No window, no curtains, a sorry lack of lace. I used the commode—it wasn't linger-worthy.

Two rooms remained. I opened the door to the right and found Ted and Aviva's bedroom. Their bed was miles wide. Through the window, I could see the bouncy castle, its turrets slumped like revelers after a long night. A stray balloon hung listlessly over the bed. On one bedside table shone the genuine Gejiu tin figurine of a running mare and her frolicking foal, which I'd presented to Aviva at the party. "Look at that," she'd exclaimed and showed it off to her guests. I saw pinned beneath the galloping hooves the family tree that Ted had drawn, with an added bold line that descended from Ted and Aviva. It ended at a single point: *ELI*. My poet heart hiccupped. My son heart flinched.

But the best was waiting directly across the hall: my bedroom in all its glory. There wasn't any window where Father and I slept. Would my dreams be different if I could wake to a tree and sunlight? I turned the knob. It was stuck. Turned it again, no give. The door was locked. I was barred from entry. After all my careful conduct, it didn't seem fair to a fellow. I ran at it shoulder first and jammed my collarbone. I heard a noise coming from behind the door or maybe my brain was shaken. A low hum, a secretive sound, like the murmur of conversation. I listened for a while but nothing told me what it was.

Foiled, I returned to the kitchen and rooted for scraps that even a beggar wouldn't miss: broken crackers, apple slices turning brown, stumpy orange plugs that tasted faintly of carrot. I went downstairs, through the garage, and into the rectangled yard. A last band of light fell across the castle, making its pink sides blush. Brown grass showed all around, and the bushes looked dry and dusty. The one tree, at the rear of the yard, had a trunk just big enough for love. Someday I'd bring Lisbet here to meet my new family and carve our initials into the tree. I saw thin scratches at its base and stooped for a closer look: *ELI.* A name in brief, faint as a whisper. I'd seen no photographs in the house that might've been him, which was odd, come to think of it, but not so bad for me. I knew from experience that it was hard to compete with the dead.

A low fence enclosed the yard, little more than a gesture. On either side, the houses crowded close. I could see into their yards and they into mine—already I was feeling possessive. Three houses down I saw another bouncy castle, this one red and blue. I heard a dog barking and then another, very loud, and I scooted back against the house, dogs being not my favorite. Cousin Deng had told me that every American family had a dog, a cat, or a rabbit. I later discovered just how wrong he was. It was guinea pig, not rabbit, and not every one but most.

Next door, a window winked. A man's face appeared, then vanished. I heard a door open, and he walked into his yard. He looked like a countryman, though it was hard to tell since he was wearing a cap pulled low. I stayed out of sight against the house and craned my neck to observe him. The man turned in my direction. Yes, I was right, he was a countryman, no mistake. Of the older variety, but he still had vigor. He marched back and forth across his yard, swinging his arms and pumping his knees and making grunting noises. When he was finished, I saw him look up at Ted and

Aviva's house, to the window of the locked room hidden behind its curtains. He stared for a long minute, then he tugged at his right earlobe and blew the window a kiss. If I'd have blinked, I would've missed it.

I'd GROWN SLEEPY AGAIN. I crawled into the bouncy castle and lay there drowsily, listening to a bird calling for its mate. Fruity scent, the sweet sweat of children. A blue fuzzy sock turned into a thumb mitten. The light was pink-suffused, the walls above me ripply smooth, same as I imagined a woman's box to be. I curled and dozed, dreaming of houses colorful and vast. When I awoke, I didn't know at first where I was. I thought I should go and check on Father and prepare his supper as always, and then I remembered that I'd left Gejiu and re-homed myself overnight. I rolled onto my stomach and squirmed halfway onto the grass.

"Two weeks," I heard Ted say. "That's what I told his father."

"*Two* weeks? *Two?* I thought we decided one." Aviva's protest set my worry fish darting. What would I do if they sent me away? I was the eggs; they were my basket.

"Two," Ted said. "He'll need time to find a place to live."

"Good luck with that," Aviva said. "There's nothing left to rent. Unless he wants to move to Bakersfield. Or Barstow. Does he have any money, do you think?"

It was dark outside. Their window was open. I could see them clearly in the bedroom light.

"His semester costs like three thousand dollars. He said a bene-factor gave his father the money. Apparently he's shown a lot of promise."

"What will he live on?" Aviva said.

"He must've brought funds to get himself started. The school would've required that he demonstrate support. He's not allowed to work on a student visa."

Start-up funds. What an excellent idea! You'll think I'm being sarcastic but I'm not. To keep an open outlook always serves a gentleman best, and though I hardly qualified for gentleman status, I was a *poet pupa* with principles of my own. It was true that I needed start-up funds, given how little I had. I'd planned for the Bank of Uncle to make an initial investment, but the chances of that happening seemed to be thinning a bit on the ground.

"I can barely understand what he's saying," Aviva said. "The British accent is plain weird. Do you think he understands us? He looks as blank as a baby. No, I take it back. He looks like the Cheshire cat."

Thanks to Miss Chips, I knew the reference—all grin, no substance, like businessmen everywhere, also politicians. Perhaps I'd overdone my endearing smile, but I'd be wrong to fault myself I was younger then by almost twenty years and in a compromised strait. When your pockets are empty and you're aiming hard to please, it's easy to confuse a grin with a rictus.

Their voices had grown faint, so I belly-crawled out of the castle, oozed over to the house, and flattened myself against the deck.

". . . your father," Aviva was saying.

"I don't want to talk about it," Ted replied.

"You never do! You never want to talk about anything important. You can't leave me to deal with him alone. You haven't spoken to him in months!"

"His fault, not mine," Ted said.

"Please, for once, can we leave blame out of it?"

I couldn't hear Ted's answer; they were moving about the room.

". . . old," Aviva said.

". . . immortal," Ted said.

". . . help," Aviva said. ". . . attention."

Their voices faded. I tucked away what I'd overhead, storing it for later. Sometimes information was as valuable as gold. I hustled down the side path around to the front of the house.

"I'm home!" I called as I rang the bell at the orange door. I had two whole weeks to change their minds, plenty of time for persuasion.

4.
Boardinghouse

Top, tail. Again. Top, tail. Again. I'm prepping green beans one by one. The pile at my left hand bristles with hatted beans. The pile at my right grows from mound to hillock to mountain. From left to right, I snap their ends as they travel. Cook shouts from the kitchen, "More beans, faster!" I shout back, "Go fuck yourself," and hear their laughter, Cook's loudest of all.

It's seven o'clock, the dinner hour. As waiters rush past me, I smell oil, chili, and garlic. The growing din and the rising heat of bodies tell me the restaurant's full. They come by the score for Truly Mongolian Green Beans, the signature dish at Pop Up Veg Out Nicely. From my station near the back, I hear the kitchen door swinging and the front door moan. "Shut the door!" somebody yells. "It's frickin' February!" The door slams shut. The line outside won't budge. They'll wait an hour for a counter seat, longer for a table, even though there's another Chinese restaurant right next door and three more down the block with the same dish on the menu except that those establishments don't call themselves a pop-up or source their beans from a local farmer who does his own graphics. Somebody posted a photo of Cook's "fresh interpretation of a classic," and the crowds came running. I can top and tail five thousand beans and not a scrap falls to the floor. There's nothing to it, really. The aunties had me doing this from the time I was old enough to perch on a rusty pail.

You're worried for me. You, whoever you are. Citizen of the World (since you're reading this), sympathetic to a boy flying high on a dripping mop. *He's supposed to be in school. Has he given up his studies?* Because school was the pathway up and out, the playing field leveler, the closer of gaps, my best shot going forward. Every afternoon, five days a week, I went to my Intensive English Program, and I would've spent myself exclusively on placing pesky articles and producing proper pronouns, not to mention learning the bendables like *i before e except after c*, had I not needed food and housing.

Uncle and Auntie, Ted and Aviva, they did their best for me, or as Ted told me in front of his wife, "what circumstances allow." A pained expression on his face and Aviva nod-smiling. For two weeks they fed me and took me to see the sights and let me sleep on the scratchy sofa and drive the crapmobile—their only car, unwaxed, unbuffed—with Ted instructing me on how to park on a hill. The bedroom door stayed locked. Ted gave me his transit pass, front-loaded with plenty of budget, and told me to keep it so I could ride the bus and the streetcar and the subway with a tap and a beep and a stride. Every day he went off to work, and I hoped he'd invite me along to his big, beautiful department store filled with shiny things, but he always left without saying a word. On the seventh day, with classes soon to begin, Aviva reminded me that I had one week left as their guest. I told her not to worry, sure she would change her mind. On the twelfth day, she asked me sweetly if I'd found a place to live, maybe student housing? City College didn't provide. When Aviva went for groceries—*the fourth time this week!*—Ted came downstairs to give me some items he claimed he was getting rid of—collared shirts, a fleece jacket, a navy blazer that showed off my wrists nicely, not a moth nibble among them. The moment was ripe to ask again if he needed help at the store.

"Ah," Ted said. His Zheng mustache went hopping across his lip. "There is no family business anymore. It was sold."

"Sold?" If there wasn't any store, where did Ted go every day when he said he was going to work? How did he afford that nice blue blazer or his trio of racing bicycles that hung in the garage?

"The year my mother died."

"But that was a long time ago!"

Ted looked embarrassed. "I'm sorry I didn't tell you sooner. I don't like to talk about these things. The store was my mother's; she called it her second child. Her parents had started the business, and she grew up in the place. After they passed, she took it over. She never missed a day of work. She felt responsible to the neighborhood to keep it going, and the folks who shopped there—they all loved my mother back."

"Then why'd you sell it?" I couldn't imagine giving up the fount of the family fortune had I been given the goods.

"I couldn't keep it up and didn't really want to. I'm a journalist; I used to work for the local paper, but I don't anymore."

"What about your father? Didn't he want to keep the store?"

The thin line of Ted's mouth jerked in displeasure. "He wanted it sold. He didn't help my mother run it when she was alive and he couldn't wait to get rid of it later."

"So where do you work?" I asked. "Where do you go every day?"

"To the library or a café or out to meet with people. I'm freelance, which means I write articles for lots of different outlets. And I help other people write their books. That's called *ghostwriting*."

"Ghostwriting," I tested the sound of the word. The aunties enjoyed invoking ancestral ghosts to make us offspring behave, but Father didn't subscribe. Piety is one thing, he said, empty threats another. *Don't ever think of Mother as a ghost. She's as real to us as this table, this chair, this body. This heart*, he said, a black-smudged hand placed over his cotton vest.

"That's right," Ted said. "I'm paid to put words in other people's mouths." Ted would never place his hand over his wounded heart. He was *guo ba*, crusty pot-bottom rice. He wrote words for other people instead of speaking for himself. But he'd described his mother with a pride that gave him away. Father showed that kind of pride when he talked about me to others. Try as Ted might to cover his feelings under that *guo ba* crust, I could tell that he was happy for his mother that she'd had her devotion.

"The store didn't last long after we sold it," he said. "My mother had a lot of loyal customers, but the new owners didn't have her personal touch. The big grocery stores drove them out of business."

Whoa, what? I thought he said *grocery* stores. Surely he meant *department*?

"No, grocery. That's what my mom sold, mostly. She kept a little nursery out front where she sold plants and flowers. She was great in the garden."

"I thought it was a department store that sold many beautiful things."

Ted burst out laughing. "Who told you that? It was a corner grocery store. A convenience store, that served the neighborhood."

Damn the aunties! They'd gotten it wrong again. I stammered an explanation of how they'd been both boastful and envious at the riches they'd imagined his department store had reaped.

Ted shook his head and grinned. "What other crazy stories did the aunties tell you?"

That your son died, along with your mother, in a violent, American death.

I didn't let those words pass my lips. Like Ted, I knew how to be silent.

AT THE TWO-WEEK MARK, "Time's up," Aviva said. I packed the sparkly suitcase. Ted slipped me an envelope behind Aviva's back. "For emergencies," he muttered.

"Take care," Ted said. "You're always welcome to visit."

"Call first," Aviva said, and she ushered me out the door.

Luckily, I'd made a friend; his name was Eddie Low. We met the first week of the semester, my last few days of living with Ted and Aviva, before the green bean era began. My cash was gone, my purchasing power nil. At Ted's invitation, every day I brought to campus lunch provisions from the silver fridge, but by late afternoon, my stomach was messaging that it was time to eat again and so I cruised the outdoor tables hoping to score some vittles. I'd observed that the students bought way more than they could consume, due to picky palates or body slimming or big-picture thinking, I didn't know. What they left behind amazed me: bonanza burgers, half cartons of curry potatoes. Gulpable lattes, still warm and frothy. I ate it all, unembarrassed. Had it not been for me, those fine rations would've gone to waste. I didn't permit myself to pick through the garbage. I'm a practical sort; I could've done it, but I had a certain delicacy of feeling for my fellow human beings and I knew it would distress some, especially the ladies, to see me upside down in the trash, so I followed strict rules for my own method of local sourcing. Anything left on a tray was fair game: it was either me or the seagulls, and they had other options. I didn't loiter near diners or ask, "Are you finished with that?" If they offered, I accepted, but hungry looks were out of bounds. I'd discovered the patty melt, a food invented to spread happiness like mustard, but even the butt end of a patty melt, conspicuously protruding, wouldn't tempt me to lawless behavior. A life without principles, Father had taught me, is only for rats and aunties.

I was reaching for a morsel—cornmeal crust? Ciabatta? My vocabulary was improving fast, especially concerning menu options—when a jocular voice interrupted.

"Gaah, no! Scrounge, don't scavenge."

Eddie Low, tracksuited and shiny. I pegged him at first for a countryman—razored hair, spectacles sliding—but no, on second look, he was strictly ABC. REI beanie, DC trainers. The alphabet gave him away. American-born Chinese liked ads all over their clothing, a look that Cousin Deng derided until the day he'd shown up with *VERSACE* across his chest. Fake, my friends assured me, but they didn't know Cousin Deng like I did. In fact, he'd told me he'd gotten Versace to pay *him* to wear it. Brilliant, that. The stuff I learned at his knee.

Eddie Low, on the other hand, wasn't made for Euro styling. He had a moon face and a drum of a belly, sausage fingers, suet neck. Tipped over, he would've rolled till he hit the curb. I wished I could carve off some of his glorious fat and stick it right on me. For all my tireless efforts, I wasn't gaining gravitas, hadn't added hew or heft. One look at Eddie made a serious impression.

"Don't eat that skanky stuff when you can use the scrounge line," Eddie said. "You know about scrounging, don't you?"

Well, I didn't, so Eddie showed me. Inside the student center was a long table set aside for food that people had purchased but weren't going to finish. They left it there for the scroungers. *Reduce food waste*, a sign said, hand-printed in shapely letters. Penned by a girl, I guessed, though some girls were more disarranged than others. Lisbet's handwriting, like her life, was shore-after-tsunami.

"I'm not generally a scrounger myself," Eddie said, "because my mom cooks for me, but I really believe in the shared economy. Needs get matched up. Everyone comes out ahead."

Not every theory that Eddie espoused either at that moment or in our many talks to come made sense to me at first, but that didn't bother Eddie. The beauty of the bull session with Eddie was that agreement wasn't necessary nor was talking, an excellent arrangement, especially in those early days when I was doing a lot more listening than speaking. Eddie was one who could carry a tune by himself.

"If you don't want to pay for a meal—you don't have the money, or you embrace the synchronicity of the thing—you come and help yourself. I feel good about not wasting food, and you get Cool Ranch Doritos."

I had some in my mouth, delicious, and hunted for patty melt while Eddie further explained.

"For the shared economy to work, you need total transactional transparency. It's all about efficiencies of need and fulfillment." He stuck out a hand. "Eddie Low. Business major."

"Shelley," I said. "*Poet pupa.*"

"Very cool," Eddie said. "You from China?"

I confirmed.

"You doing Intensive English? I hear it's a great program."

Confirmed again, under asterisked protest. *Great* was a relative term, the Chipping-Highworth Program being the gold standard. My classes so far had been easy. There were seventeen students in my group from all over—Spain, Turkey, Pakistan, Moldova. Brazil and Colombia. Korea and Japan. We'd been through orientation and had taken a placement test, on which I'd scored third highest. The goal was to make us proficient in spoken and written English; we weren't there to earn a degree, though some of the students hoped to transfer to an academic program, an aim way too costly and ambitious for me. There were several countrymen in the group who hoped to make that jump. Their families were wealthy and they didn't have to scrounge, but none of them scored as high as I did.

"Yeah, I've seen them," Eddie said. "The rich-y rich ones driving their fancy cars. My advice is, don't hang around with the other Chinese students. You'll talk to them the whole time and never practice your English." I didn't have to be told twice, especially since they'd taken one look at my windbreaker with the torn pocket and my shaggy locks in need of a cut and decided, like my cousins before them, that I didn't belong on their newsfeed. Eddie said he was fluent in Spanish and spoke some Cantonese, "enough to keep my grandma happy. You'd like my Grandma. Also my mom. She cooks for me and my crew anytime we show up." I took that as a promise.

Eddie's favorite subjects were history and anthropology, the foundations, he claimed, of a successful business career. He and his girlfriend, Paloma, the best coder on campus, were building an app for locals and tourists that was already scoring impressive market share. "All you need to grow a user base is an understanding of human nature. It's an easy proposition if you've got the right data set,"

Eddie said. Since my data set didn't include housing, within days, I was knocking on his door.

FOR EIGHT NIGHTS, I slept on the floor of Eddie Low's apartment and worried about where I'd go next. During the day, I attended class and then hurried by bus to the Outer Mission District, where some of my fellow classmates who were also strained for funds had told me there was work to be found sub rosa. I secured my job at Pop Up Veg Out Nicely, the fourteenth restaurant where I inquired after employment, because one hour earlier their dogsbody had quit. The dinner crowd was gathering; they wanted their green bean fix, and the owner's son-in-law, who'd been left in charge for the day while the owner had a rest at the nearest casino, decided he liked the cut of my jib and hired me on the spot, promising to pay me at the end of the week if I lasted that long on the job.

At closing time, five thousand green beans behind us, Cook allowed me to thank him for the honor of priming the canvas for his culinary arts by letting me purchase a bottle of potent spirits with a share of the funds Ted had slipped me—three hundred bucks, which I'd counted and divided, half to my underpants, the other half to my shoe. We toasted good food; we toasted pretty women. I asked Cook why the dish was called "Truly Mongolian" when he used Tianjin chilies and Sichuan peppercorns, those regions being as different from the steppes as Gejiu from San Francisco. Cook guffawed and made me promise I wouldn't give away his secret, which was to sprinkle fresh grated horseradish as a last benediction, a final kitchen kiss to wake up what he called "the limp-dick American palate." He threw his bulbous arm around my neck. "All of life," Cook confided, "is improvise, improvise, improvise." He said that the boardinghouse where he lived with other countrymen like us might have an extra bunk for rent, and before I could say "scratch my back, I'll scratch yours," I had a place to live. The Chinese groove, you see, had floated me like a feather from green beans to whiskey to roost.

The boardinghouse teetered on a street named Paris, which if that wasn't poet-like, what is? Twelve of us lived there, maybe fifteen; sometimes it was twenty. There were six sets of bunk beds arranged in two rooms, the model of democracy: one man, one vote, one bed, aside from a few exceptions. Some of the guys who worked nights slept by day and rented their mattresses at sundown, which was fine by Mrs. Yap as long as half of their windfall blew its way into her pockets. I never met Mrs. Yap, a Chinatown lady who owned real estate all over town, a confidante of the mayor, they said, and a voice for the little people since she, unlike the greedy developers who were taking over the city, provided affordable housing. This kind of talk was beyond my comprehension. I only knew that I didn't feel so little trying to fit the whole stretch of me onto the narrow bed. I paid seventy-five dollars in cash at the start of every week to a well-barbered fellow who had me count out my dollar bills and lay them on the table instead of handing them to him directly because, he said, he was careful with his immune system, not wanting to stress it out. The others told me he was married to Mrs. Yap's daughter and that I shouldn't be fooled by the big show he made writing down complaints because he never did anything about them.

It's true there were pests of one kind or another, some two-legged, some four-, some six-, and we didn't have a showerhead, only a rubber hose, but the windows opened and the front door locked and the roof didn't leak—not that anyone knew of, since for three years, they told me, there'd been scarcely a drop of rain— and that was enough for me. I couldn't allow myself the luxury of distress. *Everything's going great!* I wrote to Father, care of Cousin Deng. I kept my missives sunny and brief, leaving out any mention of my ejection from Ted and Aviva's house, and the restaurant job, and the boardinghouse with its resident creepers and peepers. Now that I'd made it to Peach Blossom Land, I put Father and his sadness behind me, in the past where they belonged. I told myself that, with Deng looking after him and me sending him assurances that I was on my way to my big American success, Father had everything he needed.

Two nights before my departure, Father had asked me to tell him again the dreams I was taking with me. "I want to write them down so I can look at them when you're gone and think of you and Mother and all her hopes for you."

"Right," I said. "Well, it's just the three things. First, I'd like to get better acquainted with our American relatives. Second, I'll find a pretty Chinese American wife. And, third, of course, I'm going to make a lot of money."

"Family, Love, Fortune," Father said proudly. "Three Achievables. Three worthy goals." He felt in his pockets for a scrap of paper and a pen, but the drink had taken hold of him and he couldn't manage. He fumbled his cigarette. His eyes were smeary with tears.

Family. Love. Fortune. I wrote the words for him, feeling queasy that what I'd just told him wasn't exactly true. I didn't want to become merely acquainted with my relatives in S.F.; I was bound and determined to find a better family to join. I had no intention of seeking a Chinese American wife, for Lisbet was the only girl I wanted. Hadn't I promised to write her three splendid poems? I'd given my solemn vow, immutable proof of my love.

But Fortune, i.e. riches, in that I was secure. Though I'd never return to make our broth and clean our shoes and sweep our single room, I'd figure out a way to set up Father in a many-roomed apartment filled with shiny things where he could stay up all night talking with new friends who'd keep him from feeling lonely. If, from time to time, he was mourning my absence, he'd need only to take out the list of Three Achievables and gaze upon it and know that I was happy.

So I rose every morning and did my homework at the library and visited the scrounge line and went to class in the afternoons, cutting out early to rush across town to display my green bean prowess. After midnight, I'd return to the boardinghouse full of Cook's good food and with just enough money in my pocket to pay my weekly rent. Before sleep, I'd take out a photograph of Lisbet sitting on the grass at Honghe University with a book in her hands and her bangs like brush strokes inked across her eyes that left an inscrutable impression. I'd wish her good night and tell her that I was in San Francisco developing into a worldly fellow and that, any day now, as soon as I could, I'd write her the poems I'd promised. I didn't know her whereabouts nor she mine, but I did have the arrogance of youth—how I miss it!—to believe I'd see her again. In that, I was right, though in so much else I was wrong.

5.
Lisbet

W E MET ON A SPRING MORNING IN THE CENTER OF Gejiu the year before I left for Peach Blossom Land. Miss Chips was living in Mengzi, a city one hour away where there were lots of foreign students. She taught at Honghe University, named for the Red River Valley, and twice a week came to Gejiu, which she said reminded her of a European alpine town because of the way the city looked with a large lake in the middle against a backdrop of hills. Every other Saturday, she invited my friend Yu and me to tea, sometimes in Mengzi, often in Gejiu. Yu was number one in the class; I was second best. Miss Chips followed the usual practice of posting our scores after every quiz, essay, and test so that we could see who was studying hard and who was failing. Invariably, Yu topped the list, and I was a point or two behind her. Yu chose the western name Tulip, because the Chinese characters for *tulip* were close to her given name. But because we'd known each other since we were young schoolmates, I called her Yu and she called me Xue Li.

Yu and Cousin Deng had become sweethearts that spring when he spotted us together and asked me who she was. *What a beauty!* he'd exclaimed. He pointed out her classical features—a perfectly oval face, arched eyebrows, sparkling eyes, and graceful gestures. She wore her hair gathered in a neat, low bun. She might've been marked by the harelip she was born with, but an early surgery had corrected it. Only a trace of a scar remained. *Best of all,* he told me, *she speaks really good English. That'll come in handy for me someday. I owe you one, Cousin.* I was surprised that Cousin Deng already spoke of a future with Yu; there'd been a parade of girlfriends before her that was the envy of his friends and the pride of the aunties, who assured his mother—the richest of the relatives living at the *lao jia* and so the biggest auntie of all—that her son's popularity meant he'd have his pick of the crowd. But in Yu he found something special. Before and after class, I'd see them whispering to each other and laughing softly, just as Father and Mother had done. *Someday,* I thought, *I'll find that kind of love.*

"I'd like to introduce my niece, Lisbet," Miss Chips said. We were standing near the entrance to a public garden. A storm had blown through, stripping the trees around us, but gray clouds were vanishing into a widening blue.

"I'm very pleased to meet you," Yu said impeccably, earning her a Chipsian nod. I, on the other hand, received a stern look for my open-mouthed stare.

"We're waiting," my teacher said.

When Miss Chips told us that she was bringing to tea her niece from California, I'd pictured a blond in a bikini on a surfboard, a

run-of-the-wave image that nevertheless produced in me a hum-
mocky moment which I'd handled with aplomb under my covers that night. The girl smirking at me couldn't have been more
different. She stood slouched, one hand in her pocket, as if she
couldn't be bothered to employ it. Her hair was black, not blond,
and slashed into short, uneven layers. Her green-brown eyes, out-
lined in charcoal against her pallid face, looked like the shiny seeds
of a secret waxy fruit. The sharps of her swiveled eyeteeth mim-
icked the narrow point of her chin. She looked vampiric and she
knew it. She'd painted her mouth blood red.

"Nice to meet you," I managed, putting out my sweaty hand.
Yu giggled. It was obvious to everyone that a bewitchment was
taking place.

"Lisbet, like you, is a student. Her school didn't suit her, so I
proposed Honghe."

"And Bobby approved since my mother was going to kill me
for wrecking her car again," Lisbet said. Her accent was like a half-
ironed shirt: starched in the middle, collar and cuffs limp. America
had uncrisped her. She'd been raised in the house in Sussex where
Miss Chips had been born. Her mother now lived in Los Angeles
"where no one enunciates," Miss Chips said.

"Who's Bobby?" I blurted.

"Bobby is married to my mother," Lisbet said, amused. "Why,
were you going to fight him?"

"Darling girl," Miss Chips said. "Don't tease. Tulip and Shelley
are going to teach you Mandarin."

My dear old teacher couldn't have uttered sweeter words. My
wits gathered; my windpipe unknotted. The dialogue lines we'd
memorized flowed like the Honghe River.

"I'd be pleased to meet with you. Would you care to schedule
a date?"

"Are you asking me out?" laughed Lisbet.

"I suppose he is," Miss Chips said. "I encourage you to accept."

Lisbet was in a program on the university campus on Chinese language and culture. On the days Miss Chips came to teach in Gejiu, Lisbet accompanied her. She was thrilled to join us. She loved Mengzi. She thought Gejiu was brilliant. She liked her study program with the other international students, but best of all, she said, were the afternoons she spent with Yu and me. After our grammar lessons, Miss Chips sent the three of us off to practice our speaking skills.

"I'd like proper forms of speech from each of you," Miss Chips would say, giving us money for the teahouse. For the first hour, we were to speak only Mandarin; for the second hour, English. "Speak slowly enough to be understood and, above all, don't be tedious."

"Does the old lady pay you to sit and talk to the girl?" Cousin Deng grumbled. We were late meeting him for coffee. He didn't like that Yu had less time for whispering and kissing. *It's going well with Yu,* he'd told me. *Any day now, I'll be getting into her pants.* Though I'd listened to plenty of his girlfriend stories and contributed a few of my own, I asked him not to tell me about making it with Yu. She was like a sister to me.

"She's smart and knows a lot," Yu said. "She makes our lessons fun. She loves to travel. She wants to sail around the world."

"Drop the lessons," Deng said. "Your English is good enough."

"I want to go further," Yu said. "I want to work for a global company. Our teacher says I have a gift. She's promised to teach me French. Lisbet speaks it too."

"Nobody in America speaks French. When you and I marry"— Yu blushed—"we'll have a big family of girls as beautiful as you and move to L.A. and be famous."

"I'm not going to live abroad. My parents need me. Xue Li can go," Yu teased. "He's looking for adventure."

"Look at those circles under his eyes," Cousin Deng said. "He's in love with the girl. Too much"—he jacked his hand—"is keeping him up at night. Forget about her. Let Yu find you a willing Chinese girl, not that ugly ghost." Her pale flesh disturbed him. He compared it to fish belly.

"I think she's brilliant," Yu said, imitating Lisbet perfectly. The two of us cracked up.

Deng didn't like being left out of the joke. "You're a novelty to her. A cheap amusement. She wants the excitement of being fucked by a foreign guy, then she's going to run back to the white guy who's waiting for her at home."

"That's not true. We haven't even kissed." I didn't mind admitting it. I had no doubt of our future.

"Then what are you doing with her?"

"Talking," I said.

Underneath the table, Yu gave my hand a squeeze. I'd confided to her how much I liked spending time with Lisbet.

"That girl's going to play you," Cousin Deng warned. His concern for my happiness was touching. Yu was like my sister, and Cousin Deng was a brother.

WITH LISBET, EVERYTHING WAS different. Before her, I'd followed Deng's advice: proceed to bed with a girl—he meant a couch, an alley, an empty pedicab—or move on to another. I'd slept with a few—nothing like he had—but Lisbet was the first girl with whom I didn't rush. *To promenade*, Miss Chips said, *is to walk slowly with pleasure*. That's how I felt with Lisbet.

For weeks, we lingered in the teahouses, making up word games to test our vocabulary and try to make each other laugh. Yu no longer joined us; she was spending time with Deng. There were big gaps in our understanding that we filled with pantomime. Lisbet used her whole body to speak, leaping up from the stool to imitate one of her teachers or crowning her head with her hands. She was asking about a woman she'd seen wearing the white headdress of the Bai minority people. *I thought white was the color of mourning, but she looked so completely happy it made me want to cry.*

Our birthdays were a day apart. We discovered that, at age seven, we'd each been cleaved in half. Lisbet's father, younger brother to Miss Chips, had died the same year as my mother. Our memories poured out. My mother had liked rowing on the water; her father had built boats. My mother had wanted me to learn English; her father had sailed the world. When she spoke of him, her face glowed like *Jin Hu*, Golden Lake, the most beautiful spot in Gejiu. It had appeared during huge rains some sixty years ago and swallowed half the city.

We went to the night market, where I bought her boiled peanuts and crispy beetles on sticks. Unlike the foreign tourists, she didn't squeal with disgust when she tried them. She bought me a ball cap, "Houston Dolphins." She said it was a total fiction; no such team existed. *Don't buy into all that American dream crap. It isn't real.* But when I asked her which she liked better, England or America, she said, *The U.S. is the bomb. It's my mother I hate.*

She wanted to be a singer. She had a pliant voice that reminded me of Father's, suited to singing ballads. Instead, she belted out rock tunes that she wrote herself, saying rebels didn't croon. Her eyes, she taught me, were a color called *hazel*.

"My mother died on an iron-shoe night," I told her. "Not a body-on-fire night." The memory cut deep. She'd been sitting with her back to the wall, her eyes resting on Father as he spun her a tale from his day. At just the moment when the swift-footed heroine was about to outrun the greedy man who'd cheated her father, Mother put a hand to her mouth and gasped. Then she slumped over and died. "It wasn't supposed to happen in the middle of a story. Father wasn't prepared."

"My father was killed when a building crane collapsed." She pointed at a crane in the distance erecting modern Gejiu, raised her arms high, and slammed them on the table. "They had to scrape him off the sidewalk."

We both sat silent, picturing the bloody mess.

"That's why I'm here," said Lisbet.

As THE DAYS GREW longer, I took her to *Jin Hu*, where Father used to walk with Mother. Often there was music playing or a balladeer along the path where young couples strolled in shy romance. Birds flew between the trees and the air smelled of lake. Children ran to vendors, who sold sweets and drinks, or sat atop a father's shoulders to get a closer look at the tall figures with giant puppet heads who paraded past, bowing and waving. One day, as we walked in a lightly falling rain, we saw a young couple on a bench sharing an umbrella. The boy was reading aloud to the girl, and she looked up as we passed. I could see she was wondering if we, like they, were in love.

"What's he reading?" Lisbet asked. Books were her foundation. She especially liked Russian novels, the big, fat ones like my mother had read though of course in different translations. Father had kept Mother's books in a carton tied with string until we had to move and didn't bring the books with us. I couldn't recall the names of any of them, but when I told her that my mother had loved the same books as she did, Lisbet recited a long list of possibilities, the syllables flowing like strange-sounding music off her tongue.

"He's reading her a love poem," I said. I wished I'd brought an umbrella so that I could draw her close.

"Did you see her face?" Lisbet said. "She's *luminous.*"

I had to ask her what it meant. "I was kidding," I confessed. "He's reading to her from his chemistry book."

Lisbet elbowed me with a laugh. My heart flew open at the touch.

"My aunt read me poetry from the earliest I can remember," she said. "That's why I started writing songs. I've got those beats in my head."

"*I've* got beats in my head," I hastened. "I love poetry, same as you."

"Really? You never mentioned it before." Her smile was skeptical, but her face brightened.

Headless, heedless, I didn't hesitate. "Someday I'm going to be a poet."

"Oh! I'd love to hear your poems."

"Not now but maybe later. When I'm ready." I tried to look mysterious, but I liked her so much that honesty overtook me. "I haven't written any yet. I'm not sure how to begin."

"You should try. You're good with words, you know." Her lips seemed to glisten. My heart beat bravely, making the treetops swim. I saw the giant puppet heads bow in my direction, urging me to take a chance.

"How many poems shall I write to you?" I asked.

She laughed, and I was mortified that I'd said the wrong thing, but then she touched a fingertip to lift a raindrop from my lashes— she was bolder than me in love.

"Write three. Three splendid poems. One for your mother, one for your father, and one for me."

"All for you," I declared.

ON LISBET'S EIGHTEENTH BIRTHDAY, the day after mine, I picked her up at the station and we went straight to the park. She wore a new dress of slithery green fabric. I bought us sweet cakes and water and spread a plastic bag on the sooty bench, though I knew she liked being careless, even in a pretty dress, and wouldn't mind a little dust. She sat down and stretched her milky legs in the June sun. I perched on the bench beside her. I had something big to ask and was almost afraid to speak. I told her that Father and I had talked the whole night long, he soaked in tears and whiskey, I in my mother's love, about my leaving for San Francisco. I'd be the first Zheng in sixty-five years to leave Yunnan.

"Don't tell me this," Lisbet protested. "I like you in Gejiu."

"My family is no good, and I can't make any money. I have an uncle in the U.S. who's very rich. I'm going to live with him." I sketched San Francisco in the air, the hills and the famous bridge. "Clang, clang," I rang for her, a cable car climbing.

"You're talking like the students at Honghe, the ones born here who want to leave China. Meanwhile, the international students want to come here and work. They all sound the same, thinking there's someplace better."

She'd seen the world, or more of it than I had. Didn't she want the same for me?

"Don't compare yourself to me!" she said with a grimace. Her nose was turning pink in the sun. Her eyes looked very green that day; perhaps it was the dress. "I've tried to tell you, I'm a horrible mess. You know that, don't you?"

"Father wants me to go. He knows it's best for me."

"Like my mother. She can't wait to get rid of me, then she misses me and begs me to come home. I go running back but I never last long." She turned away and uncapped her water bottle. After a long motionless second, she sipped.

"It's not like that with Father. He wants what Mother wanted for me: to learn English and become a big success."

"I'm sad, that's all," Lisbet said, turning back. "I've been happy here. This place feels more real to me than anywhere I've lived."

My hopes jumped for the treetops. Sure, Gejiu was Tin Capital of the World and Alpine-like as a picture, but I knew what she was really trying to tell me. It was love, not tin, that turned the ground solid beneath her restless feet.

"When I leave—"

"Oh, don't talk about that, Xue Li. Not today."

"Will you come with me?"

She buckled halfway over as if I'd landed a punch. Spilled water streamed about our feet. I bent to help her, frightened, but she pushed my hands away. When she finally straightened, bottle crunched in one hand, the other gripping the bench, her nose shone garishly pink in her blanched face.

"I can't. I'm sorry. I can't make those kinds of plans. I wish I could, but I can't."

My lips felt thick as thumbs. I swallowed half my throat. I wished to run to the lake, dive in, and sink to the bottom.

"I'm sorry," Lisbet said. "I'm really going to miss you."

We sat in silence, the sun beating down. Later, when we left the park, she took my arm and kissed me.

THE NEXT TIME WE met, her dark mood had vanished. She seemed buoyant, as if I'd never upset her, and my hopes rose again that she'd come with me. In the days that followed, we saw each other often, always parting with a kiss. When I wasn't with Lisbet, I took care of Father and handled jobs for Cousin Deng. He knew he could count on me to do whatever he asked, and it put a few jiao in my pocket. *You spend more time with her than you spend with your father. Somebody's got to pay for all those sweets and tea.*

On a fine July day, I went to see her in Mengzi, head up and hopeful. By then I'd convinced myself that we couldn't live without each other, and I was planning to ask again for her pledge. My bus arrived late; Lisbet wasn't waiting. I walked up and down, searching, until I thought to go look for her on campus. She lay like a downed kite, arms flung wide, on a patch of grass in the shade. She felt dizzy in the heat, she said, and had to rest. She knew I'd find her.

"Most guys go running around in circles. You go straight to what you want. I love that about you."

I lay down beside her, thinking that perhaps today our kisses would lead to more. She draped an arm over her eyes. She was wearing a white blouse, long blue cotton skirt, and red embroidered slippers she'd bought in the tourist market. She drew her knees under her skirt but stayed where she was, eyes hidden. Couples strolled by giving us curious looks. I half expected a college worker to come out and scold us for lying on the grass. I'd chase him off if I had to, but Lisbet was a foreign student and could do as she liked. Sweat along her hairline and at the part in her hair gleamed through the black. She smelled of grass; I smelled like diesel fuel. I'd scrubbed my face and hands after leaving the station, but the stink stayed in my clothes the way it clung to Father.

"I have this feeling that there's some other life I've missed," she said.

That was my feeling too! Our futures awaited, intertwined.

"I know. The future. You talk about it a lot." She spoke into the distance, as if she'd sent her thoughts away and was reluctant to recall them from their travels. "Is it possible that this other life, this other existence is behind me? Not in front of me, like yours, but behind? Like I accidentally veered away from what I should be doing."

"It's sad that your father died."

"No, that's not what I mean. There's nothing to be done about that." She uncovered her eyes but stayed pinned in place, peering straight up into the trees. I'd seen melancholy settle on her before but not like this, like a pall above us, blotting out the light. Her lassitude alarmed me. I wondered if she was ill.

"Nothing feels right to me," she said. "I don't know where I am. I don't know what country I belong to, or who my family is."

"Your family is Miss Chips!"

"Not really. I wanted to think so, but it's not working out that way. She's been really sweet to me, but I can't be what she needs. That little bit of home that she's missing."

"You have to make the choice to be happy." So Miss Chips had told us, and she was right. Father had chosen to live inside his sadness. I wasn't going to stay there with him.

"I'm glad you think so. That means you'll be okay." She sat up slowly. "I'm leaving," she said. "The term's over and my program is finished. My mother wants me home, but I don't want to see her. Bobby keeps calling, but I don't want to talk. I've got to go quickly; I'm leaving at the end of the week. I have some money of my own, enough to get me to Bangkok. From there, I'll decide where to go."

Before she was through, I was shouting. "How can you leave without warning? I'm not a souvenir like those shoes you're wearing. You can't just throw me away."

"I'm sorry," she said, "I'm sorry," but she made no promise about when we'd meet again. She tried to say goodbye; I refused her final kiss. Deng had been right. She was as white as fish belly, but I was the one who was gutted.

6.

Lunar New Year

A MONTH INTO THE SEMESTER, I STOPPED BY THE Program Office and saw a note with my name pinned to the bulletin board. Ted had telephoned looking for me. I didn't have a mobile phone and had given him the office number in case he and Aviva came to their senses, remembered their duty, unlocked the bedroom door, and begged me to move in. Ted's message was second best. He invited me to join them for a Lunar New Year lunch.

Their street was awfully empty for eight o'clock on a Sunday morning. Gejiu would've been teeming, the celebration lasting for days, but all was quiet at Ted and Aviva's house. I paused, happy to be back where I belonged. Between my restaurant job and third-class sleep, I was plain exhausted. I knelt on the ground, seized with sudden emotion, and touched my fingertips to the pavement. I felt my eyes moisten. Four weeks at Mrs. Yap's boardinghouse made Ted and Aviva's home seem like a luxury mansion. What a callow youth I'd been last month, looking down my nose at the meanness of their abode. When I'd first arrived on their doorstep and seen block after block of saltboxes set like stumpy teeth in a narrow jaw, every last house appeared identical to me, but now I saw that each showed off its particular distinctions: the orange trim on Ted and Aviva's windows, an arched entry on the house to the right, and across the street, an odd bit of roof covered in Spanish tiles and a balcony twinkling with lights. The house to the left had a curved picture window and the stairs on the opposite side. I saw a figure through the glass, the neighbor I'd seen marching; he was passing through the room, talking to a younger man who stood in the window. The younger man was pointing to the street. I hoped he hadn't witnessed me with my knee to the pavement, wiping my eyes on my sleeve.

Ted's bagged newspapers lay askew on the walk. He had three delivered daily and read them front to back. "Old habits die hard," he'd told me, "especially when there's nothing to replace them." I gathered them up, climbed the steps, and rang the bell. Five minutes passed. I rang the bell again. I went halfway down the steps and peered up at the living room windows. Aviva's face appeared and her mouth dropped open. Footsteps sounded; the front door cracked.

"What the fuck," Aviva said.

ONCE TED LET ME in and Aviva left the room to brush her teeth and take a shower, I was able to relax. They weren't expecting me quite so early, Ted said, but he was glad to see me because he'd been anxious to know how I was faring. I took this to mean that he wanted his transit pass back. I'd been using it all over town to pay my Muni bus fares. The card worked like magic because Ted was paying the bill.

"You keep it," Ted said, glancing over his shoulder. "Just don't mention it to Aviva. She might . . . misunderstand. She wants to help but she's not down with the details."

I repocketed the card, thankful once again for the Chinese groove. Though he wasn't a countryman per se, Ted knew the art of Oriental silence, that language of the exquisitely unexpressed. Aviva returned, wearing a strained smile. I presented the gifts I'd brought—a big net bag of oranges, and cookies I'd purchased on a busy street from little girls in green dresses who'd demanded that I buy at least a dozen boxes or they'd be standing the whole day in the cold. Shocked at their plight, I'd spent my last dollar. Half the cookies went to the scrounge line, where they were quickly devoured, and I'd given a box to Cook, who'd tasted one and fed the rest to the pigeons. It occurred to me that the smiling girls pictured on the boxes didn't look anything like those shivering peddler kids in their ugly green dresses. No, those smiling girls were like Auntie Aviva, who was acting happy when she wasn't. I bustled to cheer her up, pulling out a pan to make her sunny-side up eggs, exactly as she liked them, and setting up the coffee. My cooking skills had gotten even better since starting my restaurant job, and no San Franciscan stayed grumpy for long when handed a perfect pour-over.

She sipped the coffee and sighed. "I'll be human again in a minute. Thank you, Shelley. This looks amazing."

"I've been practicing," I said.

"Your English too," Aviva said. "I understand you better. How's school going?"

I told her school was going great. I'd made a friend named

Eddie Low, a business major who loved to write; he was helping me with my studies. I thought it best not to mention that my attendance record had its gaps since I cut the last hour of class every day to get to my job on time.

"So you found a place to live?" Ted said.

I was reluctant to divulge. The very nice shirts he'd given me had been stolen at the boardinghouse, also my new trainers—I was wearing some castoffs I'd found by the restaurant bins. I'd taken the pink sparkly suitcase with most of my clothes to Eddie's so it wouldn't disappear too. Bit by bit, I'd spent the emergency money. Everything I earned went to food and rent. But I didn't want to admit I was struggling to keep myself afloat. I'd already learned that their pity had a limit, which was exactly two weeks.

"It's a beautiful day," Aviva interrupted, deftly sparing me, and herself, from embarrassing truths about my living situation. "Let's enjoy the gorgeous sunshine." We trooped outside. The bouncy castle was gone, but the tree near the back fence was full of pink blossom. I glanced at the window of the locked bedroom and saw for the first time that the curtains were open. I wished I could fly up and peer in. I wanted desperately to know what was in that room.

"Our poor plum tree is confused," Aviva said. "It's been so warm it thinks it's spring already." She raised her arms to the sun. She wore wide-legged pants and a loose silk jacket with red and gold designs. Flippered fish or feathered birds. Something she saw as exotic in honor of Year of the Ram.

"It blooms in February every year," Ted said, "and every year, you chalk it up to confusion."

"This awful drought! At the library the other day, my coworker referred to 'the rainy season,' and it sounded positively mythical.

Well, we've done it to ourselves. And China is making things worse.

"Ah," Ted said. "The problem is China."

"You know what I mean. I'm not a China hater. Look who I married!"

"An American," Ted remarked.

"I'm not *blaming* China. I'm just saying they've got to do better. We *all* do, if we want to save the planet from cooking itself to death. Anyway, Shelley doesn't mind, do you? You don't take umbrage."

I whipped out my little black notebook, the one Miss Chips had required us to carry at all times. *Your repository of remarks, your inventory of invention. A logorrhea log for recording new delights.* I passed it silently to Ted. Equally smoothly, he extracted his pen from his pocket. From our first day together, he'd been drawing pictures in my book. He wrote the word *umbrage*, illustrating it with a cartoon of a googly-eyed bridge rearing back in offense at a boy raising a middle finger. In his doleful way, Ted liked to include a joke. He'd even taken it upon himself to make sure I knew my way around the gutter. Hence, words like *rubber* and *pussy*, their vernacular meanings displayed. Miss Chips would've laughed good and hard, especially at those illustrations that proved useful when I studied my notebook in my lonely bed at night.

Aviva announced that she needed her phone; Kate was going to call about meeting us at the restaurant. Thinking of the locked room, I volunteered to look for her phone in the house, but Aviva narrowed her eyes at me and sent Ted to fetch it along with her sunglasses.

"I miss the rain," she carried on, keeping me by her side. "I grew up in Ohio. We had thunderstorms and lightning that split the sky open. We lived in the suburbs and you didn't have to go far to hit farmland. Daniel and I—that's my little brother—we used to ride our bikes past the edge of town. It was always exciting to get caught in a downpour. We'd pedal home, yelling our lungs out. You felt alive. That's the part I miss."

Ted returned with her phone and glasses and a newspaper for himself. She put on her shades, which turned her bee-eyed and scary. He left again and came back with low chairs for us to sit on, placing mine nearest Aviva's. Newspaper open, he retreated into silence.

Aviva wanted to know, what was the air like in China? Was the pollution as awful as everyone said? "It depends on where you live," I said, which was obvious, though you'd be surprised at how often Americans had to be told. "My province, Yunnan, is the most beautiful."

"Huh," Aviva said. "I don't remember that. Crowds, yes. There were so many people I could hardly walk."

It was beautiful, I assured her. Kunming, our capital, was the City of Eternal Spring.

"That's where your father was born, right?" she asked Ted. I leaned forward, eager to hear, but he didn't look up from his paper. She aimed her glasses and beetled at him, and still he didn't flinch. She couldn't make him talk about his father, Henry, at least not while I was present. That was another kind of locked door.

After a second, Aviva returned to happy family stories. Her brother was bigger, taller, and stronger than she was but did every-thing she told him.

"Like the rest of us," Ted remarked, rustling his paper. He was listening all right, the bleb on his ear as good as an antenna.

"He still lives in Columbus," Aviva said. "He was smart to stay. He and his wife and their two girls have a five-bedroom house and a huge yard with a gazebo. He helped my parents before they passed." She sighed. "Sometimes I wish I'd never left."

"But you did," Ted said, coming out from behind the paper.

"I did," Aviva said, resolutely. "There's no gazebo here, but we can always rent a castle. If nothing else, I've taught Shelley how to bounce."

"Something tells me that Shelley was pretty good at that already. Where'd you say you were living?"

"Leave him alone, Ted. Spare him the interrogation. He can't help it," she said to me. "He always wants to be interviewing someone."

"You do have housing, don't you?" Ted persisted. "You found a suitable place?"

"A group house; it's great. The rent is low, and everyone is friendly. A guy I work with found it for me."

Ted frowned. "But you're not working, right? Because you're not allowed to work on a student visa."

"Only for pocket money. It's more like helping than work."

"Oh, well, that's all right," Aviva said.

"I won't need the job for long," I added. "I plan to become a poet."

Ted looked amused. "How is that going to help? Poets are poorer than I am."

"Are you sure?" I asked, thinking of Cousin Deng's avowal that creatives in the U.S. were highly valued, same as financiers and basketball players.

"Believe me," Ted said. "When poets make money, pigs will fly."

"Oh," I said dumbly. I'd been hoping I could switch soon from kitchen crew to poet. Like the shower hose at Mrs. Yap's billet, Ted doused me cold.

"Are you okay?" Aviva asked, seeing my chagrin.

"Too many excellent cookies!"

I excused myself to use the bathroom and spied to my recovered delight that the door to the locked bedroom was open a full inch. I crept down the hallway, held my breath, and opened the door wider, taking care not to step inside lest I be spotted through the window. I saw a single bed and a large pinned-up flag that said "California Republic" under a big brown bear. There were framed photographs on the bedside table—not scattered throughout the house as might be expected, but in sanctified, private display. A fish tank stood against the wall, the blue and orange fish inside darting about in a frenzy. Everything else about the room looked frozen. The fish tank filter made a guttural noise, source of that humming sound I'd earlier heard through the door.

"It was Eli's room," Aviva said. I turned around, abashed. Was she going to throw me out?

"Go ahead," she said, motioning. I hesitated. She stepped in and invited me to follow, and, cautiously, I entered. I noticed drawings tacked to the wall, which she told me Eli had made. "He always had a pen in his hand, just like his father." She picked up a sketchbook and showed me a page filled with pictures. *Eli Cheng*, the cover said in big black letters. All I remembered from meeting him in Kunming on my thirteenth birthday was that he was a quiet kid with his nose stuck in a book.

"We keep this room for ourselves," Aviva said. "I'm sure you understand." She sat down at the foot of the bed and smoothed its checkered spread. "When we first lost him, Ted would come in here to sleep. Can you imagine? Tall Ted, scrunching himself into this little bed?"

I didn't know what to say, so I sat down at the other end of the bed and quickly stood back up because it seemed disrespectful to sit on a dead boy's bed with my big-knuckled hand on his pillow.

"It's okay. You can sit," Aviva said. I remained standing. She brushed her hand on the blanket. Her strange quietude, so different from her usual state, prompted me to wonder. This might be my chance to ask the big question burning in my throat.

"What happened to them?" I said.

"There was a robbery." She spoke calmly. She and Ted had gone out for dinner with friends. Eli was with Ted's mother at the store. It was a Thursday night, almost closing time. They'd let Eli stay up late as a special treat because he loved working at the store with his grandmother. "That's her. Diana." She pointed to a drawing on the wall of a woman in an apron holding up an apple. "Two men came in with a gun. For some reason, nobody knows why, they used it. Eli died first, in the ambulance, and Diana at the hospital. By the time we got there, she was gone."

I swayed and knocked into the bedside table. One of the photographs fell to the floor with a crash.

"Oh! I'm sorry; I'm really sorry," I said.

Aviva stood and picked it up and looked at me with pity. "It's a shocking story, I know. I've never found a good way to tell it."

We looked at the photo. It was Eli and Diana standing in front of a window under a big red sign with white letters. "I see my father in him, and Diana too," she said. She put it back on the table—everything in the room had its special place—and showed me a couple of comic books that Eli had made, six panels to a page and the pages stapled together. He'd drawn little armies of orange fish and blue fish like the ones that swam in his tank.

"The fish were for me, actually. It was a gift from Ted. He set up the tank for me when Eli was born so I'd have something to watch in the middle of the night when I got up with the baby." She shook a few flakes into the water and we watched the fish surge. "I've replaced them ever since. I carry out the dead ones and carry in the new and we don't talk about it."

We went into the hallway and Aviva closed the door behind us.

"I can think of a hundred other ways we could use this room, but as long as he's not ready, I'm willing to wait," she said.

"I'm sorry they died." I was anxious to be out of there before Ted came into the house.

"Don't worry," Aviva said. "He probably knows we're in here talking. He'll be relieved that I told you so he won't have to tell you himself."

I WASHED THE BREAKFAST dishes and swept the kitchen floor. Kate called; they were leaving for the restaurant, Leo's favorite, on Geary.

"Wait. I forgot." Aviva left the room and returned brandishing a red envelope and her wallet. "How much should I give him?" *Ahh*, I thought and got my smile ready. *The good Chinese wife knows her New Year's customs.*

"Five bucks sounds right for a little kid," Ted said.

Five bucks went into the envelope, sealed up for Leo.

KATE WAS WAITING FOR us outside, hugging herself for warmth. She was taller and slighter than Aviva with long hair that blew around her face. She, too, was dressed for the occasion in a red blouse, black skirt, and silver chain. She teased Ted for wearing his same old button-down shirt; hadn't he bought new clothes or gotten his New Year's haircut? Inside, Leo was throwing plastic straws and Orit was unwrapping him another. They looked a matched set, small and sturdy, a pair of circus ponies, confident in their maneuvers. He was four, Aviva told me, turning five this summer. Between the two mothers, Leo looked more like Orit, though his hair was darker and straighter than hers and his eyes were more like Kate's. When he spotted us, he ducked his head, refusing to say hello. Kate bent to them both and kissed Orit, and this time, I didn't stare. Aviva had told me that Kate and Orit were married at city hall in San Francisco under special circumstances, and now the rules were being tested. They all hoped that someday equal rights to marry would become the law of the land.

Ted handed a menu to Kate. "You choose for us."

Kate protested, they should choose together, but the others insisted that Kate take charge. She spoke to the waiter, and I was impressed because her Cantonese wasn't half bad. She told me that she'd learned to speak it from her grandparents who'd emigrated from Toisan. For me, it was a side dish language—nice to sample but not the main meat. Kate was Chinese. I forgot to earlier mention. She was ABC, born in Los Angeles to second-generation Chinese American parents who'd grown up in Chinatown. I'm sorry if I confused you. Take all the time you need to make the necessary adjustment. Believe me when I say that I didn't neglect to tell you out of teasing or spite. When someone is telling *me* a story, I naturally assume that the people in it are the same race as I am, for isn't it human nature to imagine the story and picture like kind? Please forgive my clumsiness, also my starting and stopping. I'm not like Father, who used to tell his stories as smoothly as oil spreads in a pan, though Father wasn't burdened with making these fine distinctions because everyone he described was a countryman start to finish. It's awkward to have to stop and pinpoint: this person is such-and-such, that person is fill-in-the-blank, but that's the world we live in. You can't avoid labels. By the way, Orit was white and, like Aviva, Jewish. You might've guessed from her name. Orit Hazan, Kate Choy, Leo Choy Hazan. Jews, I noticed, sometimes held themselves apart. They knew what it was like to be treated as different. Orit grew up in Israel, which was another thing altogether. Have I left anyone out? Ted was Christian, I think. He didn't go to church, but his mother had. Leo was mixed-race; Orit was his mother and younger than Kate. His father was Chinese—an unknown Chinese stranger. Imagine the auntie discussion that fact would've provoked! In Orit's word, *Talmudic.*

Lunch arrived, a seafood extravaganza. I dove in, glad to be shed of the sadness locked away in Eli's room. There was rich soup with crabmeat and scallops, clams in bean sauce, a whole fish steamed with scallions. Sea cucumber for Kate and me; nobody else would touch it. Leo dropped his chopsticks; I got him a clean pair. He worked them as well as any countryman's kid.

"How's your father?" Kate asked Ted. "I was hoping he'd join us."

"Ted wouldn't let me invite him," Aviva said. "They're not talking."

"Oh, no," Kate said.

"Henry asked Huntington to find Ted a job and Ted got furious. They haven't spoken since."

"Your father gave you a house and now he's handing out your resume?" Orit said. "Are you sure he isn't Jewish?"

"Ha," Aviva said. "I *wish* he'd given us the house. We overpaid him for it."

"Worst mistake of my life was buying that house," Ted said.

"Yeah, I feel sorry for you," Orit jibed. "Since it's worth a million bucks."

"Henry shouldn't have talked to Huntington without asking you first," Kate said. "I'm really sorry he did that."

Ted looked grateful. "You know what he's like. He won't stop pushing."

"But now that Henry's gone and done it," Aviva said, "why not call Huntington? See what he has to offer."

"Can we just shut up about it?" Ted snapped.

"For two years, my father didn't talk to my brother," Orit said. "I'm convinced they made up so they could go back to yelling at each other. I'm glad Leo's father is out of the picture. It makes life a lot easier."

"I almost agree with that outrageous statement," Aviva said. Orit looked pleased.

Leo decided that he liked the chopstick game. He dropped his pair to the floor again, ran to me, and tugged on my sleeve to ask me to get him another. Kate zipped over and returned him to his chair.

"I'll visit Henry on my own," Kate said.

"Kate is Henry's *favorite*," Aviva informed me. "He wanted Ted to marry her. Please, Kate, make Ted and his father sit down together. You're the only one they listen to."

Kate laughed. I think it was a laugh. Maybe the clams in bean sauce had thickened in her throat. "My mom was the same with Ted. Whenever he came to visit, she'd give him my brother's bedroom and make Stu sleep on the sofa."

"She always insisted the guest should be given—"

"—the most comfortable bed in the house." Kate and Ted exchanged a smile. I wanted Aviva to take note of the bed-versus-sofa point, but she was looking bored, as though she'd heard it all before.

"This was back in college," Kate told me. "I spent so much time at Henry and Diana's, I practically moved in."

"Then his father learned you were queer, and that puts an end to this story." Orit stuck her arm across the back of Kate's chair.

"Not quite," Kate said, annoyed. She sounded protective of Henry.

"Who told Henry? You or Ted?" Orit asked. She was smiling, but there was auntie in her aspect, a sharp, inquiring note.

"My mother," Ted said. "She'd wondered all along."

"Really?" Kate said. "You never told me that." She laughed more freely. "God bless Diana. I really miss her. She was the only Chinese person I knew who could say the word *lesbian* out loud."

"My mother made a big effort to understand people," Ted said. "She would meet you on your terms. My father's incapable of that."

"He's just trying to be helpful," Kate said. "He wants to be of use."

Aviva scoffed. "The last thing Ted wants is help from anybody. Especially from Henry." She boxed up the rest of the food and pushed back from the table. "I'm taking the leftovers to Henry. You don't have to talk to him. I'll do it."

Leo had had enough. He slid from his chair and started running between the tables. A waiter tilted around him, dishes sliding on his tray. Kate moved fast, but I moved faster; any waiter on the move was my brother-in-arms. I grabbed the kid, expecting him to shriek, but he caught hold of my shirt and laughed. I brought him outside to wait for the others. Facing me, he grasped both my hands, climbed my legs, and flipped himself over so he was hanging upside down. When I set him right side up, he looked proud. He did the trick over and over, not saying a word, until Kate and Orit took him home.

In stony silence, Ted drove Aviva and me back to the house.

"Are you not going to talk to me?" Aviva said.

"Did you have to bring up Huntington? Can't you keep anything quiet?" Ted said.

"Let's not do this in front of Shelley. No offense," she added.

None taken. A sponger couldn't afford.

A silver Lexus was parked in front, and a man waved from the curb.

"Speak of the devil. Huntington's here," Aviva said. She greeted him warmly and went into the house. Ted introduced me to his friend and said they'd grown up together.

"On this very street," Huntington said. He punched Ted's shoulder. He was elegantly attired and slim as a cigarette. "I have to live here, but you don't. When are you going to move?"

"Huntington's a city supervisor," Ted said. "He represents our district."

"That I do," Huntington said. "Home ground. District Four, the Sunset, also known as the Outerlands. But you can live anywhere. Get yourself out of this gloomy fog. Go where things are happening. Where the excitement is."

"We can't afford it," Ted said.

"That's what I've come to talk to you about."

Aviva reappeared and said she was going to Henry's. I offered to go with her and started back toward the car, but she stopped me.

"I'm sure you have things to do. We've kept you long enough."

I shuffled my feet, *Could you please keep me longer?* But she was in a hurry. She told me where to catch the bus, forgetting I'd taken it to get to her door that morning. I glanced back to wave my thanks and saw the neighbor in his window, witness to my dismissal.

I returned to the boardinghouse, where a fistfight was brewing, two guys yelling loudly over a box of meat. I waited till others muscled them outside, then I went to my bunk and got ready to go to work. I didn't dare lie down in case I fell asleep. The day had begun with me kneeling on the sidewalk in front of Ted and Aviva's house, but I'd recovered and stood tall and shown them what I was made of. Only the neighbor man had witnessed how humbly I'd bowed my head.

The neighbor man. Who was opening the door to Aviva, her arm extended straight out in front like a cookie-box girl on the make. The bag of restaurant cartons dangled from her hand, and the neighbor man had dipped his chin like a dog about to drink.

The neighbor man.

Henry.

7.
Nature

I'D BEEN SLOW TO NOTICE WHAT WAS RIGHT UNDER my nose because the truth of the matter was hidden in plain sight: father and son lived side by side, Henry in the saltbox, Ted in the saltbox stretch. All this I said to Eddie in a fervent state.

"Dude," Eddie said. "Idiom overload."

"I'm killing two birds with one stone." My teacher, Professor Luo, had informed us that the midterm would include a list of common figures of speech, none of which Miss Chips considered Essential Locutions.

"I'll take you to meet my grandma," Eddie said. "You can ask her about Henry. She knows all the gossip."

Grandma's gossip would have to wait because, back at the boardinghouse, I was sent packing. The landlady's agent had given away my bunk to a countryman who promised him 18 percent more rent plus plush toys and kitchen parts that fell off the truck he drove, and so once again I found myself with no place to live. I hurried to the bus, late for green bean service. Cook didn't berate me. Didn't threaten me with the cleaver or heap insults on my head. When I tried to explain, he shuffled mournfully to the cooktop.

"Hey man, I'm sorry," I repeated to Cook's back. The job was the only thing holding me back from disaster. Cook drew a rag across the backsplash, erasing a speck of oil. The lunch crew had cleaned it, but Cook liked a spotless kitchen. "I'll stay late tonight, clean extra well. Whatever you need, I got it."

Feeling uneasy over Cook's moping mood, I pulled on a baseball cap, *Cache Creek Casino*, and donned a white apron. The owner had handed out a whole stack of the caps after a run of luck at the tables. He gave Cook a shiny key chain that bore the lucky number 888 and had a nifty attachment that could butcher a pig, snap a selfie, or stir a lady's drink. Cook kept it in his pocket. When he wasn't cooking, you could see his knuckles working inside the pocket to coax good luck out of the golden whorls.

The owner's son-in-law came in, and the waiters scooted out the swinging door. He was a pudgy chap who was always running a ChapStick round his scaly mouth, his lips turned lizardly by bouts of nervous licking. He swayed on feet he kept too close together for him to be dangerous. Whatever scolding he had in store for me wouldn't involve blows. Even if he hadn't been wearing a suit and tie, I would've pegged him for an amateur by the state of his febrile hands. There wasn't a nick or burn on them.

"Mr. Zheng," he called to me. He looked like the teacher's favorite who has to tell the other kids to line up and be quiet when all he really wants is for the biggest kid to slap him five and invite him to kick the ball.

I went right over. There was no point in running away. There was a steaming pile of ox squat in the road and I had to tread through it, but the road was a road, taking me somewhere better. Of that I was certain.

"Sorry, but I need that apron. The cap too," he said.

I reassured him that wasn't necessary. I'd be on time tomorrow; in fact, I swore up and down that I'd never be late again.

"Come on," he said. His whole head was sweating. "Give me the cap and the apron. Mr. Song"—that was the owner—"Mr. Song is letting you go."

A preposterous declaration. All I could do was laugh.

"I'm not kidding." His face turned bright red. "I'm under boss's orders."

His words didn't land, but his seared cheeks checked me. The laugh died in my throat.

"Mr. Song can't afford to keep you. He lost money at the casino and has to cut expenses. I'm speaking on his behalf. On behalf of Mr. Song. I mean, sorry to have to, you know. Given the situation. The newest goes first. Do you know what I'm telling you? You're fired."

I was used to getting thumped—the Gejiu cousins—but this was a kick to the kidneys.

"Don't fire me!" I pleaded. "I'm a poor student. I need this job badly. You don't want me living on the street, do you? I'm loyal, hardworking—ask anyone. They'll tell you."

A fit of furious lip-licking took hold of my dethroner. His soft hands flapped like butterflies that knew that, by nightfall, they'd be dust. I thought of how, when I was young, I hated seeing Father bow his head and shrink himself smaller to ask for a meal or credit. After Mother died, Father lost his job as chief engineer at the bus depot because he couldn't get out of bed. Eventually, his boss took pity and let him clean the buses of piss and shit and vomit, and then it was all Father could do to try to keep us housed and fed. Now, watching the son-in-law squirm before my protestations, I understood why I hid myself when Father groveled: desperation shames both wheedler and wheedlee. But that didn't stop Father from begging, which was the other lesson he taught me. A high squirm factor meant it was time to press my advantage.

"Who's going to help Cook?" I demanded. "He can't work his magic alone. He needs a right-hand man. Go on, ask him—I'm the best on the planet." Cook had his back to me; I saw his shoulders twitch. I waited for him to step forward and insist on my behalf— all those drinks I'd bought him with Ted's emergency money—but though he rattled his pans noisily, Cook didn't come to my rescue.

The son-in-law sighed. His brow furrowed.

"Me," he said sadly. "I'm the new green bean man. The employment agency where I worked got sold, and I haven't been able to find a new job. So I have to fire you and take over your duties. I come cheap. Basically, for free."

Poor bastard. We all knew that he and his wife had been removed from their apartment by a lawyered-up landlord who had developers circling, their tongues hanging out to get their crews in the building so he could raise the rents. With nowhere else to go, they'd moved in with her parents, upstairs from what used to be a laundromat but was now occupied by a coffee craftsman who sold his blond roast for twenty-two dollars a pound. The smell of roasting beans made the son-in-law nauseous. Mr. Song ridiculed him, saying that his son-in-law threw up his breakfast every morning just like Mr. Song's daughter, who was expecting a baby boy. I hoped the kid liked green beans and coffee.

Feeling sorry for the guy, I tutored him in topping and tailing, adjusted his cap, and tied on his apron, trying to raise his confidence for his big night ahead, but I couldn't bring myself to watch from the other side of the glass. I waited for Cook in the alley, smoking a cigarette the dishwasher gave me and drinking a beer from the cooler. After last service, we went down the street and this time Cook bought the drinks, one after another.

"Lost your job, lost your bed," Cook said forlornly. Tears splash-washed the whalehead toes of his Crocs. "What will you do for money? Where will you go for a home?"

I had no answer. I downed another drink. I couldn't go back to Eddie's. His roommates objected to stepping over me every morning on their way to the K-Cup coffee. They didn't want a fifth roommate, especially one who was broke.

"Why doesn't that uncle of yours give you a place to stay? He has a family duty! He's turning his back on his own."

"They have an extra bedroom, but it's occupied by sadness. It used to be their son's. He died, aged nine. Now it's no one's."

"The dead shouldn't rule the living," Cook grumbled. "Why get up in the morning? Why fuck, why piss, why eat?"

"When Mother died, Father curled up like a caterpillar. He didn't speak for weeks. He would've given up altogether, but he had me to raise." How he'd cried! It'd been up to me, seven years old, to make him wash and eat. Eventually, he started talking again, but the little stories had stopped.

"He raised you, you raised him," Cook said. "The living do for the living."

"Have you ever lost anyone?"

Cook gave me a pitying look. "Don't you know where genius comes from? Suffering. It's the only path to art."

Cook tried to hand me a palmful of wrinkled bills when we parted. I refused them. He insisted. Back and forth the money went along the Chinese groove.

"You're a good boy," he said, more tears rolling. "Go home to your father. A father misses his son."

I tried not to picture Father's sad face. Truth be told, flight had brought me freedom. Freedom from the aunties, freedom from Father. A feeling of relief that I'd left his failures behind.

Cook wiped his face on his sleeve. By morning, we'd be strangers, but he'd been a king of kindness. I grabbed him under the armpits and staggered him to a bench where he could sleep until morning. He tried again to hand me money. I accepted one bill, the minimum groove requirement for Cook to have a peaceful night. I draped his jacket over him and helped him tuck the rest of the cash back into his pocket, the very pocket where he kept his key chain with the storeroom key hanging. I closed my fingers around his triple eights, removed the key, and hied off to the storeroom, where I slept for the next three nights, my head on a sack of rice, until Mr. Song discovered me and threw me out with a curse.

THE 44 O'SHAUGHNESSY BUS wouldn't roll until morning, so I shouldered my backpack and set out on foot for Golden Gate Park. At least I had Eddie's sleeping bag strapped to my pack. He felt bad that he couldn't house me, but I assured him, while rallying myself, that I was good at bouncing. Eddie's girlfriend, Paloma Sze (Chinese American; might as well spell it out), offered to let me sleep in her Mini Cooper like various neighbors living in their cars, but no way could I hinge myself into thirds. Besides, she needed it at unpredictable hours since in between her classes and internship and working on the app with Eddie, she drove for Uber and Lyft.

I walked with solid steps, trying to stay warm in the predawn dark. Mission Street was quiet, the bars and restaurants closed for the night, and the shop windows pinioned behind metal grates. I saw two burned apartment buildings that had been in the news, their rent-controlled apartments destroyed and the residents gone from San Francisco. The signs above the stores were written in Chinese, Spanish, Japanese, Korean, and a bunch of alphabets I didn't know. To cheer myself up, I debated which language I should study next. Spanish would be helpful, now that I'd become an *hombre de California*, and after that, Russian? Arabic? Portuguese? Lisbet had told me that Portugal had beautiful seaside towns. I pictured her standing against an azure sea. I often searched her name using the school computers, though I knew I wouldn't find her until she came looking for me. She didn't post and she didn't follow. Maybe she was —

A hand grabbed my ankle. I heard a shout as I sprawled. Heart racing, I clambered to my feet, expecting a hit from behind. I had my fists up, courtesy of the cousins, and I wildly looked around, trying to keep my balance. Two dark gray bundles blocked half the sidewalk. As I regained my breath and peered into the dawning light, the bundles assumed a familiar appearance. They were people, sound asleep. I'd seen figures just like them all over the city, individuals down on their luck, or sometimes whole families living on the street. Not what I'd expected to find in Peach Blossom Land. One of the figures shifted in his sleep, causing the other to stir. His hand lay open on the sidewalk like a torn package. The shout, I realized, had come from my own chest, which tightened in pity. Perhaps the man touched me in a dream thinking that he knew me. Like everyone else in every quadrant of the city who came upon the fallen, I silently stepped around them and hurried on my way.

It was five miles from the Outer Mission all the way to Golden Gate Park. Just past the park gates, pocket meadows beckoned me down a path that meandered beneath the trees. I saw

tarps, tents, and sleeping bags arranged in a circle and people standing around. Two youngsters offered to sell me medicinals, which
I declined since I was beggared and wanted my wits about me.
The fellows—both white, one maybe sixteen, the other younger—
asked me to watch their belongings while they went to the grocery
store across the street. I have an honest face. My open mien means
that I've often been asked to dedicate myself, however temporarily,
to the care of property and person. Cousin Deng trusted me; so did
friends and strangers. I was sometimes the lookout guy, sometimes
the watchover. Was it my eyes, pointing in different directions,
that prompted their reliance? When you're born with wide-angled
vision, you've a duty to use it wisely. With such a gift, Mother had
told me, I had a lot to offer the world.

I squatted in the damp grass and ate some of the food I'd brought,
a generous helping of Cook's epic green beans and a dozen onion
pancakes. The cloud cover lifted and the air got warmer and I finally
got sleepy. I figured my new chums wouldn't mind if I lay down
in their tent, the better to secure it, so I crawled in and promptly
slumbered. When I awoke, they were sitting outside on overturned
milk crates, counting their money. Six bucks in loose change and
a twenty-dollar bill from a generous lady whose grocery cart had
rolled away in the Whole Foods parking lot and banged into the
Tesla parked next to her Mercedes. They were the only ones who
saw the accident happen. She gave them the money and sped away.

A shadow fell on the grass between them. The younger one
looked up, anxious.

"You should've asked for more," I heard a man say. His shadow
was big; he was bigger. I saw streaked teeth, a red beard fading to gray, a line of black around his neck, dirt or leather. He
wore a ponytail and dark glasses. He spread his hand, examined

a fingernail, and nibbled it intently. His hand was so large that it almost covered his face.

The older one stood. A couple breaking bread nearby quickly picked up their backpacks and moved to the end of the meadow.

"She gave us all the cash she had," the older one said. "What'd you expect me to do? Walk her to the ATM?"

The man shook his head. "How many times have I told you? You live in a credit economy. What'd she have in her cart? The good stuff, right? Bagels, lox. Brunch fixings. My mouth is watering just thinking about it." He stretched his mouth wide. His teeth were in ruins. "You held valuable information. Learn to use what you got. Next time, barter." He looked at me. "Who's this guy?"

"Shelley," I said, holding out a hand.

"You got any money, Shelley?"

I said no. I had only a sparkly suitcase, stored at Eddie Low's.

"But you know about the credit economy."

"Oh, sure," I said. Barter and credit weren't exactly the same thing, but Father always told me it was good to stand in other people's slippers, the better to tell their stories. "Money isn't everything. You do something for me, I do something for you."

"You hear that?" the man said. "Chinaman knows how it's done. You want to know anything, ask a Chinese. They've always got a scheme going. They're better than us at working our own system. You planning to stay, Shelley?"

"Just for a short while. I'll soon be making an advancement. I'm a student," I explained.

"A student of life, am I right?" he said, grinning. "What do you think, boys? Should we let him stay?"

"He watched our stuff," the younger one said. The man turned and kicked the crate he was sitting on. The boy tumbled to the ground. The crate flew again, straight into the tent where I'd been sleeping.

"Whose stuff?"

"Your stuff," the boy said. He got up slowly.

"Here's your money," the older one said. He held out the twenty and change.

"Where's the rest of it?"

"Got you breakfast," the boy said. He handed over a bag and a six-pack of soda. The man hesitated, then thrust it all back at the boys.

"Go ahead, you take it," he said, though he looked hungry himself. "Growing boys. You need it."

I offered him the food I'd brought from the restaurant.

"A barter," he nodded. He said his name was Ron. "Come back later. We put the tents back up after dark."

I WANDERED COLD AND hungry through the park. I didn't want to sleep on the ground with Ron and the boys, but I had no one else to turn to and nowhere else to go. If I went to campus, I'd be sleeping on a bench until rousted by campus police, a humiliating prospect. I pictured the long night ahead and the bundles of gray I'd mistaken for rags on the sidewalk. I, too, was now among the fallen.

A cleanup crew was pitching garbage into big black sacks; they told me that there'd been a running race and to take what I wanted from the clothing that had been shed. I grabbed a sweatshirt, track pants, and a pom-pom-festooned cap along with crinkly silver blankets that I hoped would keep me warm. Seagulls wheeled overhead, so I knew I was close to the ocean, which meant, I realized with a lurch, that I was close to Ted and Aviva's house. My feet had carried me in the very direction that I secretly yearned to go.

In ten minutes I could be standing on their doorstep. I began walking faster and then broke into a run. They'd be sitting in the kitchen, Ted reading his three newspapers and Aviva making herself a cup of her nightshade coffee. I'd cook them a beautiful dinner of whatever I found in the silver fridge. I closed my eyes and thought of all the food on those laden glass shelves—chicken and beef ribs and black cod perfect for steaming—and the three of us would laugh as I told them of my adventures.

But before I got to the boundary line where the park stopped and the saltboxes began, my cold feet stopped me. I looked bad. I smelled worse. When Ted asked, I'd have to tell him that I'd been missing class, bumming meals, sleeping on sacks of rice. How could I face him after boasting that I was on top and sailing smoothly with everything under control? He'd open the orange door, and I'd see the disgust on his face. Loserhood would clog the Chinese groove that ran between Ted and me faster than sludge in a pipe. I turned around and walked deeper into the park.

At nightfall, I went back to the meadow. Ron and the boys sat on the ground forking stew from a can. I gave each one a silver blanket; in exchange, Ron let me sleep on a tarp near their tents. The cops might come and clear us out, he warned. If that happened, move slowly, keep my hands high and open, and walk to Haight Street, where I could spend the night in a doorway. I climbed into Eddie's sleeping bag and fell fitfully asleep, expecting the cops to show up at any minute and chase us down the road, but nobody noticed us at all.

8.
Saltbox

FOR SEVERAL NIGHTS, I SLEPT IN GOLDEN GATE PARK, going to school at daybreak and returning after dark. I scrounged on campus and brought food for Ron and the boys. When my teacher, Professor Luo, noticed I was coming to class with my sleeping bag on my back and twigs stuck in my hair, a counselor was assigned to address my "personal concerns." She said I wasn't to be ashamed about my situation since a number of students across the college were experiencing homelessness. She gave me phone numbers and websites, but she couldn't give me housing. I registered her sympathy and kept my mouth shut. I wasn't going to be like Father, who shared his troubles to anyone who'd listen. But when the ground got colder and the nights grew longer and I fell behind in class, I knew I had to act.

I rang the bell at Ted and Aviva's. It was a Sunday afternoon. I wasn't carrying an armload of oranges or a sack of cookies baked by green-frocked girls. All I had was a smile, which dresses the lowliest beggar, and a handshake warmer than an oven.

"Shelley!" The door opened; Aviva was smiling back. "Good, you're here," as if I'd been summoned, which I suppose I had been, given what happened next.

"Ted's not here," Aviva said. "Shelley, this is Henry."

The old man sat on a kitchen chair with his pants rolled to his knees and his feet in a tub of water. He peered up at me and I stared back. I could've been looking at Father thirty years gone. He had Father's low forehead and broad, flat cheekbones. A fleshy nose, the Zheng men's proud protuberance, and a two-day bristle. He was shorter than Ted or so he appeared, folded. His hairline was exactly like Father's, encroaching upon the open expanse of his face as though dragged forward. His ears looked enormous, way bigger than Father's. They stuck out below the rim of the flat tan cap on his head. His eyes zeroed in on my wandering eye with the pull of a guy wire. He pointed to his right earlobe, where the Zheng family mole was clinging. With his other hand, he beckoned me over. I shuffled close to him, a little nervous, but oh, the surprise! He smelled like Father, of hair oil and bus dust and dried-plum candies. He motioned me to bow my head and when I did, he pinched my earlobe, fingering my matching bump, same as his and Ted's and every male cousin's in our linked-for-life lot born into Zhengland, schooled in family origins, ranked by aunties. There was no doubt about it: Henry and I were blood.

"You look as I did when I was young. Dumb and dumber," Henry said.

"How do you do?" I didn't know whether to address him in Chinese or English, but I opted to go with the lingua franca. He'd been sent here young, much younger than me, at sixteen, Father had said. His Chinese was likely as rusty as Ted and Aviva's downspout.

"My toe is killing me." He lifted a dripping foot. His left big toe looked like a tiger had bit it, chewed lazily, left it oozing. "I can barely walk. She—" he jerked his head "—wants me to go to a doctor."

"It's infected," Aviva said. She was quite calm, clearly used to this business.

"I don't need a doctor. I just need a little help until I get moving again."

"I work, Henry. Plus, I have other obligations. I can't be your cook and your maid. You have to hire someone. Did you call any of those agencies yet?"

Henry stood, stepped out of the tub, and toppled sideways. Old-man limbs and footbath water flew. I tried to catch him and ended up on my butt. Aviva roared exciting words that Ted had entered in my notebook. We got him dried off and arranged on the living room couch. He had a bruise on his cheekbone and a swollen knee. Aviva wrapped a stretchy bandage around his elbow.

"You made things worse," she said. She didn't call a doctor; she knew he'd refuse to go.

Henry moaned. "Tea," he uttered. I hurried to the kitchen with Aviva hard behind me.

"He's been here for two hours!" she said. "I'm going crazy. I almost called Kate to come help me. She's the only one he listens to. Where's Ted? *Where's Ted?* He has the perfect knack for sensing when his father is coming over. It's like, 'I've got to go out,' then, '*Bing, bong.* Henry's here!' And Ted's nowhere to be found. It all falls on me. I feed him, I listen to him go on and on, I look at his awful feet. I've got work to do! I've got dinner to make. I can't spend all my days taking care of Ted's father. He won't hire outside help, and he won't move to assisted living, not that I want him to—after my mother, Ruth, died, my dad stayed on in the house, and that's what I'd want for myself, so I get it. But he's not independent anymore. It's an impossible situation." She looked at me. "And Ted, well, he's adamant that I keep Henry away from you."

She moved nearer, standing so close that I could smell her sweat. A man, even an old one, isn't easy to lift.

"Henry has this idea," she said in a whisper. "He's been wanting to send to China for one of the relatives to come take care of him. He knows people who've done it. They summon family members to be their live-in help. It's always some poor, unmarried woman who moves here to cook and clean house and see them through to the end. Ted is appalled. He thinks it's exploitative. He says his father turned his back on the Chinese relatives a long time ago, that he never did anything for them during the bad years, and he doesn't get to just snap his fingers and send for one of them to rush to his rescue. So now this is their latest fight, only it isn't, because it all goes back to the same thing. If Diana were alive, Henry wouldn't be alone."

I saw to my alarm that tears were forming. I didn't know how to talk to a crying lady. But maybe her upset was the opening I needed.

Aviva took hold of my forearm.

"I'm so tired of it. I really am," she said.

I patted her on the shoulder and told her to go rest; I would sit with Henry. She did as I suggested; that's how defeated she was, though first she gave me a sharp look, finally noticing my dishevelment. Her nose wrinkled. Maybe she noticed my pungency too.

"My God, you look terrible," she said, stepping back. "Is everything all right?"

"Soon to be," I said, and I urged her down the hall. When the door to her bedroom was firmly shut, I brought Henry his tea and said, "When shall I move in?"

IT WAS ALL SETTLED by the time Ted came home. In fact, his timing was perfect. I had Henry sitting up in the kitchen chair. One foot was soaking and already better since I added salts that I found in the bathroom. I was cradling the other foot, just like I'd done many times with Father, and carefully cutting Henry's toenails, which were as hard as the horn on the Year-of-the-Ram's head. Father's feet were far worse, being the peds of a laborer man. They protested his lowly status even more than the aunties, erupting in corns, calluses, cracks, and calcifications. Boils, bunions, red-hot ingrown spikes. Maybe, like the nose and the beauty spot, dilapidated feet were part of the family package. *My son has healing hands*, Father told the neighbors, and they brought their feet right over. I knew when to cut and when to dig. I had a special way of rubbing that brought sighs of satisfaction. Henry was making those very noises when Ted walked in.

"What are you doing?" Ted asked me. "Get up. Get up." He jerked me angrily by the arm.

"It's okay," I said, removing his hand gently. "I know about feet. Father has them." Ted's face turned bright red. He was embarrassed to see me in my crouch. He didn't want me taking on a task he wouldn't do himself. Maybe he thought it was a job for Aviva, though I doubted it. She wasn't that kind of wife.

"*Ye Ye*, you better not use this toe for a week. It needs time to get better." I was rapidly calculating to myself that inside of a week, I could be settled with my own bedroom and the key to Henry's house. Maybe I'd keep it on a triple-eight key ring like the one that Cook kept for luck.

"Don't call him that!" Ted said.

"It's fine by me," Henry protested. "Calling me *Ye Ye* is very respectful."

"He's not your grandson! He shouldn't be calling you *grandfather*."

"Okay, okay," his father said. He wiggled his toes in my hand. "Xue Li, you call me Henry."

I saw no cause for Ted's outburst, though I was touched that he didn't want me exploited—a word and a concept that Miss Chips had made sure we learned. Still, it was up to me to restore family balance. Now that I had my meal ticket, I couldn't let the train leave the station without me.

"It was my mistake!" I emitted an apologetic laugh. "Thank you for reminding me that I'm in America now. I'll call you Henry, not *Ye Ye*, and I'm not Xue Li, I'm Shelley." I glanced up at their faces. The room felt filled with rocks.

"Ladies and gentlemen! Introducing *The Henry and Shelley Show*!" I clambered to my feet, threw my arm wide, and took a deep bow.

That did the trick, at least for the one who mattered, my nick-of-time benefactor, Henry. He gave a deep chuckle: "*The Henry and Shelley Show*."

I returned to my squat and drew his other foot from the water. Aviva and I had done good together—our double soak of Henry had tenderized his toes. Patting his tootsies dry, I proceeded to de-flesh him using her favorite paring knife, the one with the polished handle, which had just the right balance for trimming dead skin and slicing the claw from his nails. Soon I had a second little pile going of Henry parts that he no longer needed, and Henry, watching approvingly, leaned back in his chair with a grin.

"You see this?" he said to Ted, sounding a lot like Ron from the park. "This boy knows what to do."

Ted made an angry noise and stomped out of the kitchen. I hated making Ted unhappy, but I was being practical and he wasn't. A fine blue jacket and three hundred emergency dollars didn't beat a saltbox. From where I was crouching, exploitation looked like an excellent option, there being no others in sight.

"You know, he kept you from me," Henry said. "He didn't tell me you were here. I had to keep asking: 'Who's that young man hanging about in the yard?' 'Oh, that's a friend.' 'A friend?' 'Well, a visitor.' Finally, I asked her. 'Well, that's Shelley,' she said. 'One of the Chinese relatives.' So then I figured it out. Why the big secret? 'Oh, no secret, but he's a student, you see. Far too busy to take time from his studies.' I kept on asking. 'Let me meet the boy!' He refused. He said I'd take advantage. It was very insulting. My son has a word that he should apply to himself. What do you call it? *Paternalistic.*"

I knew the meaning all right. *How's your pater?* Miss Chips used to ask me. And, *Pater was a linguist. He was mad for the right word.* Miss Chips, her pater, and I had that in common. Nothing gives pleasure as much as choosing the right word.

Henry was still complaining. "'Don't be paternalistic. It's my life. Let me make my own decisions.' He never listens to good advice. No one's allowed to be paternalistic to *him*, especially his father."

"Is it true?" Aviva said, returning to the kitchen. "Is Shelley moving in with you?"

"What choice do I have?" Henry grumped, like a midlevel boss who's ordinarily mild but growls when the big boss is watching. "At least someone in the family is willing to help."

Aviva narrowed her eyes at me. "Well, aren't you a clever thing." Then she relaxed. "I think it's brilliant. A brilliant solution. You can help each other." *And give me a break*, she was thinking. But I still had Ted to appease.

"I feel bad that I caused hard feelings. Please tell Ted that my lessons won't suffer. I'm number one in my class."

That was true.

"And since Father asked me to look after Henry, I can now fulfill my promise."

That wasn't.

"Oh, sweetie," Aviva said. "This isn't about you." She looked at me intently. "Don't you understand? This has nothing to do with you. I already told you. It all goes back to the same thing."

"What do you mean that your father asked you to look after Henry?" Ted asked, reappearing. He'd been eavesdropping from the hallway, one of my signature moves.

"Well . . ." I made a moue of embarrassment. Miss Chips had taught us *moue. A useful expression between scoff and grimace.* It was part of our unit on What the French Have a Word For That's Better Than in English. It was a long lesson, to Miss Chips's disgust.

"Perhaps I shouldn't say, for Father's sake."

"We're all family here," Aviva said. Curiosity had wedged her mouth ajar. "Families should *talk.* How else can we support one another? Openness is good." Her eyes looked unnaturally bright while Ted's had darkened.

I shuffled my feet, fiddled my fingers. "It was Father's biggest dream that I should come to San Francisco, but the trip cost a lot. Father had to borrow the money. He asked all the relatives. No one wanted to help. Finally, one auntie gave Father a generous loan. She's Henry's cousin twice removed, so Father is very grateful to Henry's branch of the family. He instructed me to help look after Henry."

There was no auntie who made such a loan; Father's boss was the sole soft touch. But Ted had no way to fact-check my story, which is every sponger's bluff.

"You didn't mention your aunt before," Ted said suspiciously. "You said the money came from your father's boss at the bus depot."

"Some of it did. The rest came from Auntie. I was waiting to mention it until I could thank *Ye Ye*—Henry—in person." I cast a demure expression, the fault being mine, not Ted's.

Ted frowned and was silent. I held my breath. Either way, I was moving into the saltbox, but it'd be a lot easier if Ted didn't object.

The moment stretched longer. "It's Chinese custom to look after our elders," I said.

"I know that," Ted said crossly. He looked at Aviva. She emphatically nodded her head. As I said, we made a good team, Aviva and me.

"I think we both can see that Shelley could use a little help right now," Aviva said. "This works well for everybody."

"Okay," Ted said. He rounded on his father. "But you need to pay Shelley a decent wage. Not just room and board. Think of what it costs to live in this city."

"Of course!" Henry said. "I was going to offer. You didn't give me a chance."

"And you should repay this aunt the money she loaned to Shelley's father. Shelley's airfare should be part of the package."

"Let's not go overboard. One thing at a time," Henry said.

Whew! I didn't want Henry to go looking for a fictional beneficent auntie.

"I'm going to check on you," Ted warned Henry. "God knows you've got the money." Funny how Ted no longer objected to my working on a student visa, now that I was taking care of his father.

"You can empty that basin outside," Aviva said. "There's a storm drain next to the curb." She took me outside and showed me.

"Good job," she said. "You got them talking again. In my family, we talk about *everything*. We don't stay bottled up. We end up screaming at each other, but at least it clears the air. Those two keep a barrier up between them as high as the walls in this house. Well, if a person isn't willing to share his feelings, he never finds out what the other person thinks."

I felt sorry for Aviva, unschooled in the Chinese groove. Ted and Henry knew exactly what the other was thinking, even if we didn't. They had their private history, father to son to father, but whatever their grievances, I'd managed to slip between them.

"Here," Aviva said, handing me a bottle of cleanser. "Give it a good scrub. And throw that knife in the garbage. There's no way I'm ever going to use it again. Are you done yet? Can you take him home already?"

I went back inside to bring Henry home.

"You're making a mistake," Ted said to me. "Nothing you do for him will ever make him happy."

But I was jubilant. I had a place to live and soon I'd have money. In my imagination, Lisbet shimmered. With the promise of a full stomach every day and a warm bed every night, my worries were quickly fading. After all, how much trouble could one old man be?

9.

Henry's House

I FELT AT HOME IN HENRY'S HOUSE THE MINUTE I GOT there, a common occurrence for spongers worldwide. You walk in the door and instantly recognize your old life lurking in the shadowy corners: in my case, cracked tiles, dim lighting, the smell—so familiar!—of malehood. I'd have to work hard to scrub the loneliness out of the place.

"Okay, okay," Henry said, clutching. "That wasn't so hard, was it?" With him pulling on the handrail and me shoving him palm to bum, we'd gotten him up the outdoor stairs and through the front door. He shuffled into the living room and dropped into the larger of a pair of worn armchairs, first pushing aside a book. Coffee table, end table, pillowed couch were covered in printed matter. I'd never seen so many books, journals, magazines, and papers outside of the library at Honghe U., where Lisbet used to study. Scores more books, bricked with knowledge, bulged from crowded shelves. The drapes were open in the picture window, and more books were stacked beneath the sill. I was in an aerie for the erudite, a room of words and wisdom. Exactly what I needed to ignite my poet flame.

"We made it," Henry said gleefully. "Good job engineering our escape. She was ready to call the nursing home to come and haul me away. Ha! We showed them. Did you see the look on Ted's face? If you want to call me *Ye Ye*, you go right ahead. Come on now. Grab that footrest. Move it closer." He pointed at a kind of high footstool with a pillowtop of its own—an ottoman, I later learned it was called, though I'm not sure why; it was too ugly to have been designed by the beauty-loving Turks—which I pushed this way and that until it was right where he wanted it; then he heaved his legs up, wallowed his rump, and settled.

"My daughter-in-law wastes a lot of effort trying to get my son and me to talk," he said. "She ought to know by now that we don't have anything to say to each other. She used to insist on dinner once a week until we put an end to it. On Mondays, Tuesdays, and Wednesdays, I'm watching the markets. Thursdays, too. Every business day is important. Friday evenings, I'm ready to relax. I could do with a little company on Fridays. Not Fridays, he says, they're too tired after working all week. Could you call what he does 'work'? She works, not as hard as she used to. She started out as a teacher, that was good. Then she became a librarian, still important, but easier, you know, sitting at a desk stamping books. Teaching's the harder job. I taught high school students for forty years. I got an award, twice. But they're tired, he says. They're always tired. You'd think he was the old one, not me. How about Saturday night, I said, or Sunday dinner? No, not the weekends. That's when they see their friends. So Monday nights it was, sheer torture. She'd cook a big casserole full of chickpeas and lentils or something she'd stewed all day and send me home with the leftovers. I'm not complaining. It was nice of her to invite me. But she thinks I'm over here moldering, that I haven't got a life of my own. I do, they just can't see it. Old people in America, they turn invisible to the rest. Not like in China."

Had he been to China lately?

"My wife looked into it. We were planning to go. Didn't make it before she died." His gaze on me sharpened. He was wondering how much I knew. I told him I was sorry about his wife and his grandson, and his shoulders relaxed now that it'd been said.

"Who wants to go anyway? From what I hear, the traffic's awful. If I want to see tall buildings, I can look at the TV."

"The relatives would be happy to host you in Gejiu." The excitement that would bring! They'd vie for the honor; they'd pull out all the stops.

"Not interested," he said. "Now listen. I don't like to be worried after. You'll learn that about me. I don't like to be waited on hand and foot. My daughter-in-law has an excess of need to be somebody's mother, but like I said, it's a waste. In my own house, I can do what I want. Go look in the freezer. I put some soup in there last week. Split pea from Safeway. Warm that up and make us a couple of ham sandwiches and pour me a bourbon. Two fingers, lots of ice. Bring it all out here and set up a couple of TV tables. You can help me to bed after."

Maybe every fellow who lives alone has a yammerer inside him waiting to burst out. A yammerer and a martinet, eager to give orders. He said the liquor cabinet was in the kitchen, furthermost top on the right. The key was on a silver ring tied to a red cord hanging from a hook on the back of the door to the cupboard under the kitchen sink or if I couldn't find it there, I should look in the shoebox where he kept loose items that, last he remembered, he'd placed on the closet shelf. The liquor cabinet was tricky; the door had to be jiggled, and if that didn't work, I should straighten a paper clip to unjam the lock. He'd had the lock installed to keep repairmen out. "Plenty of those guys like a shot while they're plumbing."

I knew enough to check the cabinet door before I went hunting for the key. If Henry was anything like Father, he wouldn't have bothered to lock it after his last imbibe. Even misers like to get to their bottle in a hurry. Sure enough, the door of the cabinet was hanging wide open.

"I found the key," I said as I delivered his drink. "It was right where you said."

"You and I are going to get along great."

Five minutes later, he was snoring.

THE PEA SOUP STUCK to the spoon and smelled like dirty socks, so I glopped it into the garbage and made a Chinese soup with ingredients I found in the cupboards and fridge. While the soup simmered and Henry slept, and after a quick snack of half a box of Ritz—*Family Size!* the box proclaimed but then there'd have to be a family that wanted to cracker together—I examined the books on his shelves. Cookbooks in two rows bristled with slips of paper. The rest was history and biography and dense encyclopedias of people and cultures long dead. On top of a round table beside the couch was a congestion of framed photographs, like figures trapped in a crowd. The best was a black-and-white picture of Henry and Diana standing next to a wedding cake, she in a long white gown with a pearly sheen, he in a slim dark suit. She had an oval face and eyes like Ted's, small and serious. Henry's suit gave him an air of sophistication that his countenance belied—he was looking with awe at Diana like an astonished chappie who couldn't believe his fine luck. In another silver frame, Ted and Aviva posed on the steps of the big domed building I recognized as city hall. Aviva was clutching a bouquet and squinting into the sun, and Ted looked startled—*What am I doing here?* Kate was in the picture, beaming. The city supervisor friend of Ted's, Huntington, clowned behind him, a tall green bottle balanced on the palm of his hand. From the palm of his other hand rose a tower of red plastic cups. He was ready to pour the groom a drink if only Ted would let him.

All the other photos were of Diana—with an elderly couple, probably her parents; with a group of lady friends; with a boy in the park, at the beach, at the zoo. Eli. I wiped the dust with my sleeve and saw, stuck between the table and the edge of the couch, a picture that had fallen. It was the same photo I'd seen in Eli's bedroom: Eli and Diana, standing in front of a store window under a big red sign with white letters that read HONG'S FINE FOOD MARKET. Eli looked like Aviva, with a rounded face and curly hair, though he had Ted's grave expression. I couldn't make out if he possessed the telltale earlobe rivet, trademark Zheng, marker of our measure, but I was glad for Ted that his son had been a serious sort of lad. It meant that people knew they were related.

"This is delicious," Henry said, after he'd slurped his soup. A string of cabbage hung from his chin; I handed him a napkin and told him I'd been cooking all my life including a recent professional stint.

"My wife was a wonderful cook," Henry said. "She collected recipes like other people collect paintings. She would get them printed and hand them out at the store. She was a very intelligent woman. Perceptive. She took Ted to the library, got him his own card. 'Watch the other kids around him. They look to see what he's doing, then they do it too.' He was three when she said that.

I got excited. Maybe he was special. 'Of course he's special. He's your son. I'm not saying he's a genius. Don't be thinking that. But his little mind is whirring.'" He rocked forward in his chair. "She could read him like a book. I thought he might become a lawyer or a teacher, like me, but she said no. 'He observes,' she said. 'He stands outside the fray.'" He pushed his bowl aside. "Too bad he gave up before he really got going."

"What was your subject? History?" It was an obvious guess. There was scope on those bookshelves, also an air of doom.

"American history. My most popular class was a senior seminar on the Spanish-American War. Teddy Roosevelt. You've heard of him?" he asked.

I hadn't. Miss Chips had said there were too many instances of U.S. foreign interventions to give us a comprehensive list.

Henry grumbled, "You've got some learning to do before the citizenship exam. Luckily, I can teach you." Citizenship exam! He was singing my song, laying out my future. Practically pelting me with petals from lovely Peach Blossom Land.

"I'll tell you about Teddy Roosevelt someday. He was one of our greatest presidents, a man of extraordinary talent. Now they call him a racist, but the times were different then. Ted's named after him. It didn't do him any good."

HE'D LEFT HIS CAP at Ted and Aviva's house; he asked me to go back and fetch it because he was planning to visit the casting ponds and he had to have that cap. I helped him to bed and went next door.

"Oh, Shelley!" Aviva cried for the second time that day. "Is it working out okay? I'm breathing again, knowing that you're there." She turned to Kate and Orit, who were sitting with Ted at the table cracking walnuts into a wooden bowl. "Shelley has swooped in like a fairy prince to totally save us. He's going to look after Henry."

They loved the idea. "Communal living makes so much sense," Orit said. "The whole community cares for the young and the old."

"Oh, God, let's not hear about the kibbutz again," Aviva said. "It's unnatural, all those people trying to live in one place."

"I want to hear," Kate loyally said. "You loved growing up there." She brushed walnut shell from her hands and offered me the bowl.

"My childhood was idyllic," Orit said. "Some of my friends from the kibbutz have started a collective on ranch land in L.A. It has shared spaces and private quarters and a big kitchen garden. There's a school on the property for the kids. They're creating something amazing. We're going to visit for Passover. Kate and I might move there."

"You can't do that!" Aviva said. "Think of the failed experiments of communes in the sixties. You've got to have your own home. Ted, tell them."

"I'd hate for you to move," Ted said to Kate.

"We haven't decided yet," Kate said.

"In any case, you're not taking Leo," Aviva said. She looked around. "Is he still watching that awful TV show?"

Orit tiptoed to the doorway and peered into the living room. "He's asleep," she reported.

"Speaking of unhealthy living," Aviva said to me, "please help Henry clean out the junk. I can't get him to throw anything away. The place is a firetrap."

"Save some of the books for me," Ted said.

"No, Ted!" Aviva looked horrified; the others laughed. "You're as bad as your father."

"I'm the same," Kate said. "I asked the landlord if he'd rent us an extra storage locker. He said no."

"The landlord wants us out," Orit said. "He doesn't like that I organized the other tenants."

"We didn't sneak around," Kate said. "We've been very open with him."

"You've got him worried," Ted said. "Orit, a housing advocate, and you, a social worker. You know your rights."

"A developer was there last week doing a walk-through of the building," Orit said. "They want to sell it, tear it down, and put us all out on the street, the latest wave to be pushed out. It'll be another Mission District apartment building taken off the market. While we were bringing our issues to the table, he was talking to developers, waiting for prices to rise. Greedy bastard. That whole negotiation was a ruse. He was planning to sell all along."

"You should do the same," Aviva said. "Delay. Make him buy you out."

"Where are we going to go?" Orit demanded. "A middle-income family with a kid and a dog?"

"I'll be sad to leave San Francisco," Kate said.

"Will you have to leave though?" Ted said anxiously.

Leo appeared, hair sticking up, sleep creasing his face. As soon as he saw us, he ran to his mothers. Aviva tried to get him to talk, but he shook his head, *no!* Then, to my surprise, he grabbed me around the waist.

"Have a snack, sweetie," Aviva said, holding out the bowl of nuts.

"No nuts," Orit said. "We don't want him getting allergic."

"You've got that backward. Now's the time to introduce a variety of foods. That keeps him from developing problems later on. How about a glass of milk, Leo?"

"No cow's milk," Orit said.

"Why don't I just give him a beer already?" Aviva said.

"No wheat," Orit said.

Leo latched onto my hand and pulled me out of the kitchen. As soon as we were away from the rest, he turned to me and asked, "Want to see the fish?" They were the first words I'd heard him say. I'd begun to think he couldn't speak at all. Without waiting for a response, he led me to Eli's room, where the door was wide open. I saw again the bed and the desk and the notebook, *Eli Cheng*. The pictures were still on the walls, including the one of Diana. I felt a stab of annoyance. They wouldn't unlock the door for me, but this four-year-old kid could come and go as he pleased.

"That one's my favorite," Leo said, his nose to the fish tank. "I call him Eli."

"Leo!" Orit called. "Time to go!"

Diana looked out at me, holding her apple aloft.

HENRY WAS SNORING BEHIND his bedroom door. I hung his cap on the hook in the hallway, finished the dishes, and walked downstairs to carry out the garbage. As Aviva had warned me, the garage was filled with junk. There wasn't room for Henry's old Toyota; he kept that parked on the street. I squeezed past bags and boxes and rusted gardening tools. A large object was propped against the wall; I tripped and crashed into it, banging my knee hard. It was the red sign that used to hang on the best corner in San Francisco: HONG'S FINE FOOD MARKET.

There was a room off the garage, smaller than Ted and Aviva's but big enough for a bed and a chair and more cardboard boxes. That's where Ted and Aviva would've stashed me, but here in the saltbox house, I was free to choose for myself. I trotted upstairs to where my bedroom was waiting.

Little touches everywhere said *Diana*, like the walls painted mango yellow, with a matching bedspread and lamp. A basket of pens and a sturdy pad of paper sat centered on the desk. The lamp glowed and the blank page beckoned. It was as if Diana knew that a trainee poet would someday arrive to look after Henry and need a place to write. It seemed she'd even left me clothes hanging in the closet, a tan-colored raincoat and two men's suits with jackets even nicer than Ted's blue blazer. I held them up: they were too short for me. I wondered whom they belonged to. Henry would never wear trousers that slim or the pressed shirts I found in the dresser drawer or the polished leather lace-ups lined up precisely that would've brought agony to his barnacled feet. Whose suitcase was that, stamped "HSW" and smelling of men's cologne?

The bathroom was a nice surprise, way better than Ted and Aviva's. The toilet seat was padded, like Father and I had imagined, and with the flip of a clever lever, it warmed my buns as gently as a kitchen gets yeast to rise. I had ample room to stretch in the tub and shower, and there were two facing mirrors for sprucing front and back. The aunties would've approved; in fact, they would've approved of the entire arrangement and taken credit for having trained me to clean, to fetch, to cook. To serve my family betters until I died, or Fate sprung me.

Stooping to put my shoes under the bed, I saw a dark shape in the shadow. I flattened myself on the floor, reached long, and pulled out a leather briefcase stamped "HSW" in gold. I was feeling a little nervous about who this interloper was but told myself not to worry. Possession of the bedclothes was ten-tenths of the sponger's code, but just to be sure, I picked up the suitcase and the briefcase, carried them to the garage, and slid them into a sliver of space between the big red sign and the wall. Then I went back upstairs and walked once more through the house, turning off the lights and marveling at the cooked air blowing from an invisible heater into every room, keeping us warm and toasty. Many nights Father and I had shivered in our beds, perforated by cold. Someday down the road, which was looking a lot straighter, I'd install Father in his own toasty house with a big pile of blankets as warm as Diana's smile.

I touched the house key in my pocket; with my very first paycheck, I'd buy a key chain just like Cook's. The streetlamp cast its light through the living room window. I picked up the photograph of Diana and Henry in their beautiful wedding clothes and placed them on the rosewood chest in the hallway. Next to them I added Diana and Eli in front of Hong's Market with its proud red sign. I didn't have any incense, but I bowed three times, promising Diana that I'd live up to my part of the bargain. I'd take care of Henry, and Henry would take care of me.

10.
SRO

GRANDMA LOW LIVED IN AN SRO, A SINGLE-ROOM-occupancy second-floor walk-up in the place called China-town. Eddie greeted her loudly in Cantonese and helped her into her armchair while she insisted we not make a fuss, exclaiming that we were much too skinny and good thing her daughter-in-law was bringing lots to eat. For an old lady, she was daringly dressed in a polka-dotted blouse, padded plaid vest, loose trousers, and a green-and-gold bow tied in a flourish at her neck. Her room was simply furnished with Chinese paintings on the walls and a small kitchen altar, though there wasn't any kitchen, only a plug-n-play pot. On top of the bookcase was a plaster statuette of the Virgin Mary, which would've looked finer in tin. Eddie told me that his father had tried, years ago, to persuade Eddie's grandparents to move to one of the neighborhoods where, back then, working folks could afford to live, like the way-to-the-west Sunset District where Ted and Aviva resided, but his grandmother chose to stay in Chinatown.

Eddie's mother, Mrs. Low, was easy to talk to. She had smiling eyes in a fat-cheeked face and a thatch of bright pink hair the color of watermelon candy. She lived close by in a Russian Hill apartment on the other side of the Broadway Tunnel. Since the passing of Eddie's father a few years ago, she visited her mother-in-law daily.

"What's that for?" Eddie asked, pointing to the straw crop atop his mother's head, which complemented nicely her lemon yellow shirt and purple pants.

"My third graders bet me five extra minutes of reading time a day that I wouldn't dare do it." She began unpacking the two big carry bags of dishes she'd cooked at home. As Grandma Low dozed, I sat under the window, nose on the meal and eyes on Grandma. I didn't want to miss my chance to ask about Henry.

Eddie laughed. "Those poor kids. Didn't anyone tell them not to take that bet? My mom plays the lottery every week. She won five thousand dollars."

"I'm a very lucky person," Mrs. Low modestly said.

"Miss Chips, my English teacher, loved to gamble. She said the Chinese penchant for gambling was the only sane response to this crazy world and we all should learn to take delight in the randomness of life."

"Online poker?" Eddie asked.

"English card games, whist and euchre. We used peanut shells for money." According to Miss Chips, bluffing was useful in many situations, and cheating justifiable when taking moral action. As sentient beings, it was our duty to learn the difference.

"I like a teacher with panache," Mrs. Low said. I told her that

Miss Chips believed that the best teachers were called to their life's work, same as artists. Hearing that, Mrs. Low invited me for lunch.

If I thought that I'd feel at home in a district named for the likes of me, I was, for once, mistaken. The tile-covered gates, the buildings squeezed together as tightly as a diver's buttocks looked nothing like my hometown city of Gejiu, which, although not as lake-lovely as Kunming or capital-soaked as Guangzhou, where Cousin Deng once took me on a forty-eight-hour business operation that required the cover of night, was a worthy exemplar of modern China. Outside the window of Grandma Low's apartment were decorated rooftops and tasseled lanterns and an *erhu* player dressed in robes and skullcap with a long queue flowing. He sat very straight like the upright instrument he held as he drew his bow across the strings, an amplifier at his black-slippered feet and a heaven-cast expression on his wizened face. Two-inch fingernails curved from the ends of his pinkies, the cutting edge of fashion from a long, long time ago.

"This isn't like China," I said. "Where are the office towers? The tranquil gardens? The subway? They're giving the wrong idea."

"It's for the tourists," Eddie said. "They buy more crap in a fake authentic setting. Look at that girl." A laughing teenage girl modeling a conical bamboo hat was arming her selfie stick. "Culture sells. The more exotic, the better, as long it conforms to the beholder's ingrained bias toward a specified set of assumptions ingested by society at large."

We were halfway through the semester. Eddie had pulled a couple of all-nighters boning up for his second-year midterms in advanced marketing and cultural studies, and the two courses had intermingled in his head like the insistent strains of the *erhu* and the blaring car horns outside.

"But they're getting the wrong idea," I said. "That girl in the hat. She thinks that China hasn't progressed in a hundred years. How will that lead to mutual understanding? It'd be better for that girl to know what we're really like."

"Then you wouldn't sell any hats. You got to find a way to monetize your ideas."

"I'd sell a different kind of hat. A tin miner's helmet, representative of Gejiu. With a handy light in front to guide you in darkness."

"Don't bring sentiment into it," Eddie said. "To me, China's one big hungry mass of consumers. I just want to make my killer app like everybody else and figure out a way to tap into that market." He and his girlfriend, Paloma, were working hard on their app, called Five Minute Local, which, depending on your GPS location, served up audio tours of interesting places nearby. Eddie picked the sites, wrote the scripts, and recruited friends to narrate. Paloma and a couple of her fellow geeks handled the coding.

"You ought to help us. You're Chinese. You've got the inside track."

I told him if ever a single countryman could speak for a billion people, I was the man for the job.

MRS. LOW ARRANGED THE meal and Eddie set the table, insisting I should rest. He knew that between my schoolwork and taking care of Henry, who got up three times a night, I didn't get much sleep. Soon I began to nod. Through the open window, I heard the old-man *erhu* player singing a romantic ballad that Father used to sing to Mother in his beautiful sonorous voice. On fine-weather days when Father wasn't working at the bus depot or Mother at the travel office where she tap-tap-tapped on a computer—it was she who'd taught my tiny hands how to fly over a keyboard—the three of us would walk in the park, Father warbling, Mother linked to him arm in arm while I watched the people coming and going, the hangdog fathers and scolding mothers and mulish children— Father said to study the troubled families because they made for the best stories—some pitiable, some antagonistic, all of them a fascination to me when they turned up later in one of Father's creations. Hearing that same ballad prodded me wide awake. What lies I'd been sending home to Father! I couldn't bring myself to tell him that I was now tending to Henry as I used to do for him and so I sent pretty falsehoods instead. I said I was very happy living with Uncle and Auntie and *Ye Ye*; they'd bought me a new bed, the softest I'd ever slept in, and I was getting fat from Auntie Aviva's fine cooking. My studies had gone so spectacularly well that I'd be graduating early and joining Uncle as his right-hand man at the family emporium on the best corner in San Francisco. The black fish churned at my deception. To stop him from knocking against my rattled ribs, I pictured Cousin Deng reading my emails to Father, the two of them backslapping over my steady progress.

I stood and looked out on the street. Chinatown wasn't home, but the tea shops and vegetable markets and the near-countrymen shouldering their way down the crowded sidewalks brought me back to Gejiu. I listened again to the player's plangent song and as I let it flood me, I decided that homesickness, too, was a kind of pleasure, a countryman's ache for what's known.

Mrs. Low joined me at the window.

"Bill!" she called to the *erhu* player. "Come upstairs for lunch."

MR. BILL LEE LIVED on the floor below. I found him in his room putting away his *erhu*. When he lifted the skullcap off his head, the shiny black queue came with it. It was fake, like Eddie said, and underneath was the snow-white hair of a long-retired gent. His colorful street clothes, like Grandma Low's, gave him a rakish air. We walked slowly up the stairs, I carrying an extra chair and a high metal stool from the stairwell landing. "That's our huff-and-puff station," Mr. Lee said. He told me he was eighty-four, same as Grandma Low. His wife had passed and his son lived far away.

The table was so laden we barely had room for our bowls. For the first fifteen minutes, I concentrated on the noodles. The noodles and the dumplings and the soup and the fish, glorious in its crunch. The food was simple, the dishware mismatched, and we were squashed around the table on seats of different heights—I perched, knees jutting; Eddie on a low stool, chin barely meeting the table—but it was the best meal I'd eaten since coming to Peach Blossom Land, prepared as it was with love. Grandma Low kept telling Eddie's mother to put more food on our plates. "It is all very delicious," I complimented the cook.

Mrs. Low beamed. What can I tell you? Once upon a time, I had that effect on people, and Americans—so generous!—were a terribly trusting lot. I suppose my earnest attempts in those early days to speak their difficult language helped direct their sympathy to me. I've left out the halt here, also the spit and the gargle. Mistakes were made, some of them amusing but none worth diverting our story. In those heady days of my freewheeling, fateful frolic, the year of my transformation, never to come again, I was a party in a hurry. Equal parts urgency, desire, and disorder. To dally with our tale would be to slow that young man down, and what would be the fun in doing that?

"Eddie said your uncle and aunt live in the Sunset," Mrs. Low said.

"The Outerlands," Eddie declared. I'd heard Ted's friend

Huntington call it that, never Aviva. She disliked being reminded that theirs was a neighborhood for exiles and afterthoughts, once a forgotten quarter of the city until forgotten quarters were all that anyone could afford. It was bleak out there, Ted admitted, though the mix of families added some color, by which he meant the Chinese, Koreans, Russians, Filipinos, Lebanese, and Salvadorans who lived in those fogbound blocks. Oh, and the Modi family who lived across the street in the house with the twinkling balcony lights. There weren't many Blacks. Ted said that as prices laddered up, Black families left, moving east and south across water, hills, and bridges. San Francisco had no compunction about pushing out the old to make room for the new and the poor to make room for the rich, and in that way, it was a lot like the cities back home, which were roundly criticized in the U.S. while also copied.

"What kind of work do they do?" Mrs. Low asked.

"My uncle Ted was a newspaper man. Now he writes books for other people." *A ghostwriter,* Ted had called himself. He'd drawn a picture in my notebook of a tall thin man with two eyes, an open mouth, and the word *Boo!* erupting. The man's ears were as big as tires, but his eyes were tightly shut. "Auntie Aviva's a librarian."

"A school librarian?" Mrs. Low asked. "Maybe I've met her."

"She works at the big library near city hall." She'd taken me with her one day before my two weeks petered. She told a group of squirming kids the folktale that Mother used to tell me about the cowherd and the weaver princess. She smiled at me as she performed, sending me a message—*Hey, my husband's Chinese nephew, this one's for you!*—and she didn't notice: she was boring those kids to death. When she got to the part about the Queen Mother separating the lovers by drawing the Silver River—she called it the Milky Way—across the heavens with a pin, Aviva shot her eyebrows halfway to her hairline like an old man whose ass-poking doctor has snaked a finger in. She wasn't exactly a natural. It's a pretty good story told right.

"I know the librarians at the Chinatown branch but not at the Main," Mrs. Low said.

Grandma Low motioned for me to pass her my empty bowl. Now was my chance to ask her. "Do you know my uncle's father? His name is Henry Cheng."

"Henry Cheng?" Mr. Lee interrupted. He frowned. "I knew his wife, Diana. You remember the family," he said to Mrs. Low. "Sam and Lilliann Hong. Lilliann's father had a vegetable stand right here on Stockton, but Sam had bigger plans. They bought a store in the Sunset District, Hong's Market, Forty-Sixth and Noriega, when their kids were little. For a long time, they were the only Chinese out there. They lived behind the store. Diana went to Mills College with my sister Gloria."

"Mrs. Hong sounds familiar," Mrs. Low said. "Lilliann Hong," she said loudly to Grandma, who nodded. "Her daughter, Diana." Grandma made the sign of the cross.

"A lot of boys were in love with Diana," Mr. Lee said. "My brother Andy was crazy about her. She was a beautiful girl, kind to everyone. She broke hearts when she married Henry Cheng. He was a schoolteacher from New York. Nobody knew him. He was older. Sour. But we all loved Diana. She kept the store going after her parents retired. She loved the place." He gave a low sigh like a pluck of his *erhu*. "They shouldn't have left the neighborhood. They had protection here."

"What happened?" Mrs. Low said.

Mr. Lee told her the story.

"That's awful," Mrs. Low said. I didn't speak. I was there to listen.

"The store closed after that," Mr. Lee said. "The police never caught who did it. Worst of all, they said maybe the store had been a target because of something the son wrote in the newspaper."

"What was that?" Mrs. Low said.

"He wrote an article about the store that said his mother was often there by herself at night. The police said she was a target. The robbers knew she'd be alone." He tapped the table. "The real problem was that her husband, Henry, left her unprotected. He could've been with her, you know. He was retired from teaching by then. Sam never left Lilliann alone in the store; he always made sure he or one of the employees was with her. Henry didn't do that. He saw himself as some kind of intellectual, too good to be selling groceries. He could've protected her, but he didn't."

Stop the presses! Hold the phone! Aviva had told me none of that. I had a rush of affection for the ancient gent, my creaking, rusty casket of knowledge. No wonder Ted was so morose. He had guilt as well as grief.

"I've got that newspaper article somewhere. It was in my brother Andy's papers when he passed. That's how much he loved Diana."

Mrs. Low turned to me. "I'm so sorry for your uncle."

"When the aunties heard of her passing, they lit incense for her and paid for temple prayers," I said. This was true. They had cried for real on behalf of the family name.

"That's good to hear," Mr. Lee said. "There was a big Chinatown funeral. We packed the church. All of Diana's and her brother Leland's friends were there and everyone who'd known their parents. Henry Cheng didn't stand to greet a single one of us. We took up a collection and paid for the mourners' band. He was angry about it, said he didn't want it. But that's what Sam and Lilliann would've wanted, so Leland arranged it. Henry was furious at Leland and mad at your Uncle Ted. Leland said he blamed your uncle for what happened. That's not how the rest of us saw it. It wasn't your uncle's fault, though he had no business exposing his mother like that. He paid a terrible price. But Henry Cheng shouldn't have left her alone in a neighborhood that never wanted them there in the first place."

"Times have changed," Eddie said. "There's plenty of Chinese in the Sunset now. We've practically taken over. And this guy, Henry, wouldn't have expected armed robbery in the dairy case at Forty-Sixth and Noriega."

"It happened," Mr. Lee said.

"They sold groceries?" I said, double-checking. I was still hoping for the big department store.

"Sure," Mr. Lee said. "After her parents died, Diana made some nice changes to the place. Put in better lighting and started selling specialty products. She catered to the neighbors who wanted the fancy stuff."

"You mean the white folks," Eddie said.

"The foodies," Grandma Low said, surprising everyone. I thought she hadn't heard a word. Old people could be teary-eyed, but they also could be cagey.

"That's everyone in San Francisco," Mrs. Low laughed. She was too jolly to stay sad for long. "Anyway, it's good you're being useful to your *ye ye*. Your uncle and auntie need your help. They just didn't know it."

I cleared the table and brought hot water for the pot. If Bill Lee had it right, Henry and Ted each had reason to blame the other for the deaths of Diana and Eli. Anger stuck to them in equal measure. Or maybe, like Father, they had the habit of grief. *That's why Ted was so angry when he saw me trimming Henry's toes*, I thought. It wasn't embarrassment that caused him to snap. I could crouch all day at his father's feet, an acceptable transaction as long as Henry paid me.

But Ted didn't want me calling Henry *Ye Ye* when the only real grandson was gone.

Mr. Bill Lee went to fetch the newspaper clipping. "Diana was a modern girl. Maybe that's why she married that jerk Henry Cheng."

11.
Once Shunned, Chinese American Grocer Now Beloved

By Ted Cheng – July 17, 2009

WHEN MY GRANDPARENTS, SAM AND LILLIANN HONG, opened their corner market in the Outer Sunset in 1950, the neighbors didn't stream through the door. They weren't used to seeing a Chinese grocer outside of Chinatown. So Sam installed a big red sign on the building that announced in fancy white lettering, HONG'S FINE FOOD MARKET.

"He didn't put Chinese characters anywhere on that sign," his daughter, Diana, recalls. "He wanted folks to know: he was here to serve everyone." She remembers how excited he was the day the sign went up. Before that, he'd been working in his father-in-law's Chinatown vegetable market, and he was eager to strike out on his own. "The Sunset District was an overlooked section of the city where lots of families lived, and Dad went for it," Diana says.

With that big red sign offering a friendly welcome, it didn't take long for the locals to start shopping at Hong's Market. My mother, Diana, who loved helping her parents when she was younger and now runs the store herself, remembers the matrons of Italian, Irish, and German descent coming in often to buy Sam's fresh produce and to get cooking tips from Lilliann. Sam's early morning trips to the wharf for fresh crab had folks lining up out the door during Dungeness season. When Lilliann began renting out roller skates to teens who rolled the three blocks on Noriega to Ocean Beach and raced beside the Great Highway, their clientele cheered.

"It turned out, the store was the easy part," Diana says. "Finding a house they could buy was harder." They worked long hours at the store, and Sam and Lilliann wanted to buy a house close by, but homeowners in the Sunset didn't want to sell to non-whites. Racially restrictive covenants, while legally unenforceable, remained on the deeds for many Sunset homes, which Diana believes caused a chilling effect on sales. It took Sam and Lilliann more than three years of looking before they could buy a home. During that time, they lived with their two young children behind the store.

Covenants intending to keep out African Americans, Asian Americans, Jews, and other groups were struck down by the U.S. Supreme Court in 1948 and outlawed in 1968 by the federal Fair Housing Act. But the prohibitory language can still be found in many property deeds and neighborhood bylaws, including in the Outer Sunset.

A bill introduced in February by Assemblyman Hector De La Torre, D-South Gate (Los Angeles County), would require that racially restrictive covenants be stricken from public records at the time of the next sale. Opponents, including the California Association of Realtors, call the measure unnecessary and claim it would cause a bureaucratic mess. But supporters, including the American

Civil Liberties Union and the Mexican American Legal Defense and Educational Fund, say it's important to remove the illegal provisions.

"It is offensive to have people, minorities, have to sign documents that denigrate them," De La Torre said. "We need to wipe away the stain of that time in our history."

As an "Outerlands" homeowner, I was curious to know whether the deed to the home my wife and I purchased in 2000, the year our son was born, contains any restrictive language. Sure enough, studying the fine print on both our deed and the deed to my parents' home next door, I was shocked to discover a prohibition on sale of the properties to "people of the Negro or Mongoloid race." The clause was a stark reminder that, not so long ago, my Chinese American parents and I, and likely my Jewish wife and son, were unwelcome.

When I showed the language to my mother, she, like so many of her generation, told me to ignore it. "A lot has changed since then," she said. "I'll always appreciate how the neighborhood embraced us." At age sixty-three, she still handles the nighttime shift on her own. She doesn't mind the late hours because that's when her customers have time to stop and chat. "The people in this neighborhood, we look out for each other," she says. The products are different now—sustainably sourced coffee beans and curated craft cheeses—but the big red sign endures, a testament to the pioneer spirit of Sam and Lilliann.

12.

Spongers Worldwide

F OR ONE GLORIOUS MONTH, HENRY AND I LIVED LIKE emperor's sons, enjoying our private palace. He started sleeping ten hours a night; his toe life returned to normal. He resumed his qigong practice at the local rec center and his fly-casting sessions in the park. He marched around the backyard and combed the library sale for bargains and helped me apply for a driver's license that said "California" across the top, replacing my Gejiu special. I purchased a lucky key chain in one of the many Asian markets on Irving Street nearby. Every weekday, Henry traded stocks on his computer. He could sit for hours hitched close to the screen, humming and clicking away. A big haul was eighty dollars. *I never bet big. You bet big, you lose*, he told me. *Slow growth is for pussies*, Cousin Deng sang in my head.

Under his tutelage, my English improved greatly. Ted still wrote in my notebook and Eddie coached me too, but Henry made me his mission. Over dinner every night, he demanded discourse that he would then appraise. At first I didn't know what to talk about, not being a storyteller like Father, but slowly I began to tell him about Miss Chips and Lisbet and Yu. Thinking of Yu got me talking about Cousin Deng and his keen sense of business. Deng had his fingers in a whole lot of pies, but what he really wanted was one great idea and the financing to launch it. He'd take care of the rest. *He sounds like an operator*, Henry said with a chuckle, and I said the compliment fit, if an operator was a guy who knew how to make money.

Eventually, I got around to talking about Father and Mother. I told Henry about how, when Mother was alive, the three of us hadn't needed anyone else and so it didn't matter that the relatives froze us out. But once she was gone and Father fell silent, I used to hope that Father and I would be invited to live at the *lao jia*. I hadn't expected to sadden as I spoke, but my eyes grew moist and my voice faltered. Henry patted my hand and taught me a word that sounded like what it meant, *wistful*. I was learning that the telling of a tale changes the bearer as much as it changes the hearer. Father's stories always ended on a happy note, so I returned to lightness, saying, *Fate was unkind until it delivered me to you.*

Henry told me that he didn't believe in fate; as an American, he believed he made his destiny manifest, and now that my verbals were improving, I, too, could be my own master. *Look what a little steady practice can produce.* I was happy as a lark that Henry had taken me under his wintered wing. Ted had refused the job, along with all my aunties. Father, though he might've tried, was occupied by sorrow. And so we passed our evenings together, one happy ending after another.

I suppose I should've realized those halcyon days wouldn't last. Aviva demanded a daily update on key Henry components (feet, bowels, marbles) so she could judge whether I was doing the job right. She had a penchant for telling others what to do, which I didn't mind since it meant she found me useful, and she was the one to please.

Don't neglect school, Aviva instructed me often, usually right after asking me to pick up a few items for her at the store. I assured her that I had everything under control. In truth, I was cutting classes in order to spend time with Eddie and Paloma, which could've gotten me into trouble, but a friend of Paloma's who worked in the IT office changed my attendance record from spotty to spotless, and I kept my test scores high. The three of us were working on their app, Five Minute Local, which had gotten funding from a crowd of complete strangers, American goodness abounding. I'd recorded a tour in Mandarin of Mrs. Low's favorite Chinatown spots, and it'd already been downloaded over three hundred times, which Paloma said was pathetic but which inspired me nonetheless. My next big step would be to read my poems to Lisbet, as soon as I wrote them and as soon as she came looking.

"Come to this party tonight," Paloma said to me. She adjusted her beanie over her long black hair. She had a thick horsetail that frizzed on foggy days. Today it flowed because the day was bright and sunny. She was tall and firmly muscled, the opposite of Eddie— they made a stylish couple. He was wearing his usual track suit and a new pair of Nike Airs, part of his revolving collection. Paloma wore a striped green cardigan from her grandpa's closet and her mother's round-collared dress.

"Glenna Oh will be there," Eddie added. Glenna was a friend of Paloma's whom he wanted me to hang with. I liked her a lot, but I dreamed only of Lisbet.

"You know I have a girlfriend," I said.

"What kind of girlfriend disappears off email and never bothers to write?" Eddie said. "You should meet somebody new."

"She'll get in touch. When she's ready."

"What's taking her so long?" Eddie said.

"She's on a search. She wants a different kind of life."

Eddie made a face worthy of an auntie. "She's an outlaw. She fled the scene. You're wasting yourself, pining for her. Is she really worth it?"

"I love her!" I said. They both startled at the word. Eddie blushed and stole a glance at Paloma. She softened for a second and laced her fingers in his. To my envious eye, they were perfect together.

"See? You know what it is to love," I said.

"Maybe she'll turn up," Eddie conceded. "Or maybe she'll stomp your heart into a thousand little pieces."

"We'll be here, either way," Paloma said. "There's loads more work to be done. Our app sucks. We need a new idea."

It had been nine months since I'd last seen Lisbet. I thought of all the hours we'd spent together talking in the teahouse and walking in the park. She had looked at me tenderly, as only a lover would; she had kissed me into reverence. Wherever she was and whatever she was doing, she wouldn't have forgotten those special days, or me.

ONE MONTH LATER, IN April, I went next door to return a glass dish which had held Aviva's latest, a cinder block she called "kugel," and found Kate and Orit huddled with Ted and Aviva. Kate gave me a wan smile. Ted was furrowed. Only Aviva said hello.

All four were standing, too agitated to sit. I took up my customary place in the kitchen doorway.

"Who's got Leo?" Aviva said. "He was here a minute ago."

"He's watching a movie," Orit said. There were dark circles under her eyes, and she was wearing rubber sandals. Kate looked like she'd put on the wrong clothes in a hurry, pants that flapped above her ankles and a jumper I'd seen Orit wear with crisscrossing zippers like scars.

"Oh, Shelley, it's awful," Aviva said. "There was a fire in their building last night. Nobody was hurt, thank goodness, but the whole place was damaged."

"I really think the landlord did it," Orit said. "He wanted us out, and now it's done."

"You can't say that to reporters," Kate said. "We don't know anything yet."

"It's the fourth major fire in the Mission in the past three months. You think that's a coincidence?" Orit said.

"It's a real problem for the mayor. It's making the neighborhood nervous," Ted said.

"You see?" Orit said. "Ted agrees with me. It was arson."

Ted and Kate objected: that's not what Ted had said.

"You're on their side now," Orit accused Ted.

"Honey, don't say that," Kate said.

"Ted's taken a new job," Aviva informed me. "He works for the city. He's communications director for the Mayor's Office of Housing."

"Paid flak," Ted said.

"Never mind that," Aviva said. "Kate and Orit, you're moving in with us."

Kate began to protest. Aviva stopped her.

"I won't hear any argument," Aviva said. "This is the best place for Leo. He needs a familiar home. Thank goodness we have the room. You stay as long as you like."

Orit accepted on the spot. She said they couldn't afford to rent a new place, and this way, Leo could stay in his preschool.

You could've knocked me over with a kugel. Kate and Orit were moving in? Only four months ago, there'd been no room for me! They had turned out to be a pair of regular spongers, those two, and they were bringing Leo with them and their rackety little dog.

"I don't know," Kate said, looking anxiously at Ted. "Maybe it's not a good idea."

"Convince her, Ted," Aviva said.

Ted was silent. Then he looked at Aviva. "Can I talk to you for a minute?"

"I won't have Leo crashing at an Airbnb," Aviva said.

With a hard look at his wife, Ted left the room. A second later, Aviva followed, her face set and determined. I heard them clatter down the back stairs.

"Okay, got to go. Henry needs me," I said to Kate and Orit, and I dashed back to Henry's house. Henry was packing up his rod and reel to go fly-casting in Golden Gate Park, the one place he insisted that I let him drive himself. I rushed past him, hurried into the backyard, and pressed my ear to a crack in the fence.

". . . time," Aviva was saying.

"Where's he going to sleep? Are you giving him Eli's room?"

"Of course I am!" Aviva said. "It's not doing anybody any good, sitting there empty."

"It's not empty," Ted said fiercely.

"It's empty of all that matters. I've waited long enough. Our friends need us. *Leo* needs us. Look at the problems he's having. He needs a safe environment and a stable home."

"What are you talking about?" Ted said.

"He won't talk to anybody besides his mothers. He used to talk to us and now he doesn't speak. He runs away. He won't look me in the eye. He has issues, and it's going to make things worse for him if his home life is disrupted."

"Orit says there's nothing wrong with him."

"I know more about children than she does. She doesn't want to believe it, but his silence isn't normal."

"I can't have him in there," Ted said. His voice broke. "I'm not ready."

There was a long pause. I shifted against the fence, and a loose board creaked.

"Here's what we're going to do," Aviva said. "Kate and Orit will go out to pick us up some lunch. Shelley will take care of Leo. I'm giving you two hours to go into that room and say your good-byes. You can shut the door and sit in there and cry or rage or do whatever you have to do. Turn off the goddamned fish tank and let the fish strangle. When Kate and Orit return, they are moving into this house."

A strange noise passed through the fence, an utterance all too human. I thought it must have come from Ted although it sounded like weeping.

"You can't put him in that room and pretend that he's your child," Ted choked.

"That's your problem, right there. Thinking of Leo like that. It's true that being with Leo makes me think of Eli, but I'm not confused about the fact that Eli is dead. Nothing could be clearer. We lost our sweet boy and he's never coming back. But this is now. Not the past, the present." I heard her voice growing louder; she was walking toward the fence. "Our friends need our help, and they're going to get it."

I backed away, but she already knew I was there.

"Shelley! Get over here, please!"

AVIVA STOOD ON THE sidewalk, foot tapping.

"What's going on?" Henry called from the car. He was about to drive to the park.

Aviva leaned into the window. She said that a fire had damaged Kate and Orit's apartment, and they were coming to stay for as long as they wanted. "One of these days, I'm confiscating your license. But, for now, you go ahead. I need Shelley to look after Leo."

Henry broke into a smile. "Anything Kate needs, I'm here." He drove off, waving.

"At least I made Henry happy," Aviva said. "He's kinder to Kate than he is to Ted. Or me," she added tartly.

No way did I want to be stuck with the kid, so I said I had homework and housework to do.

"It'll have to wait. As of now, you're on Leo duty. Ted took off; I don't know when he'll be back. Kate and Orit are going to see if they're letting people into their building. I've got to get their rooms ready. I'll put Kate and Orit downstairs; that'll give them privacy. Leo upstairs. That's where I'll start." She looked happy as she planned. It was classic auntie behavior: the pleasurable pain of vicarious distress. Who doesn't thrill to a crisis, especially when the trouble has fallen on somebody else?

I had no choice but to follow her into the house.

"Leo! Shelley's here!" she called.

Leo careered into the room. Aviva tried to hug him; he dodged her and presented himself to me, grabbing the hem of my shirt. "Hi, Shelley," he said.

Aviva's eyebrows lifted.

"I have a bike," he said.

"Yes, it's right here. Show Shelley how you ride. But stay on the sidewalk," she called as he ran for the front door.

Up and down Leo pedaled to Henry's walkway and back. What'd he need watching for, if this was his only trick?

"Comin' your way!" Leo yelled. "Comin' your way! Look out!"

I waved my arms to stop him. "You're not doing much," I said.

He kicked his back wheel like a cowboy in a movie spurring a snorting pony.

"Real adventurers go places. They don't just go in circles."

He took off pedaling in the opposite direction, not once looking back. *Atta boy*. I went into the garage and wheeled out Ted's city bike. Ted's road bike was missing; he must have gone for a long ride. Leo reappeared proudly.

"My father took me to school every day on his bicycle," I said. "I rode with him all over Gejiu until he got sad and I had to go by myself."

Leo stared at the bigger bike. It was clear he was ready for a ramble.

"Sit here," I said, lifting him to the rear rack. I showed him how to hold his feet so they wouldn't get caught in the spokes. He listened intently and then pulled off one of his shoes and brandished his socked foot. *Leo*, his sock said, on a banner flown by a dinosaur whose cheeky smile made me laugh. Once I'd saved enough to buy myself a mobile phone and the brand-new laptop that I planned to send to Father, I'd find some dinosaur socks that read *Cousin Deng*.

I snugged his shoe back on and swung into the saddle. Leo gripped me around the waist.

"Let's go find Henry," I said.

We sailed down the street and headed toward Golden Gate Park. The wind felt wonderful blowing through my hair after the

airless rooms in Ted and Aviva's house. Happy squeals floated from
the back end of the bike. When we arrived, Leo's eyes were shining. He laughed with gusto, swinging his dino'd feet.

"Hey, where're your shoes? Did they fall off while we were
riding?"

He waggled his feet, showing off his socks again, and told me
he'd hidden his shoes on the sidewalk. He thought it was a great
joke that we'd biked off without them. Laughs came to Leo more
easily than words.

Henry was in his usual spot at the casting ponds, a ten-minute
ride from the house. There were three large rectangular pools, or
"ponds" as the anglers called them, empty of fish, where people
practiced. He'd taken me with him several times and tried without
success to teach me how to cast. Being gangly made me prone to
getting tangly.

"I tried to interest Ted when he was young so we could go
fishing together."

"Did he learn?" I'd asked Henry, my line limp on the water.

"He was hopeless."

I didn't see the point of launching a line when there were no
fish to catch, but for Henry's sake, I'd tried. It was beautiful to
watch him whip his line over the water. He'd stand on the concrete
deck between the ponds or wade in his rubber overalls right into
the weirdly green water. His face relaxed; his grumpiness subsided.
Of all the time I spent with Henry, that's where he was happy.

We waved to him; he saw us and waved back. When Henry
approached, Leo ducked his face to my knee.

"Hello there!" Henry tried to pat him on the head, but Leo
shrank from his touch. "I'm Mr. Cheng, remember? I've known
your mom, Kate, for longer than this guy's been born." He thumbed
in my direction. "What's the matter? Cat got your tongue?"

Leo signaled me. I leaned down to listen. "I want animals," he said in my ear.

"He's asking to see animals," I said to Henry.

Henry held out his rod and shook it. "Why don't you try fishing instead?"

"I want animals!" Leo wailed. I picked him up to calm him, but he thrashed like a fishing line mapping its path in the air. I almost dropped him, which gave the imp his chance. He squirmed out of my grasp and ran for the ponds. By the time I'd caught up with him, he was halfway along the concrete berm with the water right below. He might've slipped down the steep slope if a woman casting from the deck hadn't nabbed him. She looked at Henry and me, amused.

"He wants to see animals," I said weakly.

"So take him to see the bison."

I LEFT THE BIKE with Henry and walked Leo across the park road. Here was an astonishing image straight out of the Wild West: a herd of buffalo scattered on a gently rolling plain. I thought I must be dreaming. They stood stock-still, their great brown eyes watching us, unblinking. The huge humps and thunderous heads made me think of my oldest aunties, the horns as well, which were curved, short and sharp. I recalled the song about buffalo that Miss Chips taught us as part of her grammar unit, American Genocides: Past to Present, and surveyed the scene for deer and antelope too, but I saw none playing. A posted sign on the wire fence said AMERICAN BISON. You'll think me foolish to have been so agape, but bison, you see, were as strange and wondrous to me as the giant panda is to the visitors who come to Chengdu by the millions to gawp and later boast that they had. The kings of the prairie had the same effect on me. What were they doing here, so far from their natural home? Had they come seeking adventure? Did their relatives miss them? Would they stay here forever or go back home someday?

"I want up," Leo said. He raised his arms, and I lifted him to my shoulders so he could get a better look. The bison stood like statues. Not a single tail flickered. Each one faced a different direction, a lot like the humans back at the saltbox deux.

"Are they real?" I asked.

Leo nodded.

"Why don't they move?"

Leo didn't reply. He was watching in awe, motionless himself.

"It doesn't seem natural that they're frozen like that," I said.

"They run when it rains," Leo informed me.

"Why don't you like to talk?" I said. "You know how to do it just fine."

He hammered his feet against my chest. The bison didn't budge.

HENRY INSISTED ON DRIVING Leo home, saying Kate wouldn't want him to fall off the back of the bike, an alien worry to Father and me. We used to shout, as Leo did, moguling over the bumps. Father always trusted me to hang on tight.

There wasn't a car seat, but we buckled Leo securely, Henry promising to stop for ice cream from the Hippee Dippee truck, an offer he'd never made to me. I took my time biking back. They were all waiting.

"What is wrong with you?" Orit demanded. "Are you crazy? No seat, no helmet! No shoes!"

Aviva defended me, "Don't be so dramatic. Shelley's used to doing things differently."

"I'm sure it was fine. But check with us first next time," Kate said, her hand smoothing the top of Leo's head. I saw chocolate ice cream smeared on Leo's face and a toy in his hand, our own little emperor in the making. Ted stood off to the side, his hands in biking gloves and his face reddened from the wind.

"How about if Shelley takes him to the zoo tomorrow?" Henry said. "Give you gals some time to get organized." Ted flicked a look at his father but didn't contradict him. He must've come around to Aviva's behest: the spongers were indeed moving in.

"We'd be so grateful," Kate said. She knelt to hug Leo. When she stood, there were tears in her eyes. "I'm sorry. It's been a hard day. Thank you so much," she said to Aviva. To Ted, gently, "I know it's a lot to ask."

Ted cleared his throat and gripped one gloved hand in the other.

"I want you to know —" he began, and then Henry interrupted.

"Take whatever you need from my house. Books, kitchenware, extra sheets and blankets. Take Diana's clothes. I kept a lot of her things. We can go through them together." He looked like a kid unwrapping a longed-for present. Kate next door was better than ice cream, even if delivered at the price of her misfortune. He hadn't noticed how he'd cut off Ted, who'd disappeared into the house.

"You should've let him speak," I said to Henry later. I hung his cap and jacket and put away his casting gear.

"He's not used to me yet. Once he gets to know me, he'll start talking."

"Not Leo. Ted."

Henry growled, "What business is it of yours?"

"Leo's going into Eli's room. Ted doesn't want him to," I said.

"It's about time. I don't like the way he mopes. He's not the only one who lost people he loved. And he's a quitter. I don't like quitters. He left his job at the newspaper just because he wrote that his mother worked alone at night. It was a stupid thing to quit over. He was feeling sorry for himself. I told him not to blame himself, but he didn't listen. He never listens to me."

"He took that job in the mayor's office. Isn't that what you wanted?"

"Huntington brought him to his senses. That freelance business was taking him nowhere."

"Next time, let him speak," I said, thinking of the crying I'd heard from behind the fence. But Henry was thinking only of Kate.

"I want you to be helpful to the girls. Look after Leo, get him talking. He's got a real interest in science. According to Kate, he says an elephant seal weighs more than an elephant." He chuckled. "Now there's a bright kid."

What the heck was an elephant seal? "Everybody knows that," I said.

"I've got a book here somewhere." He searched the shelves and found it, *The Encyclopedia of Animals*, with full-color plates.

"Diana would've been happy. She and I always hoped that Kate and Ted would marry. Of course, it didn't turn out that way. Diana understood before I did." He shook his head. "I was a dummy. But I always knew how special Kate is."

"It's only temporary. They're not staying for good." *But I am.*

"Give him the book; that's the ticket to Leo. He'll warm up once he gets to know me."

I made dinner with a scowl.

"What's eating you?" Henry said.

"They're making a lot of work for Aviva," I said.

"Baloney. Admit it. You don't want competition crowding you out."

My hand shook when he said that, and soup slopped on the table.

"Now, now," Henry said, amused by my dismay. "Think of our two houses as the family compound. You're finally living at the *lao jia*. You got what you've always wanted."

"Not like this," I said darkly from that part of myself that we all have, the part that speaks fluent auntie.

13.

HSW

S UDDENLY I WAS TAKING CARE OF AN OLD MAN AND
a kid and a dog. Henry's hammertoes punched back, and the
paring knife came out again. Leo couldn't sleep at night; he missed
his old bedroom. Kate came over to say that Leo was asking for
me and if I wasn't too busy, could I tuck him into bed? He was
cross when I entered. *I want Shelley*, he said, pushing Kate toward
the door. I perched on the bed and told him that the biggest bison
in Golden Gate Park had called to make a bet: who could fall asleep
faster, Leo or Shelley? *Animals can't talk*, Leo said, disgusted. *That's
why I like them. They don't need words. They* growl. He showed me
his fangs and claws and asked for a bedtime story. I stretched out on
the floor and began that old chestnut that Aviva had recited about
the cowherd and the weaver princess, but Leo stopped me. *She tried*

to tell me that one. I didn't like it. He started climbing down from the bed for a bisonback ride, so I hastily started in on a different tale, one that Mother used to tell me, the story of the fisherman in the Peach Blossom Forest. He travels far from home to a distant land where everyone lives in prosperity and peace. I had the bright idea to speak in Mandarin so Leo would fall asleep faster, but the switcheroo didn't work. He asked me to start over and speak more slowly so he could try the words himself. I tried to be somniferous, not an easy task for me, but I did my best to bore him.

Eventually, Leo's eyes drooped and his questions stopped and he fell so quiet that I rose to put my hand on his chest to make sure he was breathing. He looked peaceful sleeping in Eli's bed. His pillow was bunched beside him in the shape of a smile, and I thought again of how wrong it was to leave a perfectly good bed empty. In fact, the whole room looked different from its earlier frozen state. The tiny blue and orange fish darted back and forth as before but now they seemed more playful than frenzied and the filter's mad bubbling a cheery musicale. Eli's portrait of Diana and all the drawings he'd made were gone, replaced by large colored pictures of animals in their baby state, hippos and zebras and cuddly polar bears. Leo had told me that the park was full of coyotes and hawks and even a mountain lion, but here were propaganda posters from the School of Darn Cute. A bright-eyed monkey watched me from a hanging scroll, so lifelike in his aspect that I almost checked *his* breathing. I supposed I sported the same simian expression every time I hung about in the kitchen doorway—avidly curious, enviably nimble. Alert to my next feeding and ready to jump if I had to.

"Thank God for you, Shelley," Aviva said when I emerged. Leo was a handful. Orit was working late, and Kate was exhausted. Aviva had sent her to bed. "His routine was disrupted, so he can't sleep, and he won't let me tuck him in though you know what a good storyteller I am. I learned a new one I'd like him to hear, a Native American tale. The Chinese folktales all end sadly."

This I knew. Once, at a gathering of the relatives at the *lao jia*, a year after Mother died, I tried to get Father to tell one of his little stories, which I'd boasted to the cousins were funnier and cleverer than anything they'd heard. Though Father hadn't told me a story since Mother raised her hand to her mouth and passed into the night, I thought that if he had an audience of more than me, he might begin again.

He refused. The cousins silently jeered me. In the old coal shed to which they later dragged me, their kicks landed hard, teaching me to keep quiet.

"Why didn't you tell a story?" I cried to Father later. "I promised them you would."

"The stories were for her," Father said brusquely. "Now that she's gone, there's no point."

"But I liked them too!"

"Then you're a fool," Father had said. "Never trust a story with a happy ending."

Aviva gave me a cup of milk and a few niblets of pretzels. "Leo's bedtime snack. He didn't want it." Bedtime snacks, a fluffy pillow. Leo had three mothers now: Kate, Orit, and Aviva. I tried not to feel cheated that I had not a one. Resentment curdles contentment like a squeeze of lemon into milk, a lesson I had lately learned from watching Ted and Henry.

"I wish Leo would talk to me the way he talks to you," Aviva said. "He used to. Orit says he'll talk as soon as he's settled. But I'm worried. As a professional, you know, not because he ignores me. I can see he's got a problem. *Problem*, I shouldn't say *problem*.

The word upsets Orit. He talks a blue streak to his mothers, but not a word to me. Apparently, he doesn't talk much at preschool either. There are one or two kids he's friends with, but in group, he clams up. Orit says he's being shy and he'll grow out of it. Kate asked the pediatrician, and she said he might be feeling anxious about starting kindergarten. We're to keep an eye on things, see how he does. I agree with Kate. It's not normal. Orit's in denial. But if he's super shy, or going mute around adults, or developing some sort of anxiety problem, what's he doing talking to you? You get more out of him than anyone. Why is that do you suppose? It's very interesting."

She could have used a vocabulary tune-up. *Interesting* was not a synonym for *maddening*. Perhaps she was growing more proficient in the feint of the Chinese groove.

"Make yourself shorter," I suggested and demonstrated my squat.

"Oof. If I could do that, which I can't, I'd never get out of it without a winch and a tow truck. What story did you tell him? It worked like magic."

"The story of the fisherman who goes to the Peach Blossom Forest."

"I never heard that one," Aviva said.

And she called herself a storyteller.

"My mother told it to me. Every Chinese schoolchild knows it."

"Well, *I* don't," Aviva said. "You're a lifesaver, Shelley. Truly. I want you to have this." She handed me an iPhone with a cracked screen. My fingers greedily closed over it, called to the smooth and white.

"I bought a new one," Aviva said. "I've added you to our plan. I like the convenience of text."

I thanked her, wise to the fact that she liked the convenience of texting *me*. All day long at the *lao jia*, people were coming and going, needing this or that. But I was happy to take what she was giving. Now I could save exclusively for Father's laptop.

"How's Henry? We've been so busy that I haven't had the chance to check. Orit gets me up for a run before work and boot camp on Sunday mornings. I love that Orit's a doer like me. She takes me to her synagogue for Friday-night services. It's been ages since I've gone. I don't like going alone. Ted used to come with me to make me happy, but he stopped after Eli died. I'm not saying I wish I'd married someone Jewish, but it would've been easier, for sure. You know, when you're young, how you can't know what will be important to you later? Oh, ha ha. You're *still* young. You haven't discovered that yet. What a treat you have in store. I'm joking."

Before the doer could dream up more doings to be done by me, I fled.

THE DOG'S NAME WAS Crouder, a furry, blurry, white terrier mix. There was something paranormal about him: he stared directly at me into *both my eyes at once*. I couldn't figure out how he did it, but the trick left me unnerved. As far as I was concerned, Crouder's whole species was invasive, and in particular, Crouder. He barked when they left him in the house by himself, so they put him in the backyard and he barked even harder. He dug under the fence and showed up at our back door where he whimpered like a baby until Henry opened wide and Crouder sauntered in, heading straight for Diana's armchair with a satisfied doggy smile. Once again, I'd been bilked by my own ilk. I'd failed to spot the sponger until it was too late to squeeze him out. Henry didn't mind him, because once in a while, Leo came looking for

Crouder, which brought Kate over. Nobody made him light up like Kate did.

"Look at his ear," Henry told me, pointing at Crouder curled on Diana's chair.

I looked. I couldn't believe it. A large black mole was tucked into Crouder's right ear flap.

"He's got the mark!" Henry said.

The Zheng family emblem. A chill ran down my spine.

"Did you see this?" I asked Ted later. I showed him Crouder's pull tab, but Ted only shrugged. He'd done as Aviva ordered and let their friends move in, but he seemed lost to himself. The book he was supposed to ghostwrite had fallen through. Kate had urged him to write his own book instead. *Tell your story. Maybe it'll help.*

I knew how he would answer. There wasn't much doer in Ted.

AND THEN, AS IF I didn't have enough to handle, HSW started hanging around. I'd found out from Henry that the mysterious personage with the mania for monograms and taste for tailored togs was Ted's childhood chum Huntington Wong. Like Kate, he'd known Henry for years. His mother and Diana had been close friends and had raised their sons together. Both women had served as church deacons, but Henry didn't go to Sunday services anymore. As Mr. Bill Lee had told me, he didn't feel like he belonged the way that Diana did.

Huntington's parents had passed, but Huntington still called the old neighborhood home. He'd married a rich Chinese American beauty from the Peninsula; they had two little girls and had lived in a luxury building on Broadway Street, the Gold Coast of San Francisco, until Huntington decided to run for city supervisor. He moved his family to the Sunset so he could run from District

Four, residency being a requirement of the office. Now he was
Supervisor Wong, native son made good. He was making a name
for himself standing up for immigrant rights and for small business
owners against protection rackets.

"He hasn't forgotten where he came from," Henry boasted.
"He told me the other day that he'd rather hang out here with me
than play another round of golf with the backstabbing ass-kissers
he deals with at city hall. That speaks volumes. Success hasn't gone
to his head."

"Why leave his suits and shirts here?" Huntington had moved
them to the bonus room downstairs.

"He's loyal. He says nobody does his shirts better than Mrs. Lum
at the dry cleaner around the corner. He never stops fighting for us
regular folks. I'm taking him to the ponds. He's asked me for some
pointers."

My Zheng proboscis twitched. I was protective of my protector,
source of my shelter and wages. I didn't trust Huntington Wong,
whose easy laughter rose from him like a courtesan's jasmine scent.
I'd figured out that Henry's slow-growth approach to the market
was producing a winning streak. On days he finished up, he cele-
brated with Maker's Mark. On down days, he imbibed an inferior
brand that gave him a sour stomach. Lately he'd been the picture of
gastric repose. As luck would have it, his money was piling up, and
I didn't want it going into a politician's pocket. To put it bluntly: I
needed those funds for myself. My semester was ending soon; I had
to reenroll to keep my student status, plus Professor Luo said that if
I continued my successful performance, there was no telling where
it would lead.

"Ask Ted to join you," I suggested. "He'd like to see his friend."
Henry and Ted hadn't spoken since the day Leo moved in. I could
vanquish two birds with a single pebble: bring Ted to keep an eye

and a hand on Henry's wallet, and get Ted and Henry talking, or at least in close-enough proximity that the Chinese groove had the chance to work its magic. The groove was conditioned, you see, to prize the family unit over anyone within. That might sound oppressive, but it has its uses. Sometimes, nothing else but custom, held in the body as a memory centuries old, can salvage the connection between a fractured father and son.

"Ted? He's not a sportsman. He'd ruin a nice afternoon between Huntington and me. He's got no respect for history and traditions. Huntington ran hurdles in high school. I was his coach. Great competitor. Full of heart."

"Then I'm coming with you," I said.

But Henry's own nose was twitching. After two months of living in the saltbox together, familiarity was breeding. It's a cost of family life. The *lao jia*, inevitably, lays one bare to the others.

"First, you're jealous of Kate's little boy. Now it's Huntington Wong."

He was right to call me jealous, but didn't I have good cause? Just when I'd gotten a *ye ye*, HSW had imposed.

"Huntington's used to having a caddy," I said. "You'll need me to handle the tackle."

That sounded right to Henry. He told me to fetch his favorite fly rod for Huntington to borrow. A man that loyal deserved Henry's thanks.

I hustled to show Henry that I was every bit as loyal as Native Son Made Good.

I'D BEEN WRONG AND I wasn't too proud to admit it. Huntington was a prince among men. As soon as he arrived, he insisted that I join them for lunch. From what he'd heard from Ted, I was a multitalented multitasker with big dreams and my feet firmly planted. It was high time we got acquainted. He drove us across town to a Chinatown establishment where the owner greeted him—*Right this way, Supervisor Wong*—and ordered special dishes served to us by his wife, a hairsprayed lady who good-naturedly ribbed her guest, *Where's your beautiful wife? We never see her anymore.*

She's looking after her mother, Huntington said, winking at Henry and me, since earlier he'd told us that his wife, Delilah, was visiting her horse in Woodside. *She has her mare; I have you,* he said to Henry with a grin. *You're what keeps me anchored.* Soon appeared the silky rock cod I selected from the tank at Huntington's invitation. He served the eye and cheek to Henry, who smacked his lips in anticipation, and the largest portion to me. Then he asked for the chef, who came out and apologized for his inferior cooking while Huntington heaped praise, a classic display of the Chinese groove. Huntington, more than Ted, knew how the groove was oiled.

Following lunch, we went to a gentlemen's fly-fishing shop, where Huntington asked Henry's advice about which rods were the best and under what conditions. They debated for a long time, Henry expansive under the younger man's attention. Huntington purchased the rod that Henry recommended, saying, *You'll have to use this for me often. I want an expert to break it in.* Then he bought Henry a new fishing vest and twelve beautiful hand-tied flies. Henry tried to refuse the gifts, but Huntington was so hurt that his old friend's father wouldn't let him show his appreciation that Henry had to relent. I was touched by Huntington's solicitous concern, which lightened Henry's step. We arrived, giddy, at Golden Gate Park.

Huntington wouldn't begin until I arranged myself beside him. *It would mean a lot to Henry*, he said under his breath, pressing an extra rod he'd brought into my hands. My first tries landed well, and I basked in Huntington's praise. He was good, almost as good as Henry. He cast his line deftly.

"It's the rod," Huntington said modestly. "It makes me look better than I am." Every few casts, he stopped to ask questions of Henry, who analyzed Huntington's mechanics flick by flick.

After a while, seeing the two of them engrossed, I went for a walk by myself. I walked all the way to the grassy meadow where I'd camped with Ron and the boys. There were no tents standing, and the grounds were deserted except for a few tourists renting bicycles at the park gates. An officer patrolled on a sad-eyed horse. Walking back, I stopped at the bison paddock and hallooed to them from the fence. They didn't turn to greet me, though by now we were old friends. Leo and I visited them almost every day, followed by a stop at the Hippee Dippee ice cream truck. The cloud cover was burning off, and the tall trees along the road, usually dark and forbidding, turned richly green in the sun. I looked straight up into the luxuriant branches, felt the solid earth beneath me and the upward pull of the trees. I'd fulfilled my First Achievable. I had a full-fledged family now and a place to call home, and once a body has a home (you know as well as I), the momentous things in life that one profoundly desires feel within fingertip reach. *Love* was next, *Love* and *Fortune*, Achievables Two and Three. Promises made, promises to keep. The sky broadened into a wash of blue. Sunlight reigned through the trees.

14.
Everything Right

E VERY NIGHT, AFTER DOING MY HOMEWORK AND helping Henry to bed, I sat at Diana's desk in my mango-colored bedroom ready to deliver on my promise to Lisbet of three splendid poems. There was just one problem: I didn't know how to start. My fervent feelings weren't coughing up the goods. The more nights that passed, the more I doubted myself. Was it possible that I didn't possess the true soul of a poet?

"There's an app you can use," Paloma advised. "You choose your theme then pick the imagery you want—you click on their pictures or upload your own. The algorithm does the rest."

"Show us a photo of her," Eddie said. "I still don't believe she exists."

I pulled out my new old phone and showed them Lisbet

on the grass at Honghe University. Her hazel eyes were cast in shadow. Her faint smile moved like a force through my chest. She was a swallow, endlessly swooping, and I was the birder, trying to spot her on the wing. I couldn't use an app to write the poems for me.

"Glenna Ohhhhh," Eddie said. "She was asking about you at lunch."

"It's almost June," I said. "Our birthdays are coming up. I'm sure I'll hear from Lisbet soon."

At Diana's desk, I sweated through the night, trying to think like an algorithm. Henry called me a lovelorn fool and chuckled at my distress. He said I'd be better off studying for final exams. I was running out of time to ask him to pay for another semester, but I hadn't figured out a surefire way to prompt Henry to offer.

One night, after another fruitless session, I saw the light switch on in Henry's bedroom. It was past midnight. I tapped lightly and he called to me to come in.

"Can I get you anything?" I asked.

He was sitting up in bed in striped pajamas. Without his glasses on, he looked softer, younger. He wasn't holding a book or magazine. He still had his watch on—he'd forgotten to take it off.

"You happy here? With our arrangement?" The words burst out of him. I wasn't the only one spring-loaded with worry. Instead of a poem, providence had arrived.

"*Ye Ye*, I'm happy here. I have two more weeks in the program, then I don't know what to do. I need money to pay for the next semester. Otherwise, I'll have to leave school." *And overstay my visa*, I thought, which Henry would never abide.

"You're a damn fool," Henry said. "Waiting so long to speak up."

I swallowed hard and nodded. I thought of Father asking his boss for the money to send me here. Over the years, I'd come to think that Father had not a shred of pride left in him, but now I wasn't sure. Maybe Father felt the same as I suddenly did, flimsy in substance and weakened by need. Hollowed-out from the inside like a melon scooped of its flesh. I wondered if the bad feeling went away in a person who has to ask again and again, or if it showed up every time, even in the daily beggar. I never wanted to learn the answer to that awful question.

"You want to stay?" Henry said. "You like it here fine?" He sounded gruff but he looked uncertain.

"I want to stay with you, and stay in school," I said.

Henry sat back and worked himself into a smile. "When I first hired you, Ted predicted you wouldn't be able to stand me for more than a week." His voice shook a little and I realized he was relieved. Since I'd come to live with him, Aviva no longer mentioned social workers or day programs or assisted living. She didn't bring him fish oil or offer to sign him up for the build-a-birdfeeder class at the senior center. I was his shield, his safety net, his cover. Along with Huntington, I was his only ally.

"He was wrong," I protested.

"Dead wrong," Henry said. His spit-shined lips twitched in satisfaction. I had sympathy for them both—for Ted, whose father didn't believe in him the way Father believed in me, and for Henry, plagued as he was by his own awful question: Was he as unlovable as his son believed?

"So I can tell Professor Luo I'll continue?"

"You take those exams first. If you do well—really well—then I'll pay your school fees for as long as you keep up your marks."

I fetched him a glass of warm milk and rearranged his pillow. As I reached across to fold down the blanket, he patted me on the arm.

"You're a good boy. Your father must miss you." His eyes clouded. "It's okay with him, is it? That you're not going home?"

"This is what he wants. He promised Mother."

Henry sighed and went to sleep.

I WROTE TO FATHER, care of Cousin Deng, to tell him that not only had I been promoted at the family department store, but my American *ye ye* was generously paying for me to continue my studies. I was living with him now, the better for my schooling. I heard back from Cousin Deng: *Gave your message to your dad. Nothing new to report. Your foreign girlfriend's looking for you.* He forwarded an email from Lisbet, and a bolt of joy struck me like a fist bump to my throat. *I've been thinking of you,* she said. I raced to Eddie's apartment, heart pounding.

"The mysterious lady checks in at last," Eddie said. "What are you going to tell her?"

"I want to see her, of course! She's in L.A., staying with her mother. She said her mother wanted her home because her stepfather left."

"You better take your exams and keep the old man happy," Eddie said.

I asked to borrow Paloma's laptop and attacked it with trembling hands. Lisbet's answer came back so quickly that it seemed like she'd never gone away. *I'm sorry I've been out of touch. I'd love to see you too.* Three times I read the message. I would've crawled right into the laptop if my nose-of-note Zheng nib hadn't gotten in the way. I danced for a dizzy second, trying to ignore the black fish of worry bobbing along to the beat. How could I confess to Lisbet that I wasn't a poet yet? Toe pruner, bean topper, world-class sponger. Loyal caregiver to an old man, a kid, and a dog, but not, I feared, a poet. I wrote back to say that I'd come as soon as I could after the term was over.

Take the time you need. I'll wait, Lisbet wrote.

HENRY DRILLED ME EVERY day, saying, *I have to protect my investment.* I took the exams and aced them. The score on my latest TOEFL—that standardized behemoth, that bugbear test of proficiency and polish that plagues every non-native-English-speaking student—still had room for improvement, but after three tries, it was climbing. At the top of my exercise book, Professor Luo had written: *Excellent work. I enjoyed your composition on urban wildlife.* I brought his comments straight to Henry, who pretended with a grunt to complain. *Send me the bill for next semester. Better to spend my money on you than on my ungrateful son.* He dug from a drawer an old magnet advertising Hong's Fine Food Market and posted Professor Luo's praise on the refrigerator door.

Leo, like Henry, asked for me every night. He sat on the blanket with his stubby legs crossed, elbows on his knees and his chin propped in his hands. The little mouth breather made listening into a sport, which I played to win. I called up from the depths of my childhood curtailed all the folktales and legends my mother had told to me. Aviva said I should tell the stories gratis for the sheer pleasure of childhood ritual handed down through generations, but Kate knew to slip me a twenty. Seeing as the fee structure was as flat as the service day was long, I spoke in Mandarin in hopes of putting Leo to sleep as fast as I possibly could. My cadence was his lullaby, my recycled repertoire his glide path to the country of conked-out, the district of doss, the suzerain of slumber, where often I joined him from my spot on his bedroom floor.

HENRY SAID I COULD have a weekend off to visit Lisbet. Kate was right next door, and he'd ask Huntington to drop by. Lisbet and I made a date. *Can't wait to see u*, she wrote.

On Commencement Day, I watched Eddie and Paloma cross the stage in cap and gown and took pictures of them smiling with their arms around their parents. Mrs. Low pulled me into a great big hug. *Are you making yourself useful, like I said?* She was thrilled that Eddie and Paloma had completed their two years at City College and were moving on to four-year universities. Eddie was going to S.F. State and Paloma to U.C. Berkeley. *You can do it too*, Mrs. Low said. *Get your* ye ye *to pay for it.* Her enthusiasm touched me. No one had ever thought of me attending college, not even Henry. Mrs. Low hugged me again and gave me a red envelope with fifty dollars in cash, enough for me to buy a ticket for the overnight bus to L.A. with munch money to spare.

The day finally arrived. I knocked at the saltbox stretch. The door flung open and Crouder rushed to pleasure himself on my leg. Before I could say a word, Aviva was off and running.

"Leo, Shelley's here!" She motioned me inside. She wore black stretchy pants that ended at the knees and an egg-yolk-yellow jacket that gave her a bilious look. Her curly hair was tucked under a Giants baseball cap. "Thank God you're here. There's been unhappiness in the house."

Leo ran into the room. "You shut up!" he yelled.

Aviva knelt and tried to hug him, but Leo dashed away. "Well, at least he said *something*. Kate and Orit are looking at apartments again. They haven't found a thing to rent; everything's so expensive. It's stressing Leo out. I've told them, listen, stay here as long as you like. Ted's made the adjustment. I knew he'd be okay once we cleaned out Eli's bedroom. We're having a wonderful time. I love all the energy they bring."

"Hello, Shelley," Ted said, coming upstairs. His arms and legs looked very brown and his face was windburned. He spent every weekend taking long solo bicycle rides over the Golden Gate Bridge and into the Marin Headlands. It didn't seem to bother him that Leo didn't speak. It gave them something in common.

"How were your finals?" he asked.

I flashed a thumbs-up. Earlier, he'd taken me aside to ask if Father had sent me adequate funds to pay for a second term, and I told him that Henry had offered to pay if I did well on my exams. *Anything to protect his investment,* Ted had said, sounding exactly like his father. He couldn't bring himself to credit Henry for kindness.

"I'll be gone a couple of nights. I'm going to L.A.," I said.

"But who will take care of Henry?" Aviva said. "We've got our hands full here."

"Shelley can take a vacation. I don't doubt he needs one," Ted said.

"You're no help," Aviva said. "You won't even set foot in his house." More than once, she suggested that he go next door and check on his father. Ted refused. He did everything else she asked of him but not that.

"I've left him dinners," I said. "For lunch, he'll go out. He can get his own breakfast. And Huntington said he'd drop by."

Ted frowned. "Huntington's been spending a lot of time there," he said to Aviva. "I see his car often."

"The UPS guy dropped off a package addressed to him at your father's the other day. I brought it into the house."

"I hope my father isn't putting more ideas in his head. I don't need another job."

"Stop feeling so self-conscious. You're more than qualified for that job," Aviva said.

"So I'm going then," I said.

They looked at me, surprised that I was there.

"Have fun," Ted said.

"You look really nice," Aviva said. "That's a nice shirt. Are you going to see a girlfriend?"

Yes.

SHE WAS WAITING FOR me on the curb in a sundress and glasses and looking smaller than I remembered. It took me a moment to believe it was really her. When I did, love came rushing back. She'd changed her hair color from black to almost white and her slippers to leather sandals. As the bus pulled up, she tucked her book and sunglasses into her bag and scanned the windows. I scrunched low and ran again through my options: handshake, hug, kiss, no kiss, cheek, mouth, elbow. I felt like anything I did would be wrong. I stared at the floor of the bus, saw Father there on his hands and knees, scrubbing. The footprints of others, the aunties' dirt. But I had gotten away from all that. I'd climbed on my mop and soared across the sea all the way to Peach Blossom Land. Blinking Father from my sights, I pulled up my socks, flattened my hair, rose to my feet, and waved.

As soon as I stepped from the bus, she hugged me and held on. She felt different in my arms, lighter in breadth, hollow in her bones, and her smell, musky with sweat, was unfamiliar.

"How are you?" she said, stepping back to get a good look. My heartbeat was so violent, all I could see of her was smile. The old Lisbet, the one sapped of spirit the last time I'd seen her in Gejiu, had never smiled so big.

"I'm sorry," I blurted. "I'm sorry for how angry I was."

Lisbet laughed. "How long have you been waiting to say that?"

"Since I saw you last. Almost a year ago."

"That's a long time to hold your breath." She didn't let go of my hand. "Anyway, we're here now. And you! Living with your rich American uncle, just like you said you would."

"He's not rich, but I'm going to be. I'm a businessman, working with a team of technology innovators to tap into the Chinese market." The words pouring out of me as if I were Aviva.

She raised an inquisitive brow, the old amusement playing on her face. There was my Lisbet, not so different after all. She tucked her arm through mine. "I want to hear all about it."

She drove us to a café in Santa Monica that overlooked the ocean. "I need the sea," she said. "I need to verge on water." We settled ourselves at a table under a striped umbrella, my heartbeat finally slowing. I listened as she told me of her travels and how, when she found a place she liked, she stayed a little while, working in cafés and bars until she grew restless and moved on. She'd intended to write to me, but she didn't know what to say that wouldn't sound false or stupid, so she just kept on going. She'd been to Thailand, Indonesia, Singapore, Malaysia. The Maldives, Seychelles, and Madagascar. Places her father had sailed to. She always knew she'd see me again. Of that she'd been certain.

"You should've told me. It would've helped."

"I was such a brat, I'm sorry. I was awful to everyone, especially my mom. Now that Bobby has left her, she wants us to try again. I feel sorry for her. She doesn't know how to be alone. She says she admires my independence."

"I'm never alone. I like it that way." I told her about Ted and Aviva and their son who was gone and Leo who wouldn't talk. And Kate and Orit living downstairs in what used to be the office, and Henry who was a miser with everyone but me.

"I'm glad it's worked out well for you. You look good. Happy."

"You make me happy," I said.

Another big smile. Without her black hair and the dark kohl that had used to rim her eyes, she looked fragile. Still, she was beautiful, the morning sunshine turning her cropped hair into a cap of light. She held my arm tightly as we walked. I thought she'd want to go down to the water, but she said the beach here was too crowded, so we got back in the car and drove north to Malibu along the coastal highway, beach towns on one side, ocean on the other. Houses clung to the sides of cliffs like orchids ornamenting trees.

"I've been to beaches all over," Lisbet said. "Zuma is still one of my favorites."

She parked the car on a narrow side street and led me across the road. She waited while I used the changing room to struggle out of my jeans and into a pair of Eddie's swim trunks that required a double knot. We walked down a beach as wide as a river, our feet ecstatic in the soft, warm sand. Lisbet had brought a blue-and-white cotton blanket, a favorite from her travels, trimmed with tassels like the tail tips of white cats. We spread it on the sand. The day was mild, not hot enough for swimming, but Lisbet said that whenever the ocean called, she followed. I watched as she stepped out of her dress. She was wearing an old bikini printed with tiny blue stars, its bottom slightly sagging. Her breasts, shifting in their triangle cups, sped up my heart again. Before I could reach for her, she ran into the water.

I wasn't a good swimmer, so I watched her from the sand. Again and again she dove. I remembered Miss Chips telling Yu and me that her niece was coming from California, and how I'd pictured her as a blond on a surfboard, big-bottomed and big-breasted, gyrating in the spray. What a lazy lad I'd been, consigning my imagination to the dull mentality of the pack. We all of us feel safe behind our walls. Lisbet was the first to unlock the gate in me. To her, I wasn't a spawn of a bastard; son of a failure; moneyless, motherless boy. I was a person with a history and a future of my own. Is there any mystēry why she was the one I chose?

She ran up and scattered water on my head, "from the baptismal font of the blessed sea," she said, and plopped herself on the sand. She asked me to tell her more about my San Francisco life. I began talking and couldn't stop. I described Cook urging me to *improvise, improvise,* and the green bean-o-rama and the boarding-house rumpus and old Mr. Lee, the *erhu* player who gossiped. Eddie and Paloma, my business partners, billionaires in the making. I showed her my key chain, *888.* I said that Leo was a pretty cool kid who couldn't go to sleep without a bedtime story. He and I went every week to see the bison in the park. That's where I learned how to fly-cast, courtesy of Henry and Supervisor Huntington Wong, the son Henry wished he had.

Lisbet listened closely to every word, her eyes fixed on me behind her dark glasses. As I talked, she ran a finger tipped with salve around her mouth. I wanted to kiss the smear from her lips and dive in the swell of her belly, but I wasn't brave enough. I told her how Aviva entered every room like a whirlwind, and that Ted was like an abandoned well, dug deep and covered by moss. Diana and Eli I consigned to the grave because bringing up the dead wouldn't raise the specter of romance, only the specter of specter.

"You describe them so well, I can see them." She was propped on her hands, arms straight behind her, like Mother used to sit leaning back to listen to Father. Sand freckled her thighs, and the tops of her breasts had turned pink.

"Can I tell you the best part? Even better than finding a family, better than having a home?"

"Tell me!"

"It's been great material for my poetry," I said.

"Your poetry?"

I jumped to my feet. I had no idea what I was about to say but if I didn't fire now, I'd never launch the rocket. The surf pounded behind me. In front of me, a mirage. I felt like I was holding back the ocean.

> *On my foot*
> *A little white dog has come to sleep.*
> *Go home, little white dog.*
> *There is another who loves you.*

Lisbet clapped; I bowed, overjoyed with relief that a poem had presented itself at last.

"You see, I never forget a promise."

She sat forward and cocked her head. "What promise?"

"To become a poet like you asked. I've been working on it since you left Gejiu."

Lisbet frowned. "I don't remember asking you that."

"You made me promise! Three splendid poems."

"Oh. I'm sorry. I don't remember."

"By Golden Lake," I said. "Rainy day? Giant puppets?"

Lisbet looked embarrassed. "I told you I was a brat."

I'd been holding fast to a one-sided promise. I would've been mad had it not been for the rush I felt when speaking my very own verse, or maybe it was Lisbet's legs now casually crossed on the blanket that were causing my blood to drum.

"It was a good poem," Lisbet said. "Short but sweet." She leaned in and kissed me. A second kiss was long and lasting. She moved my hands about her body. We went to the empty lifeguard tower, but it was locked, so we took up our things and walked a long way, past Point Dume and around to the other side. At the far end of the beach, tucked among rocks, Lisbet spread the blanket. "Come here," she said, lying back. I panicked trying to unknot my swim trunks, but Lisbet waited calmly, unpeeled from her own suit and elegant in the sun. When I finally freed myself, Lisbet handed me protection—City College standards, *yes means yes*—and that was another challenge. The sand, you see, and my fumble. Lisbet helped me put it on with practiced hands, which made me swoon harder. I closed my eyes against the dazzling light. Finally, there was something in Peach Blossom Land that was better than I'd imagined.

We returned to the car in the late afternoon and discovered that the backpack I'd left under the seat was gone.

"Damn," Lisbet said. "I forgot to lock the car. I'm sorry."

I had my wallet, but my bus ticket was in the backpack, and I didn't have the money to replace it. Embarrassed, I admitted I was broke.

"I have cash at the house," Lisbet said. She stared across the highway and pointed to the cliffs. "My mother lives up there."

The road wound halfway to the top. A white house stood in a riot of garden color, its wall of windows ablaze. Tall palms feathered the eaves, and the courtyard was still and quiet. I heard the surf pounding far below, a figment, I realized, like the roll of a rocking boat that a sailor feels on land.

"Wait here for a second," Lisbet said, and she hurried into the house. I buttoned my shirt and dashed sand from my hair, composing myself to meet Lisbet's mother. Thumping and bumping started up in my nervous belly with an added flutter of shame. I'd never brought Lisbet home to meet Father. Several times she'd asked, and I'd said he worked late, he was sick, he was busy. Was I ashamed of her? she'd said. No, of Father, but I had kept silent, hiding from her his weakness and the misery under our roof.

Lisbet reappeared. "She's not here. Come in."

The house had spacious rooms, flooding light, excellent napping couches—all that I'd imagined for my rich American uncle. From our perch I could see a long wash of blue sky and ocean that stretched as far as my eye could wander. I thought of the view from Henry's picture window of little box houses, telephone poles, and asphalt. His was lower Peach Blossom Land; this was upper.

"Bobby's in the film business. Obviously," Lisbet said.

"Where's he gone?"

"A friend's house. He calls every night. He feels bad, leaving me with my mother. He'll pay for my ticket out of here whenever I want."

"Are you leaving?" This time, I'd find a way to stop her.

She shook her head. "Maybe just for a while. But I'll be back. My mother's talking about moving. I've promised to go with her."

"Come to San Francisco. Then we can be together!"

"We can be together now," Lisbet said, and we went into one of the cool, dark rooms and conjoined ourselves again. I lay beside her as she slept, making plans for our future. Lisbet would move to San Francisco and team up with me, Eddie, and Paloma, a perfect match, since who knew better than Lisbet what a traveler might want from an app? I'd bring her around to Henry's house and introduce her to everybody and she'd see right away how good it feels to join a new family. I fell asleep dreaming of us sailing through the Golden Gate.

15.
Crossing the Bridge

I RETURNED TO THE SALTBOX AND FOUND HENRY ALONE, standing with his back against the wall next to the picture window like a soldier trying not to get shot.

"What are you doing?"

Henry gestured violently. "Stand back. Don't let them see you!"

"Who?" I asked and went to the window. He rushed at me, lost his footing, and pitched toward the glass. I caught him just in time.

"You're going to hurt yourself."

"I saw someone out there! I've seen him before, spying on the house. Now there's two of them. Get down!"

"Come sit," I tried to soothe him.

"Don't just stand there! Draw the drapes!"

We never bothered to close the curtains. I had to hunt for the pull cord.

"Keep close to the wall!" Henry said.

I took hold of the brittle cord and yanked. It broke off in my hand.

"Goddammit!" Henry roared. "Now you've gone and done it."

I got him into his armchair and brought him a cup of tea, careful to avoid the window. I'd never seen him so worked up. He sat stiffly, clutching the arms of the chair. I could tell he was in pain. When I tried to hand him his tea, he shook his head with a grimace.

"What have you done to yourself?" I tried putting a pillow behind his back but moving him made it worse.

"It's nothing," he insisted. "Put some bourbon in that cup."

"Did you fall?"

"I was moving boxes out of the downstairs room into the garage. Next thing I know, my back's like a slab of cement."

"You should've waited for me."

"I wanted to make it nice for Huntington." His eyes shifted. "He needs a place to stay."

"He wants to stay here?" In the saltbox of my head, I wrapped my arms tightly round my mango bedroom. I would never give it up.

"He'll stay downstairs once in a while. It's no concern of yours."

"But what's going on? He's got his own house!"

Henry gave me a dark look. "He's got enemies. It's not safe for him at home."

I pressed, but Henry wouldn't say more.

I TRIED ICE PACKS, a heating pad, Advil, bourbon. I rubbed Tiger Balm into his back and laid a warm flannel where it hurt.

He groaned throughout the day and refused to call the doctor. He spoke clearly and had no other pain, so I agreed to wait and let him rest. He said that Aviva had checked on him while I was gone and Kate had brought him lunch. She'd stayed for a nice long chat. Huntington had come to drop off some things; he had a key to the house.

"But what's he doing here?" I asked.

Still he wouldn't say.

I went to the market, bought groceries for the week, and steamed a fish for supper. Henry complained he was too uncomfortable to eat and he needed to watch the street. I moved him from his armchair into a straight-backed wooden seat placed next to the picture window and set up a tray table.

"There's no one out there," I said.

"There were two of them, earlier. Standing on the sidewalk."

"You sound like a crazy old coot." A good word, *coot.* Henry taught it to me, along with *oldster, fogy,* and *codger. Every last one of those is a badge of honor,* he'd said. *The first time somebody calls you that, you've won the game of life.*

Henry lit up in anger. "You think you see everything that goes on in these two houses, but you don't know the half of it."

"I would if you told me. Maybe I could help."

"Ted's useless, I can tell you that."

"I'm not bringing you another bourbon until you tell me what's going on."

He half rose, bracing himself against the tray table to look out the window again. I grabbed his arm and kept him on his feet as the table fell with a crash. "Look what you made me do," he cried.

"If you believed me, I wouldn't get so upset."

I cleaned up the mess and brought him a second supper, which he ate defiantly, daring me to disapprove. I knew not to push. He was carrying a secret he was dying to let out. After dark, he told me to cut the lights and we watched out the window for an hour. The street stayed quiet and the sidewalk empty. I could feel Henry's disappointment growing.

"It's the Asian protection rackets," he said. "They're a bunch of gangsters. They do their dirty business all over the city, especially here in the Sunset. They force small shop and restaurant owners to pay for protection from robbery and harassment. That's why Huntington needs a place to stay. I'm a safe house for him, one of several. He's been speaking out, holding meetings, demanding the city take action. The police told him his safety's at risk."

I felt seized at the back of my neck as if grabbed by a cold, hard hand. Gangs were no joke. I knew that from Cousin Deng, who took great precautions to make sure his dealings went undetected by local bosses or, when advisable, to pay them his respect. He didn't want to end up like others he knew who'd crossed the wrong party and never walked upright again. From what Henry was telling me, Peach Blossom Land had its own share of thuggery and hoodlums. Huntington had better watch out.

"What about his family? Is he worried?"

"Delilah and the girls are staying with her parents for now. Huntington's got a security detail for public hearings and such. They offered him twenty-four-hour police protection, but he said no. He's a man of the people; he wants to go freely about. He's part of this community. He needs to be seen and heard."

"Why would protection rackets bother the Sunset District? The businesses here are small."

"Who's most vulnerable? Immigrants, that's who. They can't afford trouble. They put every cent they earn back into their businesses. They don't have options, so they knuckle under and pay. The rackets know that. They prey on those who can't defend themselves. Huntington's fighting back, and he needs my help to do it."

"He was staying here with you before I moved in." That explained the suits hanging in my closet. I almost felt bad, taking his safe house away.

Henry nodded while keeping his eye on the street. "He was glad when you moved in. He said that I needed you more than he needed the bed. But things are heating up. He's been told to take greater precaution. Delilah begged him to stay here. She told him, out of all their friends, she trusts me the most."

I was proud of Henry sticking up for the neighborhood. The small business owners were Chinese, Korean, Vietnamese, Thai. Japanese, Brazilian, Italian, Greek. Russian, South Asian, Palestinian, Irish. Many were recent arrivals, fellow travelers who were the newest and greenest Ones Who Got Away. At my very doorstep was the modern embodiment of Father's ideal: his Peach Blossom Forest bearing fruit. Of course, I'd help Henry keep Huntington safe.

I went downstairs to finish readying the bonus room for the next time Huntington stayed. In the garage, I spotted the big red sign from Hong's Fine Food Market and felt my hairline prickle. Robbers killed Diana and Eli—had that been the work of gangsters?

"Was it gangsters who killed Diana?" I asked Henry when he finally let me help him retire for the night. He was exhausted, but his signs of pain had eased. "Did they demand protection money that she refused to pay?"

He shook his head, no. "In every community, there are the strong and the weak, and the strong sometimes step on the hands of the weak and keep them there, underfoot. Sam, Diana's father, understood that. He was as fearless as they come. Who else was leaving Chinatown and coming way out here to set up shop where no Chinaman had sold his fish and cabbages before? The gangs in those days kept to Chinatown. By the time they got out here, Hong's Fine Foods was everybody's favorite, including the neighborhood cops. It wasn't gangs who killed Diana. It was probably some stupid kids who made a bad mistake."

"Do Ted and Aviva know that Huntington stays over? Maybe we should—"

"Don't tell them! Don't you say a thing. She'll blab to the whole neighborhood, and Ted will make trouble. Now stop yapping and help me."

I rolled him gently onto his side and wedged him in place with pillows. "They're going to notice if he's coming and going," I said.

Henry's dismissal floated up from the bed. "They haven't yet and they won't. They're too busy wrapped up in their own problems to pay attention to me."

AT TEN O'CLOCK, I stepped outside to check the alleyway to make sure no one was lurking. Kate was just leaving the saltbox stretch.

"Welcome home," she said. "Is everything all right?" I wanted urgently to tell her about Huntington and Henry, but I'd promised to keep quiet.

"Henry hurt himself, but he's okay now," I said.

"Do you need my help?"

I shook my head.

"He's a lot to handle, I know," Kate said. "Come with me to get some air. I'm walking to Ocean Beach."

She waited while I made sure that Henry was asleep; then we walked west toward the ocean. It was June and the fog was in, dampening our hair. I'd come to like the shrouding fog, especially at night when familiar sights dissolved at the edges into spirit ships and hide-aways. There weren't many people about, and the homes we passed were quiet. Kate threw back her head and drew a deep breath.

"I love my nighttime walks. Sometimes the house gets a lit-tle . . . crowded."

"Is Leo in bed?"

"Oh, yes, ages ago. I promised him you'd come tomorrow. Did you have a good trip?"

"It was great. I saw my girlfriend. We were really happy to see each other."

Kate smiled. "I'd like to meet her."

"My girlfriend"—I couldn't stop saying the word—"and her mother are moving up here. Or Lisbet will come without her. They don't get along so great."

"That's too bad. What's she like? Is she Chinese?"

"She's a songwriter," I said.

"So not Chinese," Kate said with a laugh. "Don't worry. I won't go old school on you. I married a white Jewish woman. Not exactly what my parents had in mind for me."

We reached the Great Highway. A couple of cars passed; then we crossed the broad road and continued to the beach. The rough-packed sand felt impassive under my feet, so different from Mal-ibu, which already seemed like a dream. Down the way, a bonfire flared. A group of friends stood in a circle, laughing and drinking. Kate and I walked down to the water to watch the breaking waves.

"My dad was really angry when I came out," Kate said. "Henry was the one who calmed him down and got him to open his heart. He jumped in his car and drove hours to see my dad. He talked with him about what it means to be a father." Her voice caught. "It was the kindest thing anyone has ever done for me."

"This was Henry?" If he could do that for Kate, why rail as he did at Ted?

Kate shook her head. "I know. I can't explain it. Ted and Henry can't see their way right. I keep thinking they'll do better. I have to believe they want to. But a lot of years have passed since Diana and Eli died and things between them are worse."

"Mr. Lee, who knew Diana's parents, says Henry and Ted blame each other for what happened," I said.

"Nobody was to blame except the guys who brought the gun. Ted and Henry know that. If anything, each blames himself. Ted hates himself for the article he wrote. When he left his job at the paper, Henry yelled at him. He called him a quitter too weak to tough it out. That was a cruel thing to say. I've tried to get him to apologize, but he won't."

Of course he wouldn't apologize—he was the father. *My* father had never apologized to me for giving up, for lying down, for scarcely leaving the bed.

"It's not in Henry's nature to say how he feels," I said. "He can't put it into words."

"None of us can," Kate said sadly. "Sometimes language isn't enough."

Not when it came to family.

THE SUMMER TERM BEGAN. Many of my classmates were new to the program; most of the students from the previous semester had either dropped out or moved on. A few who'd entered close to proficient transferred to the Academic Program, where they might earn a degree. I felt a twinge that they, like Eddie and Paloma, were getting a full education, but I didn't allow myself the flush of full-blown envy. My sights were squarely focused on Achievables Two and Three.

To celebrate our birthdays, Lisbet sent me kisses and a picture of her feet propped on the rail of a boat. She'd gone to Greece with her English cousins, but she'd be back before long to rejoin her mother in L.A. *We're moving,* Lisbet wrote. *It's between Oaxaca and Bolinas. Obviously I told her it has to be Bolinas. That's just up the coast from you.*

Eddie and Paloma took me to dinner at a Yunnanese eatery on Taraval Street that Eddie sussed out especially for me as the best place in the city for Crossing the Bridge Noodles, aliment of my ancestors, pride of Yunnan Province, and the only good reason I could think of to venerate the past. I bowed over my bowl, same as Eddie, the steam curling from the boiling broth, which sent my nostrils quivering in my avid Zheng nose.

"You should see the two of you," Paloma said. "You look like you've died and gone to heaven."

"I'm consoling myself," Eddie said, slurping.

"Over what?"

Paloma sighed. "We've decided to shut down the app. It hasn't caught fire. Tourists download it, use it a couple of times, then delete it. We're not growing fast enough."

"They don't appreciate the artistry that we put into it. But we're going to make something better," Eddie said.

I had no doubt they would. There wasn't a billionaire in the Valley who hadn't first crashed and burned. Every titan of tech boasted about the colorful failure that preceded their success.

"We've been brainstorming like crazy," Paloma said. "All ideas are welcome. You'll be a founder with us, of course."

"Dude, yes," Eddie said. "We need your contacts to develop the

Chinese market. Like that cousin of yours, Deng. He could hook us up, right?"

Deng knew everybody, I assured them. His network was loyal and vast.

"Five Minute Local was fun for people to use once or twice, but they didn't stick with it," Paloma said. "We need to come up with an essential service that'll be used again and again."

"We need repeat users," I said.

"Exactly," Eddie said. "Like Uber without the jerks." He put down his chopsticks and patted his belly. "That was so good, I could almost go for another."

"You like this noodle?" our waiter asked, collecting our empty bowls.

"Crossing the Bridge is my new favorite sport," Eddie said, which made the waiter grin. He turned to me, and we studied each other in delight. He could've hailed from Gejiu, scraggly hair and honest face included. He saw the similarity in me.

"My friend!" he exclaimed in Yunnanese. "Where are you from? How long have you been here? Did you come alone, like me, or is your family with you?" He knew at a glance that Eddie, Paloma, and I weren't related, though to the Western eye, we'd been taken more than once for siblings.

"I came by myself, but I've got a new family now," I said. We chatted for several minutes, our excitement growing.

"He's going home to Kunming in a couple of weeks," I explained. "He has relatives in Gejiu. He says he'll look up Father and let him know I'm well."

"That's wonderful," Paloma said.

"Do you have a message for him?" the waiter asked.

I hesitated. I had a lot to say to Father. But not just yet.

"Tell him everything is great. I'm working for my uncle. As soon as I get the chance, I'm going to send him the laptop I promised." The same story I'd been feeding Father for months. I saw Paloma's eyebrows raise.

"Let's take a picture for your dad," Eddie said. The waiter gave Eddie his phone. I put my arm around my new friend's shoulders, gave him a hearty squeeze, and felt my father close. I had to blink hard to clear my stinging eyes.

"Hang on," I said before we left. I reached into my pocket and retrieved my lucky key chain, *888.*

"Please, will you give him this?" I unhooked the keys and pressed the charm into the waiter's hand. He promised me he would. As an extra thanks for his kindness, I insisted he take for himself the bag of ginger chews that I carried for Henry, for I knew the Chinese groove wouldn't let him accept cash. We shook hands gladly as we parted.

"Whatever you just gave him, it'll never reach your dad," Eddie said.

"Sure it will," Paloma said. "Special delivery, hand to hand. I love it. Make it personal, and people will connect."

I wholeheartedly agreed. He was a countryman, after all, and a Yunnanese to boot.

A FEW DAYS LATER at Eddie's apartment, Paloma said, "I want you to have this," and she handed me her laptop. It was covered in stickers that only a geek could decipher.

"Are you serious?" I said.

"I bought a new one with the red-envelope money my grandmother gave me. I know you've been wanting to get one for your dad."

I thanked her profusely. "Father will be happy!"

"You could keep it for yourself," Eddie ribbed. "Then you wouldn't have to borrow mine."

"No, I promised. I'm shipping it today."

Paloma gave me a sympathetic smile. Perhaps she understood that keeping my word on this one pledge to Father would shore up my pack of lies.

I went straightaway to send the laptop to Father, care of Cousin Deng. I pictured Father unwrapping it bubble by bubble. How envious the aunties would be when he showed up nonchalantly at the next family gathering with the almost-latest technology that was Dell which was almost Apple tucked under his arm. He wouldn't need to say a word. The Chinese groove would take care of that for him. *A present for the old man from his successful son, Xue Li. The One Who Got Away.*

Then I wrote to Cousin Deng to say that I'd sent my father a big surprise present. Could Deng please deliver it straight into Father's hands? Greetings to his mother. Her pink sparkly suitcase was safely stored in the closet should she ever want it back. I myself didn't need it any longer since I was staying forever.

Deng wrote back the next day. He'd be glad to deliver my surprise gift to Father, who was doing very well. His health was good, and his appetite was strong. Deng was looking out for him, so I needn't worry. Deng's latest enterprise was going gangbusters. He wanted to hear more about my uncle's business. What was my role? Who were his partners? Maybe we all could do business together. The big news was that he and Yu were getting married. In fact, they were going to be a family. Yu was expecting a baby. Deng was so excited! He was to be the father of a little baby girl.

I have a small request. I'm going to send Yu to have the baby in California. There's a place in Los Angeles where she can go. Then the baby

will be a U.S. citizen, and Yu and I can become Americans too. With all
your success, I'm sure you have the funds to help our little girl, who will
be your niece. My own investments are presently tied up. Send me right
away $10,000 U.S. I'll join Yu as soon as the baby is born, and you can
thank me in person for looking after your father during your long absence.

Ten thousand dollars! I had only $237 to my name, which until
now had felt like an imperial sum. Deng said that the total cost of
Yu's maternity package was much higher, but he'd borrow the rest.
I was family, after all. He didn't want awkwardness between us.

"What's wrong with you?" Henry asked when I went to make
our supper. "I told you that Huntington is taking me out to dinner."

"My cousin needs ten thousand dollars to help my friend Yu
have her baby. He asked me to send him the money."

"He has a lot of *chutzpah* asking for that kind of dough."

Better not to mention where Deng had gotten the notion that
ten thousand dollars was a divot in my dough bank.

"He's probably asking everyone he knows," Henry advised.
"From what you've told me, he'll make it happen. I admire the
confidence. Look at Huntington, a self-made man. Ted could
learn a thing or two. None of this moping around, letting down
his own father. You can't expect to win if you take yourself out
of the race."

The door opened, and Huntington breezed in. No knock; he
had his key. He'd stayed a couple of times in recent days, arriving
after dark, though it didn't seem clandestine to me since he parked
his car out front. Aviva had noticed and asked me about the visits.
I told her, truthfully, he came to Henry for advice.

"You look well," Huntington told Henry. He was carrying a
suit bag over his shoulder and a batch of pressed shirts. He said he'd
just come from Mrs. Lum's laundry. "Shelley's taking such excellent care of you that the rest of us look like bums."

He didn't look anything like a bum. He wore one of his sharp suits and a gray felt hat with a feather in the band. I could smell his cologne, which he'd told me was a European custom blend of oud wood and tonka. I gave him a stack of mail addressed to him at the house. He casually flipped through it and tossed it on the table.

"Man, that's a nice-looking fedora," Henry said. "Reminds me of one I bought with my first paycheck. Where's that hat, Shelley? Where'd you put it?"

I promised him I'd find it. He wouldn't remember later that he'd asked. Hats, shoes, TV remote, medicine bottles weren't important to Henry. But he always kept track of his money.

"Try it on," Huntington said. He put his hat on Henry's head. "Fits you perfectly."

"I wore a hat like this the day I married Diana."

"Then I want you to have it." Protest and persuasion flowed back and forth until I lifted the hat from Henry's head and suggested he put on a fresh shirt for dinner. He went to his bedroom to change.

I motioned Huntington into the kitchen and kept my voice low. "Henry told me that this is a safe house for you."

"That's right."

"Is Henry in any danger? Should I take him someplace else when you're here?"

Huntington glanced toward the doorway. "Can you keep a secret? The cops watch the house. I haven't told Henry. I don't want to raise his concern. He's perfectly safe. No one's going to touch an old guy like him."

"He gets worked up. I don't want him to worry."

Huntington put a hand on my shoulder. "I like how you look after Henry. He hasn't been this good since before Diana died. He tells me you learn fast. I can see that. You speak better than most

American kids. What are your plans? You're still at City College?" His hand left my shoulder to smooth his perfect hair.

"For now. I need to keep my student visa or figure out something else. My girlfriend's moving here, and I'm working on a start-up with my friends."

"This country was built by the ingenuity of people like my parents and Henry and now you," Huntington said. "Keep in touch with me, will you? At some point, you'll need a new visa. I can help."

"Wow. That would be great."

"What's your girlfriend's name? How'd you meet?"

I told him about Lisbet, English-born, Honghe-schooled, world traveler.

"Lisbet. Pretty name." Huntington looked thoughtful. "It's a little tricky, wouldn't you say? Dating a white girl?"

"I don't think of her that way. She's just Lisbet."

"Well, you're young. Anything seems possible. I envy you that." He glanced toward the doorway again. "It's exciting, isn't it? Sleeping with a white chick."

What? Creep! But a creep who could get me a visa. We heard Henry coming down the hall.

"What are you two hatching?" Henry said.

"We're going to find a way to keep Shelley here for good," Huntington said.

"He'd have a future if he studied harder," Henry groused.

"You're proud of him, admit it," Huntington said, helping Henry into his jacket. "You can't keep a secret from us." He winked at me.

Henry reached for the hat with the jaunty feather. "If they ask next door, tell them Supervisor Wong and I went out."

AFTER THEY LEFT, I borrowed a bike from Ted and went to the library to study, but I couldn't concentrate. I owed Deng an answer. If I told him the truth about the state of my savings, he'd know that I'd been feeding him a fistful of fictions, a patty melt of lies. He'd tell Father and ruin everything.

Distressed at the prospect, I left the library, walking the bike as I pondered in the dark. A shadow ran across the road. I froze. An animal with long legs and a thick, downward tail turned and stared at me. Pointed ears, narrow snout, eyes shining. My heart sped up, and the animal knew it. I jumped on the bike and sped away.

Back in the warmth of Henry's house, I knew what I had to write. *Dear Deng, Congratulations on your wonderful news. I'm happy to hear that you're having a baby daughter. Regrettably, I cannot send you the money. My capital funds are tied up in promising investments. If there's anything else I can do to help my good friend Yu, please tell me.*

16.
Silkworm

A I YA! THE LAPTOP NEVER ARRIVED. IT MUST'VE BEEN stolen en route, Deng said. Thieves operated everywhere these days in Gejiu. One couldn't be too careful. Dismayed, I called the shipping company, but they couldn't trace it. *This happens sometimes with overseas shipping,* the rep said sympathetically. *Next time, make sure you insure it. Or better yet, have someone you know hand-deliver it for you. That's really the safest way.*

I cursed those shipping-route bandits. The one honest promise I'd made to Father had ended in disaster.

Are you sure? I wrote to Deng.

No laptop. You were dumb to ship it. But your father thanks you for the lucky key chain that your friend the waiter brought.

Of all the rotten luck. I retreated to my room, came out only to check on Henry, and went back in to brood. Day passed into evening; evening passed into night. At two o'clock in the morning I was still wide awake when something interesting started up in my brain. A larva of a notion was forming, making its sticky presence known. I observed it carefully but didn't uncocoon it yet. If it had anything to tell me, I had to leave it alone. For the next several nights, I lay in my mango bed, homework neglected, poetry abandoned, conversation teeming in my head. My worm grew, grubbed, and molted, but did I have silk or nothing?

Me: Why didn't Father get the laptop I sent?

Worm: Because it was stolen in transit. You didn't have a safe way to get it into his hands.

Me: Cousin Deng said I was stupid to ship it.

Worm: It's a well-known fact that thieves are everywhere.

Me: What did the shipping company tell me?

Worm: Next time, insure it.

Me: No, that other thing.

Worm: Have someone you know hand-deliver it for you.

Me: Like the waiter at the restaurant for Crossing the Bridge Noodles.

Worm: Who took the lucky key chain, *888*.

Me: And delivered it straight into Father's hands.

Worm: There's a lesson here.

Me: Is there?

Worm: It's staring you right in the face.

Me: If you're so smart, tell me.

Worm: Me? I'm a worm. Figure it out for yourself.

Me: Technically, you're not a worm. You're a caterpillar. The name *silkworm* is a misnomer.

Worm: Remember you promised Father that you'd someday find a countryman who'd deliver a laptop from you right to his door?

Me: I've got it. It's better to have someone deliver your package in person than to trust faceless operations.

Worm: Bingo.

Me: But how would you find somebody to deliver a package for you? China's a big place.

Worm: Think. Think! How do any of these apps work, the ones that put strangers together?

Me: Crowdsourcing.

Worm: Exactly.

Me: The app helps you find someone who's going to where you want the package delivered. That person takes the package for you.

Worm: Yes, and the sender pays through the app. The company keeps a cut.

Me: What about theft? The person might steal what he promised to deliver.

Worm: You never distrust people. Why start now?

Me: Peach Blossom Land is changing me.

Worm: Or maybe you're just growing up.

Me: This is big business we're talking about. I have to get realistic.

Worm: Go back. What was the first thing the shipping company said?

Me: Insure it.

Worm: You're onto something there.

Me: The sender insures it. Another revenue source.

Worm: And the app rates both parties, a data point visible to anyone.

Me: Anyone who downloads the app.

Worm: We sell ads too. And maybe a premium version.

Me: Would there be enough deliverers to handle all the demand?

Worm: In urban locations. They're going there anyway. Some travelers are constantly on the road. Their company pays their way or they're on government business. Using our app, they can make a few extra yuan by delivering a package, no sweat.

Me: So if I have a present for my girlfriend who lives in Beijing—

Worm: —the app finds you someone in San Francisco who's going to Beijing and that person delivers the package for you.

Me: They do it for the money?

Worm: Sure.

Me: That seems too simple. Think of how business is done in China. A countryman is accustomed to more than a strict exchange for money. And remember what Paloma said? Make it personal, and people will connect.

Worm: You have a more subtle mind than they give you credit for.

Me: They who?

Worm: Stick to the question. What else might a countryman want or need? What currency isn't money?

Me: Opportunity. Access. A favor. A gesture of affection or respect.

Worm: What do the relatives always bring when they go to one another's houses?

Me: A gift.

Worm: A gift.

Me: You pay for the service but add a little gift for the deliverer, to make it truly Chinese.

Worm: A surprise, like the ginger chews you gave to the waiter—

Me: —which makes it fun. We have social features, so people can show how they played it—

Worm: —all the way to the recipient's door.

Me: "You want to send that to your father in China? There's an app for that!"

Worm: "I downloaded it yesterday! SilkwormCentral!"

Me: Ha ha. Very funny.

Worm: Okay then, SilkRoad. After the trade route that passed through Yunnan.

Me: We're going to make a fortune.

I HAD IT. I'D cracked the code, dropped the penny, switched on the light bulb. I'd spun pure gold from the dross of my mistake. Eddie would lift me off my feet; Paloma would de-screen herself to give me a thumping hug. I laughed out loud in revel at the height of my latest bounce. Like all those tech titans who'd risen from the ashes, I'd found a way to turn disaster to success. I snuggled under the covers, turned out the light, and fell asleep smiling.

17.
The Chosen Peril

EDDIE AND PALOMA HOISTED A BEER, PROCLAIMED me a genius, and got to work right away. They whiteboarded our objectives, technical and monetary. Paloma wanted a better name—something edgier, she said, something unexpected. She always thought smarter. People were tired of silly names that lost their vowels on the way to market like quarters dribbled from a child's pocket. We decided on TinRoad, an homage to my hometown of Gejiu, and a poke in the eye, Paloma said, to the snooty-minded who draped themselves in silk and velvet. Eddie registered the domain while Paloma recruited a crew of stellar engineers from City College and Cal, all sworn to secrecy until we were ready to seek funding. I went to class, took care of Henry, and showed up for Leo every night. Lisbet and I wrote often. She was returning to Malibu in September to help her mother move to Bolinas, and I was counting the days.

For Leo's fifth birthday, his mothers held a picnic in Golden Gate Park and invited all their friends. The whole crew came— white, Black, brown, yellow, the muddy end of the rainbow. The kids ran around the grass while their parents huddled under the shivering trees. Kate and Orit hired Leo's favorite food truck, Hippee Dippee Soft Ice Cream, all organic. I felt bad that they hadn't invited Henry, but there'd been no peace made between Ted and Henry. Aviva was distressed; she said they'd never gone so long without speaking, not even in that terrible year after Diana and Eli were killed, and silences had a way of stretching out until it was too late to make amends. She taught me a new word, *estrangement*.

After we sang to Leo and cake was passed around, Ted and Aviva popped the corks on sparkling apple juice and wine, and everyone, adults and kids alike, toasted the court ruling that had been all over the news. Men could marry men now, and women, women, a wonderment even Father, with his hope for humankind, wouldn't have known to dream of.

I gave Leo a ride home, bisonback-style, while the others cleaned up. We sat on the bed as we looked through his favorite book, the animal encyclopedia from Henry. His breathing slowed, and his sturdy form, usually in motion, grew soft and heavy against me. It felt altogether right.

"You're the best, Shelley, you truly are," Aviva said when I joined the others in the kitchen. "Thank you for helping with the kids today. Aren't we a marvelous group?"

"Very special," Ted said drily. "What the mayor's speechwriter calls 'a representative cross section reflecting the rich diversity of the city.'"

"What's a mixed marriage anyway?" Aviva said. "The biggest

difference between Ted and me is that he hardly talks, and I can't shut up." Everyone laughed, even Ted.

"Remember the multiracial parenting group we started?" Ted said.

"What a disaster that was," Aviva said. "We met three times before it fell apart. There was that couple—he was Taiwanese—"

"—Yuqing."

"—married to Susie, who was Jewish—"

"—and they got into a huge argument about whose parents were the bigger racists," Ted said.

"We had so many issues to work out as couples that we never got around to talking about the kids," Aviva said.

Kate and Orit laughed. "Oh, we've been there," Orit said. "There are more lesbian parenting groups than there are rainbow flags."

"We quit every one that we joined. They're better in theory than in practice," Kate added.

"We had a nickname for Eli," Ted said.

Aviva nodded, eyes shining. I held my breath. To my amazement, Ted continued.

"The Chinese were called 'The Yellow Peril.' Jews are 'The Chosen People.' So we called Eli 'The Chosen Peril.'"

Was it my imagination, or was he actually smiling? Tears appeared in Kate's eyes. For once, Aviva stayed quiet. I thought that she was holding her breath, like me, but now I see it differently, being married myself. For all her chatter and the way she filled a room, Aviva knew when to make space for Ted. Marriage is mysterious, especially somebody else's.

"We have something to tell you," Orit said. Kate looked tense. The mood changed instantly. Aviva steeled herself for news she didn't want.

"We've decided to leave," Orit said. "We're moving."

"To the East Bay?" Aviva asked, without much hope. Since the fire, they'd been scouring the listings, answering ads, elbowing their way in a frenzy of other renters as desperate as they were in their search for affordable housing. It wasn't to be found.

"We're joining the collective that my friends have started in L.A. County, near Palmdale. It's called Beit Hayeladim, the 'Children's House.'"

"Not the kibbutz," Aviva cried. "This isn't Israel. This is California!"

"It's not a kibbutz," Orit said. "It's not like where I grew up with four hundred people growing dates. Most of the adults work regular city jobs. But it is a place to live in community and raise our kids together."

"What does Leo say?" Aviva asked.

"We'll tell him soon. We think he's going to love it. The kids sleep together, learn together, work in the garden. There are chickens," Orit said.

"He's talking some," Aviva argued. "He's just starting to get used to us and you're taking him away."

Kate hastened to chime in. "We're so grateful to you and Ted. You showed us how good it is to live with friends."

"Leo doesn't know them. To him, they're absolute strangers," Aviva said.

"I know them," Orit said. "I grew up with them. When I'm with them, I feel like I'm home."

Ted was looking at Kate with concern, maybe wondering, as I was, if she really wanted to go. She saw him watching and raised her chin a fraction. "We're done in San Francisco. Or, anyway, San Francisco's done with us. We're going to start fresh at Beit Hayeladim."

"We leave next week," Orit said.

Ted put his arm around Aviva. "We always knew this was temporary." She held on, tears falling.

KATE CAME OVER TO give Henry the news.

"It's a damn stupid idea," Henry said. "I don't like you gals setting up in a commune. Look what happened in the sixties—those pie-in-the-sky *collectives* fell apart when people discovered that human beings are all the same underneath their tie-dye shirts. *I-me-mine* is how we're wired. Read your history. Socialism doesn't work."

Kate laughed. "It's hardly socialism, Henry. Think of it as a Chinese family compound. Everyone helps out."

"Butts in, more like," Henry said.

"I want you to do something for me." She was seated on the ottoman in front of his armchair, and now she reached for his hand. "Make amends with Ted."

"Me make amends! You should be talking to him. He's sore that I asked Huntington to get him a job, but he took it, didn't he?"

"Not because you said. You've tried for years to boss him. It doesn't work. Ted will always choose for himself."

"That boy's a solid wall. Can't see through him. Can't see around him. The only person who could figure him was his mother."

"Try harder. Remember what you told my father?"

Henry grunted. "He wrote that letter to Ted asking him to persuade you that Ted could give you the life you wanted—a career and a family."

"Ted showed it to Diana—"

"—he shared everything with her," Henry said.

"—and Diana told you about it, and do you remember what you did?"

"Ancient history," Henry said.

"You didn't hesitate. You got in your car and drove to Southern California to see my father. You didn't tell anyone you were going; you just left."

"Diana would've tried to stop me. Ted would've thrown a fit."

"You drove straight through to my parents' house and showed up without warning. I was astonished that my dad let you in. I think he was a little bit in awe of you, Henry."

"We talked for hours," Henry said.

"You told my dad that no matter how much the two of you wanted Ted and me to get married, it was never going to happen. You were the only person who made him understand."

Henry swallowed. He patted Kate's hand.

"You said that I was a good person and he should be proud of me and love me. 'She's your only daughter. She'll take care of you and your wife.'"

Brilliant Henry, deploying the Chinese groove. Nothing pushed open the door faster than the promise of being tended to once you couldn't take care of yourself. Look how I'd gotten in with Henry.

"He came around," Henry said. "Not right away but before your mother passed. He made good before he died."

Kate wiped her eyes and stood. "I want you to live forever, Henry."

He peered up at her. "But I won't. Is that what you're trying to say?"

I WALKED KATE TO the sidewalk. She paused and looked up at Ted and Aviva's house. "I wish you'd known Ted before he lost Eli.

He was a wonderful father. I used to watch them sitting together, drawing in their little books."

"Was Eli quiet, like Ted?"

"Yes, but they could be silly too. They used to stand in Henry's alleyway and listen for the shower running, then ring his doorbell and run away. Or they'd put on the music really loud and dance at Eli's window until Henry came outside to look. It was a big game they all played. Henry liked being teased. It hurts to think about it. Oh, I wish Diana were here. She could always bring them together."

I thought of Mother, gone since I was a boy. She'd been house and roofline and cinder block and walls, holding Father and me together. Every year that passed, her absence grew. Sometimes the hurt pricked at me; other times it roared. I missed her more now than I had when I was little. It didn't make any sense.

"Henry's going to miss you," I said.

"He didn't really listen to a single word I said."

I WENT NEXT DOOR the night before they left. Leo was sitting up in bed looking weepy.

"Let's see the dino," I said. He'd taken to wearing his favorite socks morning, noon, and night. He stuck out a foot. His bottom lip quivered.

"I don't want to go," he said.

"It'll be cool. You'll have your own chickens."

"I want to stay with you and Henry."

I lay down on the floor beside his bed, and Leo slid under the covers. I couldn't see his face, only his silhouette and his dark hair on the pillow. The fish tank burbled softly.

"You're an adventurer. Real adventurers go places. They come back and tell their friends about everything they saw, like strange animals and houses hanging halfway up a mountainside and ponds of magical green water where invisible fish swim. They learn new languages and eat amazing food and sleep outside under the stars. They don't have to talk if they don't want to. They watch with their eyes and write it down in a book or keep it in their head for later."

"I keep a lot of stuff in my head," Leo said.

"Next time you see me, you'll have a story to tell."

He rustled under the covers. "Tell the fisherman story." He named it like a countryman, *Tao Hua Yuan Ji.*

The Story of the Peach Blossom Forest, which Mother had told to me. I couldn't remember her face as well as I wished, but I recalled the sound of her voice, whispery with illness, and the weight of the blankets on my bed. She told me the story whenever I asked, even when she wasn't feeling well. She said it was a legend more than a thousand years old from the poet Tao Yuanming, also known as Tao Qian. Leo learned to say those names, listening to me speak to him in Chinese every night. Who would tell him the story after he moved away?

I took out my phone, placed it near me, and pressed the button to record. I'd send the file to Kate so he could listen whenever he liked. Then I traveled far into the forest, taking Leo with me until he fell asleep right before the story ended.

18.
The Story of the Peach Blossom Forest

[IN ENGLISH]

You good? Who you sleeping with tonight, the monkey or the tiger? The turtle, okay. That one new? I haven't seen him before. Where's the one Aviva gave you, the ugly one, the camel. Yeah, that one. Grab him too. Your turtle would like a little company.

[In Mandarin]

So there was this fisherman, he lived with his old parents in a village called Wuling, and they were really poor. Nothing wrong with that. Nothing wrong with being poor. A lot of these legends, they're about poor people. Or they're about people who can't grow their crops until somebody finds a magic spring. That's not what happens in this story. No dragon gives him a magic pearl and he doesn't find a spring. He finds something even better, the Peach Blossom Forest.

One day, the fisherman goes out in his boat and the fishing's really terrible. He's feeling pretty bad because how's he going to feed himself and his parents? He decides he better take his boat farther down the river. He rows and rows, hoping that he'll find a really great fishing spot around the next bend. He's never gone so far in his life. Then all of a sudden, boom! Right in front of him, he sees a big forest filled with flowering peach trees.

He pulls his boat up on the riverbank and starts walking through the forest. It was wintertime when he left and now it looks like spring. The whole ground is covered with petals, and more petals are drifting down from the branches like pink snow. It's like he's walking through big clouds of floating blossoms. It smells good, too, like flowers. It's warm and lovely and he's feeling really good about the place.

Then suddenly, the forest stops and he's at a spring. Oh, I guess there is a spring in this story. Water is important. Everybody needs water.

[Leo speaks.]

[In English]

Yeah, that's right. That's the Chinese word for *water.* Okay, hang on. Here you go. Don't spill it. You good? That's okay. Just wipe it with your sleeve.

[In Mandarin]

So our poor fisherman is at the spring, right? And next to the spring is a big mountain. A huge, tall mountain, too big to climb. *Well, that's a bummer,* he thinks. *No more peach blossom forest. Where am I going to go next?* Then he notices a crack in the side of the mountain. It looks like the opening of a cave, and there's a little gleam of light coming through. He says to himself, *I'm going to go check out that gleam of light. See what I can find—cave, passageway, whatever.*

At first it's really narrow. He can barely pull himself through even though this guy, being poor, is skinny. But eventually the thing widens and, what do you know, it *is* a passageway. And it leads into a green valley where he sees a whole village filled with houses and fields and trees and ponds, and he's thinking, *This is a really nice place.*

He doesn't get very far when he starts seeing the people who live there. They're walking on the paths and working in the fields and fishing. They're all dressed alike, in soft robes, very nice, and they look really happy. There are old folks and parent types and little kids playing with the animals—

[Leo speaks.]

[Continuing in Mandarin]

Animals, yeah. Guess you've learned that word too. What kind? Um, goats, I guess, and dogs. Birds, nice ones. There's a couple of cormorants, they're a kind of bird that people use to fish. Lots of ducks and chickens. They're making a lot of noise like this [squawking; laughter], and the fisherman realizes he's getting kind of hungry, and wouldn't one of those ducks be tasty about now? Because he's very hungry.

One old guy, noticing the fisherman, comes over to him and asks, "Where have you come from?" The fisherman tells him how he rowed down the river, farther than he'd ever been, walked through the forest, and squeezed through the passage. The old guy invites him to his house, and all his family gathers and they ask the fisherman if he'd like to have some lunch. They prepare a huge feast—roast duck, steamed fish, juicy dumplings, a big bowl of noodles. He eats and drinks—

[Leo speaks.]

[Continuing in Mandarin]

Um, chocolate milk—and they keep bringing more food to the table. In his whole life, he's never been treated with such kindness.

After dinner, they tell him their story, just like I'm telling you. Their ancestors escaped some mega bad times during the Qin dynasty and settled in this valley. They've lived here ever since with no contact whatsoever with the outside world, which is just the way they like it.

"The Qin dynasty?" he asks. "You've got to be joking. That was like, hundreds and hundreds of years ago." *So that's pretty cool, he's thinking. That they've been hanging out here all this time, free from the world's troubles.*

He stays in the valley for several more days. Everyone invites him into their homes and feeds him delicious meals and gives him a comfortable bed to sleep in. He's amazed that they live as they do, and they're amazed that he's found them. Everyone he meets gets along really well and nobody is poor or treated differently than anyone else. He decides he wants to live forever in this beautiful, peaceful place.

But first he better go back to Wuling and check on things. He needs to make arrangements for his old parents and maybe pay off a few debts. He decides he'll go home for a couple of days and then come right back here and settle down for good. There are a couple of pretty girls he was introduced to; maybe he'll fall in love with one of them and they'll get married and have a kid who'll play with the goats and chickens.

Right before he leaves, the old man takes him aside. "Listen," he says. "Do me a favor. Don't tell anyone about this place. It's really important. Will you promise?"

He makes the promise. He feels bad because he knows that no way is he going to keep such a great discovery to himself. All these years, everyone in Wuling has treated him like dirt, and now he, a poor fisherman, knows something important. He's going to share the news when he gets back, no question about it. But he thanks the old man for his kindness and promises not to tell.

He's not entirely stupid, this fisherman. On his way home, he marks his route, landmark by landmark, so he can find his way back. When he gets home to Wuling, he asks to meet with the magistrate—that's the head guy; they call him 'Mister Big'—and he tells him what he's seen. The magistrate is excited. He orders a group of officials and soldiers to go with the fisherman on his return. They set out on a big boat, the best the fisherman has ever ridden in, and he's feeling good because he's getting the VIP treatment.

But all the signposts he left for himself are gone. He searches and searches, but he can't find the route. He never makes it back to the Peach Blossom Forest.

[In English]

The End. Too bad. That guy blew it. If only he'd stayed there in the first place, he would've had a great life. Maybe he even would've become immortal. I don't know. My mother never said whether they were immortal or not. Peaches mean *immortal*, or at least *long life*.

Leo? You awake?

Good night, little buddy. Safe travels.

19.
Busted

A VIVA LEFT FOR WORK EARLY THE NEXT MORNING before the three departed. It was the first of August, and the summer fog swirled. She belted her cardigan into a firm knot.

"I'll be fine. Just fine. I said my goodbyes last night." She waved brightly and drove away. Ted busied himself packing Kate's car, and Leo wasn't talking to me or anyone else.

"Let's get your backpack," Kate said. "Then we'll be ready to go." I watched Leo climb the steps. Stairs had gotten easier for him; he'd grown over the summer.

"He's going to like it there," Orit said. "He can play outside anytime he wants. He won't have to wait for someone to take him to the park."

"Will he have a fish tank?" I said.

"There's a chicken coop, which he'll love. There's a fabulous garden. There's sun! I'm so tired of the gloom. There's just one problem. They've asked us not to bring a pet. They have too many."

My mind was on Leo, so my ears weren't afoot. I thought she said that there were too many kids and so they couldn't bring Leo.

". . . he's so fond of you," Orit was saying. "Henry said he's always coming to the back door looking for you."

Was she suggesting Leo stay with us?

"I'm sorry it's so last minute. We didn't know the rules." Orit smiled that smile I'd come to know so well after months at their disposal: the crease of cajolery, the parabola of persuasion. No, no! She was talking about Crouder.

"I don't want him. Can't you find somebody else?"

"He won't be any trouble. Henry said it's okay. Otherwise, we'll have to leave him at the shelter." She handed me Crouder's bowl and a box full of slobbered toys. "He's kind of like you, right? He needs a good home."

Leo reappeared, both arms wrapped around his backpack and tears streaking his face.

"Guess what, Leo?" Orit enthused. "Shelley promised he'd look after Crouder! See, he's got Crouder's bowl and all his toys and he'll put Crouder's cozy bed right next to his own. Look at how happy Crouder is! It makes me happy too!"

We looked down. Crouder was smiling up at me. He lifted his rump and settled it on my foot. Leo didn't utter a sound. When I went to his room after they were gone, I saw the animal encyclopedia sitting on his desk where I'd be sure to find it.

A DAY PASSED, AND then another. I went next door to see Ted and Aviva and found them as glum as I was. Even the fish in the tank looked forlorn, drifting more than swimming, and the bubbles glupping dolefully: *Leo, Leo, Leo.* Ted retreated into his silent state. The house felt emptier than ever.

Aviva came into Leo's room, where I was sitting at the desk, paging through the animal book. "Are you okay?" she asked.

"The fish look unhappy. Crouder sits at the back door like he's waiting for Leo."

"I miss him too," Aviva said. She sat on the bed and smoothed the blanket, and I recalled the morning that I found the room unlocked and Aviva told me the story of the deaths of Eli and Diana.

"If he hadn't lived here at all, we wouldn't be missing him so much," I said. "I wouldn't be thinking about—" I stopped, surprised. I was about to say "my mother."

"That's true, but we wouldn't have had the fun of it either. I used to listen at the doorway. He liked your stories way more than he liked mine." She was smiling to herself, looking down, and I realized she was giving me a little bit of private space, same as she'd done for Ted on the day that he'd spoken at last of Eli, their Chosen Peril. She seemed to understand, as none of the rest of us did, that yearning and mourning sometimes carried on below the surface, a very confusing state.

"My mother told me those stories when I was little," I said.

She nodded, still smiling. "But Leo is alive and well. He's going to grow up happy. We can be happy for him."

"Will he remember me, do you think?"

She told me the truth, which I have always respected. "He'll remember the stories. Maybe that's enough."

FALL SEMESTER STARTED, AND my TOEFL score inched higher. I spent every spare minute with Eddie and Paloma working on our new idea. The schedule was ambitious, but if all went well, in a year we'd apply for early funding. Eddie didn't want to bring investors in too soon else we give up too much control. He said that we'd look back someday and wish we'd have stayed forever in our poor and happy state. At the time, I didn't believe him, and I still don't know if he was right. I'm more sensible now than I used to be, but I wouldn't call myself wise. That will have to wait until I'm an old man, and even then, I've witnessed how wisdom comes and goes, as fickle as a felon.

In September, Lisbet's mother went to England, and Lisbet met her there for a few more weeks of travel. We decided that I'd visit her in Malibu upon her return. There would be loads of packing before the move, and we didn't want to wait. I closed my eyes at night thinking of Zuma Beach.

The twenty feet between Ted's house and Henry's became an impassable distance. Pretending not to care, Henry boxed up his broken feelings and stuck them with the junk stored in his garage. Now all his expectations rested on Huntington and me. Several nights a week, when Huntington stayed over, he and Henry sat up late talking politics and sipping Maker's Mark. The other nights, Henry supervised my studies. He enlisted Professor Luo to map out a plan for me that included a transfer to a four-year program. In their estimation, I had the makings of a university man.

I wrote to Father, care of Cousin Deng.

> *Dear Father,*
> *I send you greetings from excellent Peach Blossom*
> *Land. Life is wonderful here. Ye Ye, Uncle, and Auntie*

see to all my wishes. Ye Ye has decided that I should fur-
ther my studies. He's sending me to university and won't
need my assistance any longer at the family department
store. I hope to make you proud.

I'm very sorry, but the laptop computer I sent you
has gone missing, and I can't replace it right away. This
is only temporary. My business partners and I are working
on a new product that will one day bear fruit as plentiful
as the Mengzi pomegranates that you and I love to eat. I
promise I'll buy you another laptop, one that's even better.
Then I'll find a countryman who's going to Gejiu and I'll
ask him to deliver it straight into your hands. Your loving
son, Xue Li, University Man.

I heard back from Cousin Deng. He'd found the money to send
Yu to Southern California. She was staying in a house with a pair of
women who would see to her needs and comforts. *It's all very proper,*
he said, which worried me that it wasn't. In a week or so, the baby
would be born a U.S. citizen, and then Deng and Yu would marry.
You asked if you could help. Go to see them after the baby is born. Yu is scared
and didn't want to leave me. It would calm her to see an old friend. I'll be arriv-
ing as soon as I gather the funds. I visit your father on a regular basis. He's quit
his job at the bus station. He's found a new situation better than cleaning buses.

I'd been so occupied with my own concerns that I'd barely
given Yu a thought. To be alone and having a baby far from home
would be scary, even for someone as capable as Yu. I knew her father to be strict and wondered if he was angry with her for getting
pregnant without first marrying Deng.

Send me the information, I wrote to Deng. *I'm going to see Lisbet*
soon in Southern California. I promise to visit Yu and meet your new
daughter.

THAT NIGHT, HUNTINGTON ARRIVED later than usual, after Henry was asleep. His shirt was limp, his collar was open, and he looked a little flushed. He held up a fancy-looking bottle.

"How about it?" he said. I took out two glasses. He poured a drink and downed it. "Man, I've had a night." He poured himself a second and offered one to me. We stood in the kitchen sipping a bourbon much smoother than Henry's.

"I couldn't take another shot of Maker's Mark," he said. "Henry's as cheap with his liquor as he is with everything else."

"Is everything okay?"

"Oh, yeah. Don't get me wrong. I've had a *good* night. Sometimes my life gets a little crazy, but I'm not complaining. Thank you, by the way, for covering my tracks." He lifted his glass to me. "How's that girlfriend of yours?"

"She's fine," I said. I didn't want to talk to him about Lisbet.

"Crazy," he said, talking to himself. "Crazy, crazy." He drained his glass. "You done with that?"

He washed and dried our glasses and put them away. "I keep a clean house," he winked. "But it's late. I got to get some sleep."

"If you don't want anyone to know you're here, why do you park out front?" I said.

He didn't lose the smile. He had that professional touch. "You're a fast learner, just like Henry said. Don't worry. Nobody's going after an old guy like him." He bid me good night and went downstairs to bed.

I went to my mango bedroom and sat down at Diana's desk. I had two more poems to write, which I still wanted to do, to keep my word to Lisbet. I wrote a line, scratched it out, and started over. Professor Luo said that I had a talent for writing, but my knack for weighing words produced only scribble.

I must have drifted off. I woke up to shouting, stumbled to

the front room, and looked out the window. Henry was outside in the shadows, yelling. I raced down the stairs before the crazy old coot did himself serious damage. The shouting grew louder, other voices joining in. My foot landed on a wobbly Crouder ball. I flew backward with a crash, tweety birds circling round my head. By the time I clambered to my feet, Henry had his fists up.

"Does Supervisor Wong live here?" Two men stood on the sidewalk, one working a camera.

"Get off my property!" Henry shouted. "Get off my property before I call the cops!"

"We're on a public sidewalk," the man replied. He was wide-waisted and slump-shouldered and wearing a puffy jacket, more marshmallow than man. The second fellow, who had a camera pressed to his face, wore a purple fanny pack around his gut. They were two white guys who shopped at Trader Joe's. Hardly Asian gang members here to take out Huntington Wong.

Henry advanced, dukes up.

"We're reporters," the first man called. "We just want to know: does Supervisor Wong live here?" The camera clicked and whined.

"Put that damn thing away!" Henry shouted. He grabbed the camera and flung it to the ground.

"Whoa, whoa," the first man said, raising his hands. The photographer swore at Henry. When he leaned over to pick up his camera, Henry decked him. Behind me, footsteps clattered. Huntington ran past me and took Henry by the arm.

"Get the hell out of here," he said to the reporters. "You're harassing a private citizen."

"He assaulted me!" the photographer said, camera up and shooting.

"Don't say anything," Huntington said to Henry. "Go back inside and let me handle this."

"Do you live here now?" the reporter said. "Is this your official place of residence? According to county records, your former residence was sold more than six months ago. This address was listed in your last public filing. Is this your current residence, and if it is, where are your wife and children?"

"He doesn't live here!" Henry shouted. "This is my house!"

The camera kept whining, an animal set upon its prey.

"Shut up now, Henry," Huntington said.

The reporter smiled. "No comment for the record?"

Huntington shook his head. "No comment."

The photographer spoke from behind his camera. "You're busted."

20.
Uproar

"THEY'RE GOING TO FIRE ME!" TED SHOUTED AT Henry. "They've put me on leave; they've started an investigation. Do you realize what you've done? It looks like I was on the take, that I got the job in the mayor's office in exchange for letting Huntington claim that he lived here, in your house. A house in his district, where he's required to live. He hasn't lived in the district for months! We're talking fraud, corruption, misuse of public funds. I could go to jail over this!"

Henry grabbed my arm as hard as a pinching cousin. Red blotched his sagging face as if Ted had slapped him. I lurched him into his chair, not trusting his legs to work.

"He has a girlfriend," Ted said grimly. "Delilah found out, took the girls, and moved in with her parents. The house was hers; she sold it months ago. Huntington's been living at his girlfriend's place in Sausalito. Fucking idiot. He doesn't even live in the city. As if no one would find out."

"It's a mistake," Henry protested. "Those goddamned reporters. They were trespassing. They walked right onto my property without my permission. Didn't leave when I told them to clear off. They think nothing of breaking the law themselves while ruining a good man's name."

"A good man?" Ted said. "He lied to voters. He falsified records. That's called fraud."

"He's doing good for the voters! He's cracking down on the real criminals, the gangs demanding protection money. I bet you one hundred percent that it's the gangs who are behind this. They want him off their backs."

"There are no gangs threatening Huntington," Ted retorted. "There never were. That was a story he told you to give him a reason to stay. It was all a lie. He listed your address as his own on official government records. He had mail sent here; he parked his car out front. The whole thing was a ruse."

Henry bellowed and charged out of his chair, too fast for me to stop him. He shoved Ted in the chest, which didn't budge Ted but almost toppled Henry. I grabbed the back of his shirt; he dangled for a second like a thrashing kid or a sack of evicted kittens on their way to a drowning. When I set him on his feet, he fastened himself to the back of the chair and told me to get lost.

"Huntington didn't lie to me," Henry insisted. "The gangs are after him, just like he says. They've got the cops and politicians in their pockets. They extort money from the honest people, immigrants like us, the hardworking ones just trying to run their businesses, no different than—"

He blinked hard, hearing himself, and faltered. This time, he let me help him into the chair.

"No different than Mom? Is that what you were going to say?" Ted demanded.

Henry shook his head.

"She wouldn't have been stupid enough, or vain enough, to let Huntington trick her," Ted spat.

"Don't talk to me like that!"

Ted closed in, standing right over his father. "Or have I got that wrong? Maybe he didn't trick you. Maybe you were in on it with him."

No, no, he lied to us too, I started to answer, but Henry gripped my hand. He wanted to speak for himself.

"They're trying to damage his reputation," Henry said. "People will look into it; they'll find out it was nothing. They'll call out those reporters, and Huntington can sue for libel, slander, the works. I'll get my lawyer on it."

"His reputation is more important to you than mine is," Ted said bitterly. "Tell me. Did you know, or didn't you?"

Henry shut his eyes, his expression clotted by shame. Father had used to look like that after he asked me to beg an extra month from the landlord or make a plea to an auntie for a loan he couldn't pay back.

"Yeah, I thought so," Ted said. "You let him fake his address. Then you persuaded him to get me a job, which you pushed me and pushed me to take. He was your golden boy. Mr. All-American, the athlete-scholar. A neighborhood nobody immigrant's kid who became a big success. Now you have two failures on your account: me and Huntington. Shelley, you better watch out. You stay here long enough, you'll turn rotten too."

Henry's eyes flew open. "Leave Shelley out of this."

"I tried to. You dragged him in."

"He's *family*," Henry said.

"Yes he is, poor bastard."

"Henry didn't know! Huntington lied to us too," I said, desperate to get them to listen, or at least to quit. This wreck of a reunion was worse than their impenetrable silence.

But they kept on shouting, unable to give in, a brace of the vulnerable speared by the lies of that dastard, Huntington Wong. They would've fought all night if fuming, phlegmy Henry hadn't caved to a coughing fit. Ted answered his father's hacking with a final attack of his own: "I'm in trouble. You are too. You put us there," he said.

HENRY TRIED SO MANY times to reach Huntington that the extra-large buttons on his extra-large phone got extra-large stuck, as if yesterday's rice porridge had gummed up the works. Huntington didn't call back. He'd gone into hiding. His lawyer made the television rounds to answer the hue and cry, saying it was all a big misunderstanding, to which Henry yelled at the screen, *What did I tell you?*, until he heard the lawyer add that Mr. Henry Cheng, an occupant of the house in question, was "a muddleheaded old man, completely unreliable and categorically confused." That started Henry savagely stabbing again at the phone. Still Huntington didn't answer.

Then things got worse. The longtime owner of a Vietnamese sub shop way to the west on Lawton Street whose banh mi sandwiches were rhapsodized over by the hipsters invading the Sunset claimed that he'd paid Huntington fifteen thousand dollars to facilitate the expansion of his business, but his banh mi bonanza never came to pass. The money was paid but the permit never issued, leaving the cilantro-and-pâté-on-French-roll market wide open for a parvenu—white, inked, bearded, young—to swoop in and capture. The Vietnamese guy was out for revenge.

"Why can't you tell Ted the truth: that Huntington tricked you?" I said. I hadn't forgotten that look on Henry's face. Like Father bearing up under mortifying shame, Henry couldn't bring himself to say: *I screwed up. Forgive me.*

"He made up his mind about me a long time ago. He always thinks the worst of me. Maybe I deserve it."

"Or maybe Ted thinks you think the worst of him."

"You're speaking nonsense," Henry said.

They were a pair too proud to parley, too boxed-in to bend. They couldn't detect or even imagine how alike they were, both of them unmoored and bewildered by their grief. Bonded by anger, the life force of mourning. And why, after all, was Ted so sore at Huntington? Because he'd lied, or because he'd stolen Henry's affections? How would I feel if a mischief-making monkey-wrencher turned Father away from me?

"What happens now? Is there any way to fix it?" I asked.

Henry pounded his fist on the chair. "Call Huntington again. Unblock my number. If he sees it's me, he'll pick up."

He didn't.

HENRY SENT ME TO summon Ted. Aviva stood guard at the door.

"I wanted them talking but not like this. Henry's gone too far," she said.

"It was Ted who blew up at Henry. He was shouting down the house."

"He had every right. This whole debacle is Henry's fault. I'm really worried for Ted."

I felt bad for both Ted and Henry, wronged as they were by that feather-hatted shyster, but I had to stand up for Henry. I knew what it was like to fall under Huntington's spell. When you're young and broke and striving, or maybe just old and lonely, it's easy to believe the person who pretends to believe in you.

"What now?" Ted said, coming to the door.

"Please come," I begged. "Give your dad a chance to make this right."

"It's too late for that," Ted said, but he followed me just the same. Henry was standing, holding onto the bookcase, miles from his chair. Stubborn old coot. I could see by both their expressions that there'd be no truce today.

"Huntington's been forced to resign as a city supervisor," Henry said.

"I read the papers," Ted said shortly.

"I can't believe it," Henry said. "The feds are investigating him on this business of unusual payments. He may have done . . . bad things."

"I'd call accepting bribes a bad thing."

Henry struggled with the next. "I want you to talk to my lawyer. You need to be prepared in case they start asking you questions."

Ted stared at his father. "Is that all you have to say?"

"I'll pay for the lawyer." A big concession, exactly wrong.

Ted spoke in slow measure. "I hired my own lawyer. I've been placed on administrative leave. I'm barred from going into the office."

"They can't do that!" Henry protested.

"They want my computer, phone records, files of every kind. They're interviewing my boss and coworkers. Everyone's avoiding me. It's thorough, dirty, and public. Worst of all, Aviva has to deal with it too. It's humiliating."

"Let me help—"

"I want nothing from you. And when this is over, I'm leaving."

"Of course! Change jobs, good idea. They have no respect. They're terrible, those bosses."

"You didn't hear me. I'm getting out. We're selling the house. As soon as this is over, I'm gone."

HENRY SAID LITTLE THE rest of the day and evening. In the morning, I helped him shave and made him an extra-good breakfast. I told him not to worry; he would explain to the authorities how Huntington had lied, and Ted would be cleared of suspicion.

"I'll do that. I'll get my lawyer on it," Henry said reflexively, all fighting spirit drained.

"They won't sell the house. Ted was just talking. It's their home," I said. And Eli's home too. As long as they lived in that house, they kept Eli close.

"You go on to school. Don't worry about me," Henry said.

After class I went to Eddie's, returning to the saltbox at six. Crouder met me at the door with a strange whine. The lights were off. There was no sign of Henry. His chair was abandoned. His cap and jacket were missing from their hook in the hallway.

"Henry?" I walked through the house, worry rising. The door to his bedroom was shut. I opened it, heart thumping; he wasn't there. A clean shirt lay on the floor, its sleeves disturbingly empty. Drawers were open with long tongues of clothing hanging out. I dashed down to the garage, still calling. His car was gone. He never stayed out this late, even on the rare day when he drove the car himself. I ran back upstairs and went once more wildly through the house. In Henry's bedroom, Crouder bumped me twice behind the knee.

"Crouder!" I commanded. He came around and sat at my feet. "Where is he? Where's Henry?"

Crouder stretched and showed me his gums. In a family full of closed mouths, the dog was about to speak.

"Where, Crouder?"

He jumped onto Henry's bed. There, on the pillow, was a note: *Heading south. Keep an eye on the house and study hard. Good luck.*

The coot had flown the coop! Henry had run away.

21.
Heading South

A *I YA!*" TED CRIED, A TRUE COUNTRYMAN'S EXPRES-
sion. They hurried to the saltbox and scoured the house, calling Henry's name. In their rush, they left the front door open, and
Crouder dashed out. I raced after him, but he zigzagged across the
street, dodging between cars and neatly avoiding a vigorous chap
who was pedaling pell-mell. Safe on the other side, he slowed and
looked back at me, laughing. Then he turned and trotted onward
toward Golden Gate Park into a life of grand adventure. I watched
him go in admiration. That sneaky little fur ball had survival in-
stincts as well-honed as my own.

"Henry's suitcase is missing," Aviva reported.

"His car is gone," Ted said.

"He's too old to drive. He doesn't have a cell phone. Should we call the police?" Aviva said.

"He's not a missing person. He has a valid driver's license. His lawyer told him he's under no legal obligation to stay put. We have to wait until we hear from him," Ted said.

"But where did he go?" Aviva said. "Why not tell us?" She looked at me. I looked at Ted. He shifted from foot to foot.

"I was hard on him," Ted said uncomfortably. "He may have felt . . . unwanted."

"Well, I think it's perfectly childish of Henry to run off like this," Aviva said.

"He didn't do it for you," I said. "He did it for himself."

They looked appalled and then abashed. Ted rubbed a hand across his high forehead. The living room was dim in the evening light. I turned on a lamp and wished I hadn't, for it made us more aware of Henry out there in the dark.

"Do you know where he went?" Aviva asked.

I shook my head. "He didn't tell me a thing."

Ted began pacing. "Where could he be? And for how long? A couple of days? A week?"

"His note sounds like he expects to be gone for a while," Aviva said.

"Anyone know where his address book is?" Ted asked, looking around helplessly. "Maybe he went to see one of his old fishing buddies. I think there's one in Irvine and one in San Diego. They moved after retirement to be close to their kids."

"He has no friends left. He's outlived them all," Aviva said.

I fetched the address book, which was frayed and stained and full of crossings-out. Ted paged through it. "My mom kept up with a lot of people. Here's Kate's old address in Orange County.

I remember that house. There were avocado trees in the backyard. Her dad grew winter melons."

"That's where he went," I said.

Ted shook his head. "Her parents are passed. No one in the family lives there anymore."

"No," I said. "Not the house. He went to find Kate!"

Ted gaped. "Jesus, I bet he did."

"At the kibbutz?" Aviva said. "That's nuts."

"It's not a kibbutz," Ted and I said in unison. We cracked up, more in relief than in mirth.

"It isn't funny," Aviva said. "I'm worried sick. He's probably dead right now in a ditch."

"I'm calling Kate," Ted said.

She picked up on the first ring. "I was just about to call you," she said, speakerphone amplifying her distress. Without any warning, Henry had rung the cowbell at Beit Hayeladim. His car had broken down a mile from the place, and he'd hitched a ride to the gate. At that very moment, he was eating soup in the dining room and debating with several residents the origins of the kibbutz movement. The discussion was just getting started.

"You better come get him," Kate told Ted, "before he settles in for good."

AVIVA VOLUNTEERED TO DRIVE south with Ted, saying they could use the time to talk about Ted and his father and how to get Henry home.

But Ted was ready for her, the brooder shooing away the intruder. He reminded her that she'd organized a special library program, which she was supposed to lead. "The kids will be disappointed if you're not there."

"How will you bring back Henry's car? You can't drive two cars at once. He shouldn't drive himself."

I spotted my chance and jumped, monkey-agile, to claim the shotgun seat. "I can drive Henry's car back," I volunteered. I didn't tell Henry to scarper, but now that he had, his timing was perfect. I'd get to Southern California and visit Lisbet and Yu.

Ted agreed, and he called Kate to tell her that he and I would drive down in the morning. I hurried to write to Lisbet and Yu, saying I was coming to see them, with Ted as my Uber driver.

YU REPLIED FIRST. The baby had just been born! *Deng will be here soon. He's making the arrangements. Please come as soon as you can. I want you to meet my beautiful daughter.* Lisbet's message was equally happy. In a couple of days, she and her mother would be back in Malibu, and she couldn't wait to see me. There were things she wanted to say.

The next morning, Aviva was awhirl, loading the crapmobile with an ice chest full of sandwiches and an armload of presents for Leo.

"Tell him I miss him," she said. "I'll come see him as soon as this mess is over. No, don't say that. Don't call it a mess, though it is. First Huntington, now Henry. And it all falls on Ted. What's that? Is that for Leo?"

I was bringing with us *The Encyclopedia of Animals,* Leo's favorite book. Under "A," for "American," the buffalo stood. *O give me a home.* I'd marked the page for Leo.

"How sweet," Aviva said. "Let's send him a picture of Crouder. Have you got one?"

Why would I need a picture when I had the real live dog?

"Bring him over then. In the yard, not the house. I'll take a picture and print it. He can hang it on his wall."

Wished I could. Crouder was sleeping.

"For Pete's sake," Aviva said. "Get him up! This is for Leo!"

I didn't know who this Pete was, but I didn't have Crouder. I went back to the saltbox and ate a plate of spareribs and a bowl of juicy grapes. When Ted texted that he was ready to go, I returned to the saltbox stretch and reported, "Crouder's gone out."

"Gone out? Where would he go?"

"He's probably next door. He likes to go visiting in the neighborhood," I said.

"But we're next door," Aviva said.

"Ready? Let's go." Ted kissed Aviva. "We won't be long. Two, three days at the most. I'll call you from the motel in Palmdale."

"But what about the dog?" Aviva called as we pulled out of the driveway.

I shouted back, "He won't be any trouble!" We hit the road, *The Ted and Shelley Show.*

My earlier trip to L.A. had been on the bus at night. Now I had a view of California rolling by. We crossed the Bay Bridge— *full of Chinese steel*, Ted remarked; a countryman had to blush—and saw the old bridge running right beside. It was being taken down piece by piece after an earthquake damaged it years ago. Its long deck was suspended over the water, ending abruptly in midair. I thought of our *lao jia* coming apart in pieces, first with Leo's departure and now with Henry's. Could we put back together the old family home?

"There are a hundred thousand more people living in San Francisco now than there were ten years ago," Ted said. "No wonder there's so much traffic."

"Is that a lot, a hundred thousand?" Yunnan Province, feathered nest where little Gejiu bird perched, had forty-seven million.

Ted laughed. "It is for us. Cities need new blood. Though it's hard to keep up with the changes."

"Would you really sell the house?"

"Aviva and I almost sold it, years ago, after Eli was killed. She wanted to move back to Ohio. Her brother lives there, and she wanted to be near her nieces. Her brother found us a house, way more affordable than here, but I couldn't bring myself to go."

"Are you still angry with Henry?"

Ted sighed. "What am I supposed to do? I can't leave him there with Kate."

A full hour had passed since I'd eaten breakfast, and the ice chest was calling. I reached back and rooted among its riches, blessings on Auntie Aviva. Ted sipped at his coffee. Driving had unlocked in him a *maybe* sort of mood.

"Maybe we should've gone to Ohio. Maybe that would've made things easier. After."

"Father and I moved after Mother died. It didn't help. We still missed her. When she was alive, Father used to tell terrific stories, but when she died, he stopped. A year went by and then another. I kept waiting for him to start again. But he never told another story."

"How old were you when she died?"

"Seven."

"Old enough to remember her. You can hold on to that."

I told him how Father, Mother, and I would walk in the park with Father singing to Mother, and how, at the close of the day, he would make up a story for her about the people we'd seen strolling. "The stories were for Mother. He liked to make her laugh."

"I'm sorry," Ted said. "If there'd been a way for him to make things better for you, he would've tried."

"Same as Henry," I suggested. We stared out at the road.

BRAVELY THE CRAPMOBILE CLIMBED the Altamont Pass. The sky was bright blue, and I cheered as we ascended. Along the ridge, white wind turbines hailed us in friendly greeting.

"We've still got to get over the Grapevine," Ted warned, but he looked pleased as we crested. We drove down into the Central Valley and the landscape opened. Power lines outside the window rose and fell like an undulating ridge of distant mountains. Cars and trucks barreled beside us, everyone traveling way over the speed limit because that was the rule of the road, S.F. to L.A., northern to southern, the I-5 corridor, *not for the faint-hearted*, Ted declared. He seemed lighter, looser. His problems hadn't disappeared, but the rush of the highway relaxed him the way that bike-riding did. He'd brought a pile of old CDs and, to my amazement, he belted along with Bruce, Boz, and the Beach Boys, musical artists of the ancien régime.

The rest of our drive passed quickly. I told Ted about the app that Eddie, Paloma, and I were building, and he said that it had as good a chance as any other. He asked me about Lisbet—how we had met and whether Father minded that she wasn't Chinese; in theory, no, though I'd never taken her to meet him. I told him how I'd promised her three splendid poems.

"Like in a fairy tale," he said. "Aviva says that in fairy tales and legends, three is a powerful number."

"Three, not eight?"

"Like the hero has three tasks to perform to win the princess, or the boy traveling through the forest meets three helpful strangers."

I'd met helpful strangers, like Cook, Ron, and Mr. Lee, and I'd heard Aviva talk about princesses though hers were always Jewish.

"I wrote a second poem for Lisbet last night." I touched my pocket to make sure it was there. Well past midnight, I'd sat at Diana's desk staring at Lisbet's picture, but it wasn't until I'd gone to bed and relived as best I could by myself our afternoon at Zuma Beach that results had finally come.

"That sounds serious," Ted smiled.

"She likes them short and sweet."

"Let's hear it then," he said.

> *In the middle of the night*
> *I lay awake and addressed the sun.*
> *Please, come back and warm me*
> *Like a mango sweetens my mouth.*

"I take it you've slept with this girl," Ted said.

Was that what the poem said? "Should I change it?" I asked.

"She's going to love it," he assured me.

Later, he told me his own story. From the moment he'd met her, he'd felt the same way about Kate. They'd both gone to a meeting at the college newspaper's office the first week of freshman year at U.C. Santa Cruz. She was standing off to the side, and he noticed how quiet she was, although it wasn't shyness. She raised a hand to ask a question and her voice was as clear as a bell. When she looked at him and smiled, he felt charged with hope. He was a reticent guy, he said, who didn't like to be prodded. Kate's serenity made him want to act. It was always that way with Kate. She found the best in you. You knew you could trust her with who you really were.

They were friends for several months, then boyfriend and

girlfriend. He spent holidays at her home in Orange County; she spent weekends with him at Henry and Diana's. When his mom asked where he and Kate planned to live over the summer, he realized he wanted to spend the rest of his life with her. They found summer work in Sacramento. He got a city beat job as a cub reporter; she was hired by a capitol news service headed up by a veteran woman journalist whom the legislators feared and courted.

By the time they were moving into their sublet in downtown Sacramento, they'd lost their way as a couple. "We were miserable, and we didn't know why. Kate's boss set her straight. In a manner of speaking." She drew Kate into a love affair of three short weeks, then discarded her. It was long enough for Kate to know she didn't belong with Ted. It took them a year to sort through it. "It made us the best of friends, the suffering. Which, at that age, is monumental."

"She told me what Henry did. How he went to see her father."

"Yeah. He surprised me. I knew my mother would understand but not my father."

I thought of my father, source of no surprise. His days were filled with the monotony of labor, his nights with weeping and drinking. He was never going to change. Mother's loud gasp had been our last surprise.

"I miss Henry," I blurted. "I want him to come home."

"I told Kate to expect us tomorrow. He better not make me beg."

PALMDALE WAS DRY AND hot. I felt the scorch of the blacktop through the soles of my trainers in the motel parking lot. We went for a burger and a beer at a sports bar in a nearby mall. Ted wolfed his down, famished. He was spent from the drive and wrapped in his own thoughts. The fleeting fun of our journey had vanished. I texted Lisbet, but she didn't answer. We drove back to the motel, and Ted went to the room to call Aviva. I wasn't tired yet, so I took a last warm soda out of the ice chest and sat in a plastic chair on the deck of the motel swimming pool, which was hardly bigger than a barrel. I thought of Leo asleep in his new bed at Beit Hayeladim and Henry on the lam and Lisbet flying to meet me. In a few short hours, I'd visit Leo and Henry and then, at last, Lisbet.

Ted came outside. His bleak expression told me that the hopeful thoughts to which I'd been clinging were about to be uprooted. "I talked to Kate. Henry refuses to see me."

"He has to! You've come all this way."

"Kate said she'd try to persuade him. I'm to call her in an hour."

Beyond the city limits, the mountains loomed. The moon looked huge and red. We left the pool and walked away from the motel lights so we could view the sky while we waited. Ted said we were looking at a total lunar eclipse on the night of a supermoon. I felt that we, like the moon, were passing within Earth's shadow. I hadn't come to Peach Blossom Land for this. I had meant to leave sadness behind.

"If you could talk to your father right now, what would you say to him?" Ted asked.

I had no answer. It was my turn to be silent. Ted excused himself to make the call. He came back and quietly said, "Henry won't see me. He'll only talk to you."

The sky wheeled. The fat moon darkened.

22.
Runaway

BEIT HAYELADIM WAS THIRTY-FIVE MINUTES FROM Palmdale in a town called Agua Dulce in northern Los Angeles County. Ted and I made our plan. I would collect Henry, bring him to Palmdale, and go to Lisbet in the afternoon. Tomorrow, Ted and I would pick up Henry's car at the repair shop, and I would visit Yu as promised. I hoped to surprise Yu by bringing Lisbet with me. The day after that, Ted and I would caravan back to San Francisco, me driving Henry in his car. I asked Ted to come along to Beit Hayeladim; maybe Henry would change his mind and want to see him. *Drop me at the mall*, Ted said. *I know when I'm not wanted.*

Outside, it was already getting hot. I rolled down the car window and let the dry wind blow as I dipped and climbed through sharply rising hills left parched and brown by summer. The spare land cheered me—there wasn't a fishing pond in sight. Henry would be glad to come home.

I called Lisbet and left her another message. An older, narrower road, the Sierra Highway, took me through canyon country. I was only an hour from Malibu and its long blue wash of sea, and as I drove, I daydreamed of finding some nice little hamlet where Lisbet and I could settle, not with her mother or my *ye ye* or uncle or auntie but all by ourselves.

The day grew hotter. Ranches appeared, their golden hillsides stamped with the silhouettes of grazing horses. The paved road ended, and I continued on a packed-dirt track according to Kate's instructions. I pulled up to a wooden ranch gate and got out to ring the cowbell. Kate appeared and opened the gate. She waved me down a driveway to a parking area, where I saw several cars and a pickup truck beside a long, low building. We greeted each other. Orit was away for the day, Kate said, and Leo was in school; I could visit with him later. We should look for Henry first.

We found him staking plants in the garden. He stood and shook my hand in formal greeting, and I felt like I was meeting him for the first time. Kate left us to talk in private.

He walked me back to the long building, which was the dining hall, and we settled into wicker chairs on the porch.

"How are you?" Henry said. His eyes were bright with mischief. His face was browner than before, and he wore a straw hat like Farmer John in Leo's picture book. I recognized the khakis, but the denim shirt was new.

"You forgot your ginger chews." I handed him a bag.

"Don't need them anymore." He patted his stomach. "Kosher cooking. It's done wonders for my digestion."

Surely my cooking was better.

"You've stressed everyone out," I said.

He looked regretful. "I needed to get away. It's been a long time since I took a vacation. It's beautiful country here."

"Ted isn't angry anymore," I said. "You can come home and then things will return to normal."

He looked thoughtful and a little sad. "Ted gave me a lot to think about when he said he was leaving. Maybe it is time for a change. We can't find common ground. We used to do things together when Diana and Eli were with us. They were the bridge between us. Their deaths changed all that." He peered at me. "It's no use beating the family drum. Sometimes families break apart. You know it as well as I do."

It pained me to think he was right. "My exams are coming up. How will I pass if you're not home to coach me?"

He stretched out his legs. A fellow walking by called Henry's name with a smile, and Henry waved back. "You have the basics. All you have to do is practice. You don't need me for that."

He sounded so calm that I felt like I was talking to a stranger. "What should I tell Ted?" I asked.

"Tell him not to blame himself," Henry said. "It was high time one of us left. I was the logical one."

"I'VE NEVER SEEN HENRY like this," I said to Kate. "He seems . . ."

"Content," she said, bemused. I wasn't alone in being disarmed by this strange new version of Henry.

"Is he coming home with me today? We promised Aviva we'd bring him back."

"And I promised Leo that you'd say hello. Let's go wait for him. He'll be out at noon for lunch."

She showed me around as we waited. "We're on forty acres. Six families, eleven adults and nine children. We expect to double in size. We have a waiting list of people eager to join. I took a job in Santa Clarita. Orit is working part-time and helps with the children. Her parents live in Calabasas; that's only an hour away. Most of us have regular jobs—teaching, IT, the movie business. Finance and banking—that's how we got our loan. We're not that far from Santa Clarita or even Burbank, depending on the traffic. We hire workers to help us look after the property. It's big, as you can see."

We passed a rock garden, more stone than cactus. A palm tree, the goofy kind, all skinny trunk topped by feather duster, stuck up from the middle. Folks greeted us as we walked, smiling warmly when Kate introduced me. Everybody, it seemed, loved Henry.

Several buildings stood in a clearing, larger ones to the left and smaller ones to the right with curtains in their windows. I saw green lawn and a playground, a basketball hoop, kids' bikes. I thought with a pang of Leo's bike, which Aviva had kept for him, though she knew he would outgrow it. A bunch of older kids were kicking a soccer ball over dry grass. Pretty soon that would be Leo.

Their apartment was in the last residence building at the far end of the clearing. The space was small and sunny. There was no proper kitchen, since they ate in the dining hall, but they had a pleasant living room, which they shared with another family. "Their bedroom is on that end. Ours is through this door."

"Where does Leo sleep?"

"In the Children's House."

"He doesn't sleep with you?" Who told him his bedtime stories?

"He stays with the other children. They're grouped by ages. It's very cozy. He loves it."

The schoolhouse was a simple building with a wraparound porch. I could hear children's voices through the open windows. "That's the library," Kate said, pointing to a finished shed with a lantern by the door. "Leo goes by himself every day to take out books."

"Shelley!" Leo called. He ran to us and wrapped himself around my leg, his face pressed to my jeans and his long hair flopping.

"Hello, buddy," I said, shaking my leg gently.

"Mama said you were coming today," Leo said, letting go too quickly. He waved to a boy crossing the yard. "That's my friend Nathan. He goes to my same school."

Nathan ran to Leo. They walked away in a clutch, giggling. Leo cupped a hand to whisper in Nathan's ear.

"He's got a brother," Leo reported, coming back to Kate and me. "He's one of the little kids. Look at my chickens!"

He showed me the coop and pointed to the largest bird pecking in the yard. "That one is the rooster. They let me name him Mister Big. Those are the hens. We eat the eggs sometimes."

After Leo introduced me to every chicken and the goats and showed me the vegetable garden, Kate said it was time for lunch. "You can eat in the dining hall today," she said to Leo. "Your teacher said it was okay since we have a guest."

Leo frowned. "I want to eat with Nathan."

"Can you show Shelley where we all eat dinner together?"

"I eat breakfast with my moms and lunch at my school," Leo told me. "I don't like the other place. It's noisy."

"It's okay," I said, crouching next to Leo. There'd be no time for storytelling today. I breathed in his familiar scent mixed with something new. Chickens, maybe, or the sweat of his older self. "It was good to see you, buddy."

"Bye, Shelley," Leo said, and he ran into the schoolhouse.

"He was talking pretty easily with that kid," I said to Kate. I wanted a moment longer.

She nodded. "There are a couple of friends he talks to. His

teacher said he speaks sometimes in morning circle. He sings all the songs. He never did that before. He's not comfortable in every situation, but it's early days yet." She took the animal encyclopedia I brought and promised to give it to Leo.

He emerged from the schoolhouse holding Nathan's hand. He didn't stop to wave as I watched them trot away. I could see that he was happy, a little emperor rooster with free run of the ranch.

HENRY JOINED US FOR lunch in the dining hall. The meal was delicious, home-baked bread and a hearty soup made with vegetables from the garden.

"I've made a decision," Henry said. "I need your help to get it done."

"Great," I said, glancing at the time. I'd done my duty to Henry and Ted, and Lisbet was waiting.

"I want you to clean out the house. I've been putting it off for years. Get rid of all the junk. Most of what's there we never use. With me out of the way, this is a good time to do it."

"Aren't you coming with me?"

"Nope," Henry said. "I'm staying here for a while."

"Oh, dear," Kate said.

"There's plenty of room," Henry said. "I talked to your friends. I pledged a contribution. They say I'm welcome to hang out. The whole idea is to have multiple generations. I'm the old guy in the bunch."

"This isn't a *lao jia*," I said. "You're not the *ye ye* here."

"Why can't I make my own *lao jia*? You did it," Henry said.

Kate and I tried to persuade him, but he was dug in.

"Don't you want to go through Diana's things and decide what you'd like to keep?" Kate pressed.

"Shelley's in charge. He can handle it. I'm tired of my same old life. I'm going to enjoy myself."

I DROVE TO MALIBU, my thoughts as jammed as the road. Ted and Aviva would raise a clamor, but maybe a break would do them good. As for me, wasn't this a lucky stroke? Lisbet could come stay with me at Henry's house! We'd have the saltbox all to ourselves. I couldn't wait to bring her to meet Eddie and Paloma.

I found the winding road and joined a long line of beautiful cars that snaked up the mountain. The white house gleamed in the sun. I crossed the courtyard and rang the bell.

A woman answered the door. She had Lisbet's sloe eyes but none of her languor; the very skin around her mouth jumped in agitation when she saw me. Peering into the cool, dark entryway after sweating all day in the sun made my head swim. I couldn't tell which of us was trembling.

"Are you that boy? The one who's in love with my daughter?"

I shouted for Lisbet, and her mother looked delighted. "She's not here," she declared, posing, tiny fist to mouth.

In disbelief, I rushed past her into the house.

"We had a fight," she called after me, sounding languid after all. "She left."

I ran through the rooms calling Lisbet's name, but she didn't answer.

The fist opened into five red talons, a hawk swooping over my head.

"Poor, poor boy. She's run away again."

23.
Yu and Me and Ted

ENRY HAD ABANDONED ME. LISBET HAD SLIPPED through my fingers. Phone calls and messages went out to both; neither fugitive replied. Ted told Aviva that we weren't bringing Henry back, and she ordered us to drive *this very minute* to Beit Hayeladim and command him to come home.

"I'm done trying," Ted said. "He told Shelley he's staying put. Nothing we say will make him change his mind."

We ate in glum silence at the diner next to the motel, though I could barely swallow a bite. Finally, Ted said, "You wanted to visit your friend Yu today. Take the car. I'll wait here. When you return, we'll pack up and go home. It'll be cooler anyway if we leave late in the day."

"Let's just go home now."

"She's counting on you," Ted said. "Didn't you promise her you'd visit?"

I expected more sympathy than this after what had happened with Lisbet. "I don't want to go," I said. "What use could I be? Deng will be there in a day or two."

"She's just had a baby," Ted said. "She might be feeling overwhelmed. I've read about those birthing centers. Some of them sound bad. Don't you want to see if she's all right?"

"Leave me alone," I snapped. "Just because you can't get Henry to do what you want doesn't mean you can boss me. I'm tired of doing your job. He's your father. I came all the way down here, and nothing turned out right. I just want to go home!"

Ted was quiet. After a moment, he said, "You're right. We ask a lot of you. We put a lot on your shoulders. You've done things for me that I don't want to do. Don't forget, though: you get paid to take care of Henry. Nobody pushed you into it. You asked for the job. I felt sorry for you, so I went along with it, although I had my reservations. The visa issue, for one, and the fact that he doesn't care about anyone but himself. I told you it would end badly. You didn't listen."

I slid out of the booth and shouldered my backpack. "I want to go home," I said.

Ted stood. "You do what you want. I'm going to see your friend."

YU WAS IN A city called Rowland Heights on the east side of L.A. County. It took us two hours to drive there through a ganglion of highways. While Ted wove through the branching traffic,

I unlatched and relatched my seatbelt, thinking it was pinning me down, until I realized that the tightness was inside my chest.

"You okay?" Ted asked.

"I'm still mad," I said. "At you and everyone else."

Ted threw me a sympathetic look. "I'm sorry about your girlfriend. It's been a bad couple of days for us both."

"She didn't wait to tell me. She just ran," I said. All that Lisbet and I had said to each other in Gejiu and Mengzi, the language we had learned, the verses I had tried to write, meant nothing. Zuma Beach meant nothing.

"It's a shock, I know. It's okay to be angry. Don't hold on to it, though. It sticks to you hard, like rust. You know how the fog eats away at our downspout and gutters? After a while, you don't notice the good parts of the house. You see only the damage."

"You should take your own advice," I said.

"You're right, of course," Ted said. "Easier said than done."

I quit talking and counted the cars on the highway. Anger was a devilish thing. I felt terribly satisfied letting my anger romp, a quandary Ted knew well. It wasn't such a mystery to me anymore why Ted and Henry battled. When you can't believe what has happened to you, your heart gives way to your spleen.

We changed course from the 5 to the 60. We would hit Rowland Heights right before the 57. Ted was talking again; I only half listened until I realized he was talking about Yu.

"It's not illegal," he was saying. "She's entitled to come here and give birth, but these so-called maternity hotels are run by profiteers. They make money off of pregnant women like Yu who crave a better future for their babies."

"It wasn't Yu's idea," I said, remembering her dream of learning French and working for a global company so she could travel.

She always intended to live in Gejiu and take care of her parents. I wondered if the baby would change all of that.

"There was a raid reported last week," Ted said. "The women were kept inside and crowded together, hidden from the neighbors in a cut-rate operation that didn't provide good care."

That got my attention. Cut-rate operations were a specialty of Deng's.

"My cousin Deng made the arrangements. He's coming to meet Yu. They're going to get married and become U.S. citizens now that they have an American-born child."

Ted shook his head. "It doesn't work that way. He's mistaken if he thinks it's automatic."

"He's a big-picture man. He leaves the details to others."

"Of course, if you have money, you're well taken care of," Ted said. "Apparently sixty thousand bucks will get you a deluxe experience with doctors on-site."

"What does ten thousand bucks get you?" That was the amount that Deng had asked me to send him.

"I don't know. It's risky. Like everything else, you get what you pay for. Is he well off, your cousin Deng?"

"He's an entrepreneur. A creative businessman."

"Creative?" Ted said, the newsman in him sniffing. "What do you mean by that?"

I shifted in my shotgun seat. "Not all of his dealings were official."

"What is his business, exactly?"

"Sales. Marketing. Broker. Supplier. He does deals wherever he has friends in the right places."

"And he pays those friends for their trouble? Under the table, perhaps?"

"I think so, though he kept me in the dark. He always had a job for me: drive this van, deliver this message. Be on this corner when I call and don't ask questions." *Kuai, kuai, kuai!* Deng used to shout. Hurry, hurry, hurry! "Sometimes he paid me. Usually he asked for a favor."

"Sounds like he took advantage of you."

"I couldn't refuse him. He paid attention to my father when none of the others did. To tell you the truth, I didn't like working for him." A confession I'd never made to anyone, including myself. It was disloyal, and foolish, given my lack of options, to cut the cord to Deng.

"And he wants to settle in L.A.?"

"That's what he told me. He's good with computers too."

"Ambitious, resourceful, unafraid to take a chance. A model of modern China. He'll fit right in," Ted said.

THE ADDRESS DENG HAD given me was for a poorly marked apartment building on a noisy street behind a strip mall. We found the right door and heard a baby wailing. First Ted knocked, and then he pounded. The woman who finally answered didn't want to let us in, but Ted wouldn't be denied. He loosed Chinese swear words in his clumsy accent and also opened his wallet. I was impressed he'd come prepared. At a hundred bucks, the woman cracked the door. I called Yu's name down the dim hallway. She shouted back joyfully, "Xue Li! Xue Li!"

She rushed to hug me, tears pearling. She looked as beautiful as ever though paler than I remembered and awfully thin for a mother. I introduced Ted. She greeted him in her best English, which sounded halting next to mine. She blushed and apologized and said she was sorry but that since Miss Chips, Lisbet, and I left Gejiu, she hadn't practiced much. Ted told her that she spoke excellent English, a whole lot better than his Mandarin.

"Your swearing is good," Yu complimented him in her old mischievous way. The woman who opened the door, a lady with a thick neck and fleshy middle who was wearing a shirt covered in smiling bears, interrupted to tell Yu that no visitors were permitted even if I was the father. Yu just as sharply replied that they'd treated her horribly since the minute she'd arrived and she was going to talk with us for as long as we wanted and the old bitch better not interfere.

"I speak better than you do," Yu switched to English, her British accent chiming. "I can report you."

The old bitch retreated. Yu smiled wolfishly after her; I'd never seen such an expression on her delicate face. Then Yu turned and took me gently by the arm and said she was so happy to see me and would I like to meet her baby? She went to bring us to a different part of the house, but the old bitch blocked her. Yu pushed her, yelling loudly until the woman cried, "Go ahead! You'll get us all into trouble." Yu asked us to wait, she would bring the baby to us, and she squeezed down the hallway past suitcases, cartons, a broken fan lying on its side. The place reeked of soiled diaper. I spied out the greasy kitchen and, for once, wasn't tempted.

The doors off the hallway were shut. A group of pregnant ladies came out to look at us in fright. A second old bitch joined the first one and ordered the women back into the room.

"This place is unlivable," Ted said. "Are all six of those women sleeping in one room?" He'd been quick to count them, his nose for news at work.

Yu reappeared, carrying a tiny bundle. "This is my little girl," she said, stroking the baby's head. "She's five days old. I haven't named her yet. I'm waiting for Deng."

"She looks like you!" I said.

"My wee bairn," Yu said, smiling. Miss Chips had used to read to us verses by a chap called Robert Burns. Yu was so beautiful and Deng so handsome that their wee bitty bairn was bonny.

Ted asked if he could hold her. He held out his arms and tucked her close to his chest.

"Won't Deng be happy?" Yu said. Her eyes were alight with pride.

"Have you told your parents?" I said. "Your father?"

Yu lowered her head. "My father won't speak to me. He's very angry that we didn't wait until we were married."

"But they know you're here, right?"

"Yes, I told them. Deng was going to visit them and explain everything after I left, but he's been so busy making his own arrangements that he hasn't had the time. I wrote to them. My mother instructed me not to write again."

"What's she saying?" Ted asked.

I shook my head. "Her parents are very unhappy. She hasn't got much money. She's waiting for Deng to show up. When's he coming?" I asked Yu. "I'm worried."

"Pshaw," Yu said, sounding for a second exactly like Miss Chips. "Look at our darling baby!"

Ted was adjusting her blanket and cooing at her like a granny. "Hey," he said. He began unwrapping the baby. "Does she look all right to you? Shelley, clear off that table. Wait. First, move it under the window. The light is better there."

I hurried to clear off old magazines and an ashtray, raised the window blind, and moved the table into the daylight.

"Spread out the blanket." He placed the baby on the blanket. "Okay?" he asked Yu. She nodded. He gently unsnapped the baby's shirt and drew it over her head. She didn't cry or fuss but lay there quietly, her hands curled. She looked like a little frog. Her arms and legs were spindly, but her belly was boldly curved. He removed her diaper last. No question about it—she was a girl—but just to be sure, I zeroed in on the earlobe. Pink and pristine, like every other Zheng's of the female persuasion, no rump of a mole in sight. He motioned Yu to join him and the two of them bent close.

"Does she look yellow to you?" he said. Awkward! A bad American joke. "No, really," he said. "Ask Yu for me. Does her coloring look different now compared to when she was born? How about her eyes. Do the whites of her eyes look yellow?"

I told her what he was asking. Yu, alarmed, looked anxiously over her baby. She told me that her eyes did look a little yellow, and maybe her stomach too.

"May I touch her?" Ted asked, and again, Yu nodded. He pressed gently on the baby's forehead.

"That doesn't look right!" Yu cried. "Her skin looks very yellow!" Ted told her not to worry. He put the baby's shirt back on, bundled her snugly into her blanket, and laid her in Yu's arms.

"She'll be okay," Ted reassured her. "Has she seen a doctor?"

"There was a lady here; she said she was a doctor," Yu said.

"What day was that?"

Yu couldn't remember. "Maybe the first day? Maybe the second. They gave me some medicine that made me forget."

"She might have jaundice," Ted said. "That can show up a couple of days after a baby is born. We need to get her to a doctor." We didn't know *jaundice*; Ted had to explain. The old bitch reappeared and insisted that there had been regular doctor visits. All the mothers were healthy; all the babies had been examined, I translated for Ted.

"What doctor? When? Can we call the doctor now? Have you got a name for this doctor, a number?"

"Get out of here!" the woman yelled. She screeched at Yu,

"Tell them to leave! They're making trouble. He's upsetting the mothers. We're going to get complaints!"

"No translation necessary," Ted said drily. He took Yu to a quiet corner. "Would you like to come with us? We'll go find a doctor."

Eyes wide, Yu gripped his arm and nodded.

"Get your things. You're not coming back to this place."

This time, it was Ted who blocked the old bitches. Yu put the baby into my arms and ran for her suitcase. I stood like a statue, afraid I was holding her wrong.

"Relax, breathe. She won't break," Ted said.

Ten minutes later, we were on our way to the hospital, Yu murmuring to her baby in the back seat of the car. Ted was triumphant.

"You're not going back there," he repeated. "God, that place was awful. Call Aviva," he said to me.

"Shelley!" Aviva answered the phone. "What have you done with Crouder?"

I handed the phone to Ted.

"Eli had jaundice when he was born, right? Can you tell me everything you remember?"

"Will you hold her for a while?" Yu asked me. "I'm very, very tired."

I crawled into the back seat. Yu fell asleep in an instant. The baby looked up at me with the yellow eyes of a cat. Next to a real live baby, Crouder was a walk in the park.

24.
Waking Up

TED WAS THE HERO OF THE HOUR. HE TOOK US straightaway to USC Medical Center. The doctors there assured Yu that the baby would be fine after they treated her for jaundice. Yu thanked Ted over and over, and Ted, embarrassed, said that anyone would have done the same. To me, he muttered, "I've never done anything like that before. I don't know who that was."

Yu stayed overnight at the hospital with the baby while I tried to reach Deng. He hadn't replied to Yu's messages or mine. Perhaps he was en route to L.A., but after Henry's folly and Lisbet's flight, my worry for Yu was climbing. When I finally got a message from him, it was as bad as I feared. He wasn't coming for Yu or the baby. Yu's father had made trouble for him all over town by accusing Deng of corrupting Yu and ruining the family name. Not only that, he demanded of Deng's important contacts that they stop doing business with Deng, and he complained directly to Deng's mother and the aunties, who threatened to cut Deng off if what Yu's father said was true. *Yu is lying*, Deng wrote. *I bet you a thousand yuan that I'm not the father. I saw her with that asswipe Tao more than once. Let some rich American have her. She's not my problem.*

Deng didn't have the guts to tell Yu himself. He left that job to me.

Yu wept bitterly. Ted and I took turns toting the baby. We brought the two of them to Palmdale, the baby, still froggy but looking more pinkish than yellow, riding in her own swanky chair purchased by Ted. As soon as we pulled into the parking lot of the faded green motel and felt the heat rising from the scorching tops of the cars, Ted announced, "We're not spending another night here. Let's get our stuff and go." He went to call Aviva and came striding back, smiling. He told Yu: "You're coming home with us."

The drive home took a lot longer with a newborn baby on board. At a rest stop, Ted told me that he and Aviva had instantly agreed there was no way he was going to leave Yu and her baby. "They'll stay with us until she figures out what comes next. Is there any way your cousin is going to do the right thing?"

"Um, I don't know." Although he'd boasted about how he wanted a family of daughters as beautiful as Yu, I'd never seen Deng within ten meters of a baby.

"Doesn't he love this woman?" Ted asked.

He had promised her he did. Yu certainly believed it.

"If he loves her, he won't leave her stranded," Ted said.

Lisbet. Lisbet.

HENRY'S HOUSE WAS SEALED tight, as though it knew he wasn't coming home. The whole place was stale and dusty. Henry had sent me a single message: *Start clearing out. I want it done in 30 days.* I dumped my backpack and collapsed on the mango bed. Sleep overtook me before I could undress. In the morning, I shed my clothes, climbed under the covers, and fell back into a stupor. Without Lisbet, I had no reason to get out of bed. I told myself that there must be some explanation, but deep down I knew it was over. Twice she'd left me stranded. Only in a fairy tale would a fool hope for a third chance with a princess who refused to be loved.

When I awoke, I dragged myself to the kitchen and ate instant noodles, which I microwaved in the cup. Then I went back to bed, where I watched videos on my phone until I fell asleep. The next day, I walked to a corner market to buy a frozen pizza. The pizza tasted of salt and cardboard, same as the noodles. I crawled back into bed. I didn't care that I was missing class. I heard a knock on the front door and ignored it. Like any tender shoot that struggled to grow in canyon country, I'd been left parched and wanting. Sleep was my only respite.

Eventually, Eddie and Paloma came to roust me, worried because I hadn't answered their texts or even told them if I was back. Paloma had called Aviva, who'd said she'd seen lights on but that I hadn't answered her knock.

"Phew, it smells bad in here," Eddie said, walking into the house.

I dropped into Diana's chair, fatigued right through to my bones.

"You look awful," Eddie said. "Are you sick?"

"Did something happen with Lisbet?" Paloma asked.

I nodded dumbly. When I didn't say more, Paloma signaled to Eddie, and they moved quietly through the house, opening doors and windows. I heard Eddie go down the stairs to the garbage cans in the alley and Paloma washing the dishes. A few minutes later, they returned.

"She knew I was coming," I told them. "And she left before I got there."

"Damn," Eddie said. "I knew it."

Paloma shushed him. "Come on," she said, taking me by the arm. "You're sleeping at Eddie's tonight."

I went with them obediently, too tired to object. Eddie gave me his bed and slept on the couch. When morning arrived, I rolled over and went back to sleep. Through my dreamless drift, I heard the faint sounds of Eddie and his roommates coming and going, and the robot vacuum and the rev of a car engine, but nothing pulled me from the bed. I wasn't thinking anymore of Lisbet or worrying about Henry or wondering how Yu and the baby were doing. I was in a sunken state, dragged to the bottom by an under-tow of sleep.

The sun rose again. Warm sunlight streamed through Eddie's window. I felt a hand on my shoulder and struggled to open my eyes.

"I'm sorry to wake you," Paloma said, "but we have work to do."

She made me shower and get dressed and eat a bite of breakfast and join them in the living room. We had design decisions to make, she said, starting with the look and feel of the app's landing page. Eddie had updates on market sizing. We worked all morning, the two of them happily arguing about Eddie's list of beta testers and Paloma's estimation of our MVP, the Minimum Viable Product that would get us the feedback we needed. Listening to them spar with their unshakeable confidence in themselves and each other, I felt better than I had in days.

"I'm starving," Eddie announced. "Shelley, how about you?"

We went into the kitchen and made turkey sandwiches on good black bread, and I found that I was hungry. I ate one and then another and then I was ready to return to Henry's house.

OCTOBER HAD ARRIVED, AND the brilliant sunshine held the fog at bay. Sitting at the kitchen table, I made a list. I would start with the easy stuff—closets and drawers that hadn't been opened in years; Henry's books, plenty outdated; the medicine cabinet full of pills, unguents, and syrups with expiry dates from the previous century—and move on to the garage. The bedrooms and kitchen would come last. I felt good at the prospect of clearing out decades of disuse. Houses, like people, needed to be refreshed, and though I hoped he would return sooner rather than later, I had a begrudging admiration for Henry's breakaway. I had thought that transformation was a right held exclusively by the young. It never occurred to me that old people sometimes changed too.

I went to see Professor Luo, who upbraided me for missing class. I explained that my benefactor, Mr. Cheng, had urgently needed my attention, but I was back now and very sorry and eager to make up the work. It wasn't the first time Professor Luo heard a plea from an international student. Some of my classmates were homesick, some were out of money, some broke on the wheel of homework drills and tests. In my case, it helped that I paid my tuition bills on time and in full, courtesy of Henry. Professor Luo gruffly gave me another chance.

Afterward, I went to see Yu and the baby. As soon as I stepped inside, Aviva dragged me to the kitchen. I tried to take up my old listening post in the doorway, but she made me sit down with her and Ted at the table. I was part of their story now, invisible no longer. She said that Yu and the baby were out for a walk in this beautiful weather. What had taken me so long to come over? Aviva had been waiting. She wanted my full report on Beit Hayeladim.

"What's it like? It's not a cult, right?" Aviva said.

I had to ask for a definition. Ted tried to explain. "Satanic," I wrote in my little black notebook, pentagramming it for later study.

"It was very nice. Lots of kids. Families. People were friendly," I said.

"How did Leo seem? Happy?"

"He's talking more," I said. "He likes his school and his friends."

"I should've gone with you," Aviva said to Ted. "I could've checked the place out. I probably could've gotten Henry to come home."

Ted ignored the speculation; he'd likely heard it a hundred times since coming home empty-Henried.

"Kate already told us that Leo made the adjustment more easily than expected," he said. "She and Orit are thrilled. She keeps telling me not to apologize for sticking her with my father. He's wildly popular, she says. They all want to sit with him at dinner." Ted snorted. "Kate says they're one big extended family."

"Not a family," said Aviva. "A *tribe*."

With that, I ventured to ask the question that had set the black fish in my tummy madly swimming ever since I'd learned that Leo slept every night away from his mothers, in the Children's House. "The other kids at Beit Hayeladim. Do they want Leo with them? Since he's halfway Chinese and not all the way Jewish?" I asked.

"Who knows," Aviva said, "since you didn't let me come with you."

"I trust Kate," Ted said. "She wouldn't be living there if she and Leo weren't welcome."

"I hope you're right," Aviva said. "Maybe the place is exactly as advertised. Wouldn't that be great? We should all be so lucky."

My tummy fish finned to a drifting quiet. I was relieved to hear Ted's reassurance. Almost all whom I'd met in Peach Blossom Land had treated me with MVP, Minimum Viable Politeness, but there had been instances—a comment here, a shove of the elbow there, an unguarded, hostile look—when the fact of my foreignness threatened somebody else.

"Besides," Aviva added, "Orit is Jewish, and she's his biological mother, which means that Leo is a Jew." She explained about bloodlines and such.

"So it doesn't matter that he's Chinese, as long as he's Jewish?"

Aviva sighed. "It's complicated."

"Race and faith aren't equivalent, although sometimes we talk about them as if they are," Ted said. "Then there's the whole question of economic class."

"Oy," I said, unable to keep up. There were too many identities to label and sort, a hallmark of San Francisco, although I was not unfamiliar with the roll call of roles that each of us performs. After all, in Gejiu I was son to the father, father to the father, insider, outsider, countryman, and stranger. The details differed but the whole was universal: myriad multiplicity was a fact of modern life.

CROUDER WAS ANOTHER STORY. From him, I expected a sign. A paw print on the back stoop, a bark in the middle of the night. An overturned water bowl—I freshened it daily—or a pile of fertilizer. I got *bupkus*. Aviva posted lost-dog fliers around the area, but Crouder was still out there, exploring. It pissed me off that he should treat me so cavalierly. Who had fed him, cleaned the fur around his puckered arsehole, gathered his turds like crop? Some friend he was. Had he never heard of loyalty? Of nobility, of devotion? I assured Aviva I had no idea what had happened to the little mite, a technically accurate statement. Maybe he was snuggling with the bison and coyotes. The least he could do was check in.

"They've all abandoned me," I said to Eddie and Paloma. "Lisbet. Henry. Even Crouder."

Eddie was glad that I could mention Lisbet's name half in jest. "Everyone gets dumped. You'll get over it," he said.

"That's not particularly helpful," Paloma said without looking up from her laptop. Between her course load and our start-up, she was working nonstop.

"Freshman year, I was totally in love with a girl named Alyssa. She broke up with me right before she left for Burning Man with some other guy," Eddie said.

"Again, not helpful," Paloma said, the click-clack of her keyboard like the sound of a passing train. She was a genius at crushing code.

"But then I met Paloma, the best thing that's ever happened to me," Eddie said.

"So far," Paloma said, still tapping. "I know your mother loves me."

"*I* love you," Eddie said. Paloma smiled. TinRoad was bringing them closer together, a beautiful by-product of our on-demand platform with its on-trend flow.

"You're not going to meet your next girlfriend by moping every night," Eddie said. "Paloma has a lot of friends." I shook my head. "At least look," Eddie said, holding up Paloma's phone.

"Don't be a dick," Paloma said. "Shelley's not interested in dating right now."

"If he was, he wouldn't have gotten his heart stomped," Eddie said.

Paloma patted my shoulder. "You'll meet someone new. You're open to people. You don't have a cynical bone in your body. That's *why* you got stomped, of course. Anybody could have told you she was going to bolt. It's her emmo, right? She can't handle commitment, so she runs? It scared her to be in love with you. It meant she was responsible for somebody else's heart."

"MO," Eddie said, seeing my confusion. "Modus operandi. The usual way she does shit."

"I guess so. She told me she's not good at sticking by people, but I thought she was talking about her mother."

"It's *all* about her mother. That's really who she was running away from," Paloma said.

"But she promised!" I said. A last gasp of the injured. The moment the words puffed into the air, I heard how feeble I sounded.

"So now you know," Paloma said. She stood and went back to her laptop, sympathy session over. In her own sturdy way, Paloma woke me up.

25.

Yu's Warning

OVER AT THE SALTBOX STRETCH, YU AND THE BABY were thriving. The baby was rounder and sturdier and talking, so to speak, through her little tea-spout mouth. At every diaper change, her fat legs kicked in freedom. The jaundice was gone, and she was sleeping well at night. Yu was stronger too. After three weeks, she'd gained a few pounds—sing kugel's praises—and the fullness suited her. Her smooth face luminesced. The earlier stress had made it hard to get Baby to take the breast, she said, but now they had the hang of it. I hastily dropped to a knee and fiddled with my shoelace to stave off the details. Yu laughed at me and told me how grateful she was to my uncle and auntie. They had opened their home to her. They loved giving Baby her bottle. Their friends had given her loads of baby equipment and money for clothing and diapers.

"Have you chosen a name for her yet?"

Yu sighed. "I keep changing my mind. Nothing seems suitable. I wish I could ask my mother." She ran a fingertip along a wisp of Baby's hair. She'd written and called and pleaded with her parents, but they refused to answer. Deng had downright disappeared.

"Baby will know where she came from. Gejiu is in her blood," I reassured my friend. With each other and with Baby, Yu and I spoke the local dialect of our district. Her daughter wouldn't know her grandparents, Yu said, but at least we could give her the language of the memories Yu carried.

"I want her to have a western name while we're living here," Yu said. She gave me her impish smile. "Maybe I'll call her Shelley, since that's really a girl's name."

"Call her Little Tulip," I said, recalling the name that Miss Chips gave Yu.

"Ah, Miss Chips," Yu said. "I miss her. I admired the way she lived, moving freely about as she pleased. She must have been rich. A secret millionaire."

"Father didn't think Miss Chips was rich, just a very generous lady."

Yu set Baby in her angled seat and shook a soft rattle. "How is your father? I saw him right before I left Gejiu. He was with Deng. They were quite jolly. I almost didn't recognize your dad. I knew him as a gentle fellow, a little sad but mild. He seemed different that day. Of course, you speak with him regularly yourself, so you know what he's been up to."

"Deng fills me in," I said. I reached for the rattle and shook it at Baby, who began to fuss.

"Deng," Yu said with disgust. "I was stupid to have trusted him. I thought he had a better idea for me than I could have for myself."

"He'll come around," I said feebly.

Yu tossed her head. "I don't want him anymore. I don't need him. I'm happy I have Baby"—she swiftly bent and kissed her— "but Deng is nothing to us now."

"Your baby will want to know her father," I protested.

Yu shrugged. "Some fathers are worth saving. Deng isn't." She gave me a steady look of peculiar sympathy. "I always admired your father. How he raised you by himself after your mother died. Does he miss you, do you think? More than he's willing to say?"

"He's happy I'm here. He wanted me to come. He promised Mother he'd make sure my future was bright." Under Yu's unwavering gaze, I didn't sound convincing.

"When you talk to him, please give him a big hello from me and tell him about my baby. His feelings might be hurt if he finds out from somebody else. I wouldn't want that to happen. This way, he can be the first person from home to send me congratulations. Do it for me, okay?" She plucked Baby from the chair, lifted her blouse, and stuck Baby to her breast before I had a chance to avert.

"Call him soon. For my sake," Yu said.

I nodded, eager to escape. Yu's words went in one ear and out the other, which is another way of saying that the Chinese groove kerflopped.

THE NEWS ABOUT HUNTINGTON worsened, which tightened the squeeze on Ted. A second Sunset District business, a vacuum cleaner and sewing machine repair shop owned by an elderly Chinese couple, came forward to accuse Huntington of taking payments for a building permit that never materialized. Reports said Huntington had acted alone in the matter, which meant, to my relief, that Ted wasn't under suspicion for arranging an alleged bribe. But he still wasn't permitted to return to his job in the mayor's office while the authorities decided whether Ted had helped Huntington use Henry's home address. Ted was stuck in limbo, no end in sight.

To fill the time and try to make a little money, Ted went to the library every day to ghostwrite a few articles and blog posts that his friends had sent his way. But his main occupation was helping Yu and Baby. He hired an immigration lawyer to help figure out what to do in case Yu wanted to stay. He showed her how to take the bus and wheeled Baby to the park so that Yu could have time on her own. Aviva helped when she got home from work, but Yu trusted Ted with Baby more than anyone else.

One afternoon, Aviva and I watched from the front window as Ted walked up and down the sidewalk with Baby strapped to his chest.

"It used to confuse me that he avoided Leo," Aviva said. "I thought he was afraid of having a child in the house. I guess I was wrong. He was waiting for a purpose. Leo didn't give him that. Yu and Baby do."

"Because Baby is a girl, and not a boy, like Eli?" I asked.

Aviva was quiet for a moment. "It's not that simple," she said. "When you lose a child, there's no clear way through the horror. All you can do is love your darling child and stand in the pain and wait. If you can do that without losing your mind, something unimaginable happens. A little crack opens. A little light shines through. It opened sooner for me than it did for Ted. It wasn't his fault that it took him longer, though it's been damn hard to wait for him and to see him suffer. I think it's finally opened; the light is shining through. There's a little more space these days for him to feel something new."

"Since Leo left," I suggested.

Aviva shook her head. She gave me a sad smile. "No, not Leo. Henry."

HENRY INSTRUCTED ME TO donate furniture, kitchenware, the books. Piles of old papers should all be thrown out. But even I, who had no use for the past, knew that some of it was precious. There was a shoebox of letters Diana wrote to her parents while she was at Mills College. She was only across the bay, but she wrote faithfully every week, describing what she was reading, the dresses she sewed for herself, the friends she had made. She sounded warm and relaxed, the opposite of Henry. She teased her brother about his latest haircut and encouraged him to pursue his own career. "I'll help Mom and Dad," she wrote. "Hong's Fine Food Market will forever stand!" In a few of the letters, she gave her frank opinion of a girl she didn't like or a professor whose lectures she found boring, and I thought it possible, once they'd eventually met, that she and Henry had admired in each other the candor of their independent views.

Along with the letters, there were loose photographs, including snapshots of Diana and Henry in Ghirardelli Square and of Henry and Ted camping beside a clear blue lake bordered by dark forest. In the photo, Ted's fishing pole was twice as tall as Ted. There were lots of pictures of Eli from the time he was born until his last birthday—I saw a big "9" on the cake. One photograph showed a robust Henry, his face split by a huge smile. He had a baby in his arms; I thought it was Eli until I saw the date on the back of the picture and realized the baby was Ted.

I emptied the living room bookcases and borrowed the crapmobile to take box after box to the library bin for donation. Flowered curtains, tablecloths, winter coats, and picnic blankets all went to Diana's church. The cookbooks and letters I saved for Ted and Aviva for the traces they held of Diana.

The garage was a regular junkyard of camping gear, fishing gear, gardening tools, and paint. I found a deep-fat fryer and a full bag of cement. There were enough household cleaning products to make the whole block sparkle. In America, even a house as modest as Henry's could yield up mounds of stuff.

One Sunday, after working for hours, a faded bandana of Diana's tied around my head, I tripped and banged my knee hard exactly as I'd done before on the big red sign that used to hang above the store: HONG'S FINE FOOD MARKET. I sat down and rubbed my knee and thought what a shame it was that the sign should be discarded. I remembered Mr. Bill Lee telling me the story of Sam and Lilliann leaving Chinatown for the fog-swooned streets of the Outer Sunset District, and the family they had raised in the rooms behind the store when they were blocked from buying a house, and the beautiful girl, Diana, whom Mr. Lee's brother had loved. I sat for a long time in the gloom of the day's end thinking how strange it was that no one knew until they knew how life and death would proceed. In all the in-between time, the only way to carry on was to let that mystery hover. The big red sign would go to the dump; there was no more use for it now, but I had learned the family story, and maybe, someday, I would tell it myself.

Then I remembered something. From the sliver of space between the sign and the wall, I pulled out the suitcase and the brief-case that I'd put there months ago. *HSW*, stamped in gold.

I brought the goods upstairs and laid them on the kitchen table and dusted them off with my sleeve. I reached to open the suitcase first, then stopped. I needed to think carefully about what I should do with my find, but I was tired and hungry and had schoolwork to finish before bed so I left both cases by the rosewood chest in the hallway while I fixed myself a proper supper. After I ate, I sat down at Henry's computer to work on an assignment for Professor Luo. I checked my phone when I was done. There was a message from Deng: *Arrived S.F. Call this number. I brought you a surprise.*

In my thrumming belly, the black fish flipped.

26.
Surprise

ENG HAD A SURPRISE FOR ME. WHAT COULD IT BE but money? Catbird Cousin Deng, he'd come with his pockets full. One of the aunties must have died—the stout, whiskered one who'd had no children—or the ship had come in on a late-maturing operation because, in the end, despite his boasts and bluster, Deng produced results. He was sharp and he had nerve, two qualities every business builder prizes. And now, finally, he was ready to reward me for my years of service which, when I was auntie-trodden, I gave without question but now that I stood tall, a wage earner in my own right, my newly juiced cousin would be passing me the siphon to his tank of start-up fuel. I vowed to myself that whatever Deng bestowed, I would split it with Yu, fifty-fifty.

Yu bit her lip and shifted Baby. "Would you like me to come with you?"

"Don't subject yourself to that man!" Aviva put a softened arm around Yu's shoulder. With Orit gone, Aviva had given up trying to turn back the clock and make herself twenty again, which resulted in her looking heaps better—auntie appropriate and a whole lot happier sleeping in on Sunday mornings.

"Why is he here? I don't trust him," Yu continued.

"He's here to take Baby!" Aviva asserted. "We're not going to let him."

"Is he dangerous, this Deng?" Ted said. "I should go with you."

"Do!" Aviva urged him, thrilled at the combatant her husband had become. The two of them were more incensed than Yu, whose concern was all for me.

"He wants something from you," Yu said to me. "Be careful. Don't let him talk you into doing something that you don't want to do." We shared a discomfiting look, both of us familiar with Deng's powers of persuasion. He knew how to get his way.

"He's here to get rich," I assured them. "He says he changed his plan from L.A. to San Francisco because this is where the money is. Don't worry about me. I can handle myself."

DENG INVITED ME TO meet him downtown on a cloud-scraping floor of the Millennium Tower, where he was living in luxury. A business associate of Deng's purchased the apartment when it was boxes on a blueprint and ordered it filled with marble and mirrors. Deng was his new lookout man, sent to make various arrangements. The associate, based in Shanghai, Hong Kong, Macau, and Singapore with considerable Beijing contacts, had too many deals going at the present moment for him to handle personally certain particulars of his investments. Deng swelled as he said the last, threatening to burst his buttons. He was twenty pounds heavier and looked twenty times as rich, a black-headed, shiny-suited capitalist roader. I didn't feel the least pinch of envy. I aimed to become a capitalist myself, but by my own lights and not at a boss man's bidding while puffing out my chest on behalf of an enterpriser who thought he was smarter than me. One look at Cousin Deng told me: my days as his errand boy were over.

"You don't look any different," Deng said in greeting. "You're just as poor and shabby as when you left."

"I'm doing fine," I said. I wanted to pound him like the piles beneath the Millennium Tower for betraying Yu and Baby, but Yu had made me promise not to dump on Deng. He wasn't worth the trouble.

"I'd offer you some work," Deng said. "You look like you need it. But I've got a new gopher these days. He's more useful to me than you were. He doesn't ask so many questions." He strode down the hallway and opened the door. I heard Deng laugh, and Father walked out.

But what had become of the humble man whom I'd left in my cousin's care? Had Father and I passed each other on the shores of Golden Lake or sipped *pu er* across from each other at the teahouse, or even had our hands touched as we reached for the same ripe melon from Mother's favorite vendor at the end of the market row, I wouldn't have known him. *No, that isn't right*, I thought, as I stared at him, struck dumb. If I'd spotted him across the way, I would've called out to him in an instant: *Hey there! Cousin Deng!*

For Father looked a perfect picture of Cousin Deng as I'd last seen him in Gejiu. He stood, legs straddled, a cocksure angle to his head. Dark-washed blue jeans—jeans, on Father!—were slung low and long, and huge white basketball shoes swallowed his troublesome feet, certain bunion torture. He sported a satellite dish for a watch and a tan dabbed on from a bottle. His jersey shouted "TOM FORD." If only he'd worn his old gray cap, softened by years of weather, I might've seen something of my father in this stranger, but his head was bare, and I saw with a pang that his hair was black as lacquer. A deeply cut wrinkle still ran straight between his brows and his Zheng badge still sagged on a drooping earlobe— Father, like Aviva, couldn't turn back the clock altogether—but there was an insipid smile on his face like the grin of an eager youth. It made me furious to see it. *I* was the one poised for change, not Father.

"What are you doing here?" I demanded.

The smile didn't waver; it was as fixed as the new teeth installed in Father's head. Deng answered for him.

"Don't look so shocked. He's a new man, your father, and my best recruit. You're not the only guy who can carry water. He's a lousy drinking partner, but I love the way he jumps. Right, Uncle?" He socked Father on the shoulder the way he used to knock me with a friendly blow between a tap and a clobber. Father's head bobbed and the stupid grin widened.

"Xue Li, it's your father. You hardly recognize me, huh?" A nervous chuckle. "I'm happy to see you. You look good. Well-fed." He patted his stomach. He'd swapped out his eyeglasses and dyed his hair, but he was still long bean skinny with a concave curve for a belly. "Look what I have, the gift you sent me." He showed me his key chain, *888*. "It brought good luck to both of us, wouldn't you agree?"

"What's going on, Father? What have you done to yourself?"

Father looked apologetic. "You've gotten taller," he said. "You haven't stopped growing yet, eh? How are your studies going? How are your aunt and uncle? Is their health good? Is their business still expanding? I'd like to visit their store, the best one in San Francisco, so I can thank them for being your generous hosts the whole time you've been here."

Deng noticed my Zheng mustache twitching. "Yes, give us an update, little cousin. We've been hungry for more news. Do you speak like an American now, in brags and jokes? Have your poems made you famous? Did our Gold Mountain uncle put you in charge of his great big fancy store? It's been ten months since you left us. Plenty of time to capture glory. We're all ears." He stretched his mouth at either end and tugged on his Zheng marker.

"He had Three Achievables," Father burbled. "We wrote them down together." He drew a scrap from his pocket—all this time he'd saved it—and proudly read: "Family, Love, Fortune."

Family, Love, Fortune. I turned and saw my wavering self in a floor-length, brass-bound mirror, the guilty framed in gilt, remembering how I'd hidden my true aims from Father when I departed Gejiu. I'd busted out of there thinking only of the new and better family I wanted to join, and of reuniting with Lisbet and not (as I'd told Father) of looking for a Chinese American wife, and I'd failed spectacularly, at least in Family and Love.

But the Third Achievable, Fortune! It was still within my grasp. Out of all us fervid countrymen, subjunctive-savvy and TOEFL-hardened, who toiled in Professor Luo's classroom, I was the one he singled out as a university man. Not only that, I had a *new* Gold Mountain: the awesome platform of our TinRoad app, to which Eddie, Paloma, and I were devoting our ingenuity and labors until the day we scaled so high we'd be ringing the Wall Street bell. Hand over hand, I was hauling myself upward. I didn't have time for distractions.

Father tightened his hold on the slip of paper. He was waiting for me to reassure him that our long separation had been worth

every day, every week that I was absent, but I refused him the comfort. ASAP, I had to send Father home.

FOR THE NEXT SEVERAL days, I waited impatiently to get Father
alone. Deng said he needed him but wouldn't say for what. The
inching hours had me jumping out of my dermis. Paloma called;
where was I? I raced over to Eddie's place and threw myself into
niche noodling, problem-solving, mapping market share, worried
the whole time about how I was going to dislodge Father. Even if
I persuaded him to leave, how would he pay for the ticket? I didn't
have the scratch. I couldn't ask Henry—he had my tuition to pay.

"Your father's been here since Sunday; when are we going to
meet him?" Ted prodded. I could tell he was surprised that Father
hadn't called, which Father certainly would've done had I made the
arrangements.

"Deng has him on a leash. Doing what, I don't know," I said.
"I'm waiting for Deng to allow him a few hours off."

"I promised Yu I'd stay out of it or I'd go confront your cousin.
I don't know how you could've worked for the guy," Ted said.

"I was young. He took advantage of my trust."

"You don't have to be young to be stupid," Ted said. Henry's
blunder entered the room smelling of oud wood and tonka.

"If Huntington is cleared, will Henry come home?" I asked.

"I hope they fully investigate," Ted said. "I'll bet, if they follow
the money, they're going to find out that Huntington has a long list
of dubious dealings to his name."

"And Henry?" I persisted. "Will he come home after that?"

"I have no idea what's in my father's head," Ted said. "I couldn't
begin to guess."

So the groove wasn't working for either Ted or me. Maybe it

didn't work at all beyond the great border, its powers sapped when a countryman crossed the sea. Or maybe, like an algorithm, it could only do so much, never able to fully replace human-to-human, heart-to-heart, messy, muddled effort. The only thing left to try was Aviva's great cure: talking things out with our fathers. That we'd never do, especially when the fathers were nowhere in sight.

AREN'T YOU DONE CLEARING *out the place yet?* Henry wrote. *Don't be sentimental. I want a fresh start.*

I walked through the barren house. The beds, tables, and chairs were still in place, but without the books and faded pictures on the walls, the house gave little hint as to who lived there and what their story was. I went to the rosewood chest in the hallway, the very spot where I'd stood many bounce-filled months ago on my first night at Henry's. There, where I'd left them, were Huntington's suitcase and briefcase. I carried them into the living room and set them on the coffee table. I was wearing a pair of disposable gloves used for surgery or scrubbing the tub or breaking into luggage not one's own. A clean white handkerchief of Henry's was spread on the table like the page of an unwritten poem. On it rested the trusty paring knife that I kept sharp to trim the horn from Henry's feet. A tool that fine had many uses.

Switching on Henry's reading lamp and positioning myself under its glow—how I missed seeing Henry in its circle!—I first tested the clasp on the suitcase. As I expected, it was locked. But the mechanism was simple, hardly more secure than the antique-style gentleman's lock on the rosewood chest. Half-disappointed that Huntington hadn't thrown me a tougher challenge, I picked up the knife and worked it into the lock, blade up, point in. The lock sprung in a couple of seconds.

I searched every compartment to the sound of my heartbeat in my ears. There was nothing to be discovered but a pink polo shirt and a pair of fancy braces for holding up Huntington's pinstripes. No gold bars or bundles of dollar bills or a Swiss bank account number on a microchip wedged into the water-silked lining. I sat back, disappointed. I had thought Huntington more nefarious than a grinning alligator on a rose-colored shirt.

I moved on to the briefcase and felt a satisfying flurry. Now we were matching wit to wit. The combination lock, which didn't yield to a gentle tug or a questioning probe of the knife, required me to line up three little numbers. I dared not force the knife. If I were to leave evidence that I'd tampered with the lock, I might render the contents useless. I tried to imagine what secret code Huntington would've chosen. His wife's birthday? Never. His girlfriend's? Maybe. Or maybe one of his daughters'. I pictured Huntington moving about the house. The last time he and I spoke, we stood in Henry's kitchen drinking a fancy bourbon. He had raised his glass to me with an exaggerated wink, saying he couldn't take another shot of Henry's cheap liquor.

I went to the kitchen and stood for a long moment in front of the liquor cabinet. The door was unlocked. I remembered the first day I'd come home with Henry and his wending instruction that I would find the key on a red string that he'd tied to the hook on the back of the door, etc. But, in fact, Henry always left his cabinet unlocked because it was too much trouble to hunt for the key. Maybe Huntington, like Henry, made things easy for himself. How would he have done that? Left the first two numbers in the unlocked position and spun only the third, so that the next time he went to unlock the briefcase, he had only to change a single number? With an expert fly-caster's economy of motion, maybe that was exactly what Huntington had done.

I angled the reading lamp and peered. I couldn't believe what I was seeing: 8-8-9. Could Huntington really have set his secret combination at lucky number 8-8-8? Despite the interruption of immigration, the spanner stuck in the span, the diluting effects of displacement, was he still such a Chinese son? I blinked hard, breathed in, tried to loosen my shoulders and lighten my touch. After each click, I gently tugged the lock. At 8-8-8, it yielded. My laugh echoed in the quiet of Henry's house. Huntington Wong was a countryman through and through, minted by family, ruled by expectation, shaped by forces unseen.

WHEN I FINALLY MANAGED to get a few hours alone with Father, I didn't know what to say. I had a little speech prepared about my future prospects, which depended, most urgently, on my being granted the freedom and space to pursue with passion the life I wanted to lead—potent words, hallowed beliefs, foreign to a countryman and teat-milk to a scion of the U.S.A.—but how, given the look of gladness that brightened Father's face as I walked to where he was obediently waiting for me beneath the clock tower of the Ferry Building, how could I tell him the truth: that I wanted him to leave? Peach Blossom Land was *my* adventure. Not Father's and not Deng's. His place was at home; mine was on the wing, or on the mop, more like, a boy flying high above Gejiu—a story he'd apparently forgotten, though he'd imagined it gloriously for Mother.

"Let's walk," I said, avoiding his eager smile. He'd changed to dark dress pants and a short-sleeved, pointy-collared shirt, which looked as ill on him as the earlier blue jeans. The basketball shoes were gone, replaced by narrow footwear certain to cause painful eructations. Had Father replaced his feet, too, along with his hair, teeth, and person?

"I'll show you all my favorite places," I said, but, perversely, I didn't. Something inside of me wouldn't release. Instead of bringing him to my home range on the west side of the city, and showing him where Leo and I had roamed at the zoo, the beach, the casting ponds, the meadow where the bison stood, as alert and timeless as temple gods, I dragged him around to all the predictable places while spouting facts collected from our defunct touring app. It was a chilly morning, overcast and gray, but at every bridge, pier, hill, and tower, Father heaped extravagant praise. San Francisco was as beautiful as I'd said; no wonder I was happy, and Mother would've been happy too, to see me so successful. In a tourist shop in North Beach, I bought him a packet of glossy postcards that he could take back to Gejiu. "I'll bet you can't wait to go home," I prompted, "and show them where you've been."

He rocked in his tight shoes, cheap leather cracking. "There's no hurry. Deng needs me."

"What are you doing for him? Nothing bad, I hope."

"Oh, business. Business," he said, just as Deng would've done or as I would've in an earlier era. "You know how these things are."

"I'm worried about you, Father. You seem very changed. Are you okay? How's your health?"

"You see how well I'm getting along without you." His Zheng mustache gave the barest shiver.

"What about your job at the bus depot? What did you tell your boss, the one who gave us the money for me to come?"

"It's not important. Tell me about your job and your studies. How's my cousin, your uncle Ted, and his American wife? I should pay my respects to his father. The aunties warned me that the old fellow wants nothing to do with the family—too many bad memories of the war years and losing his parents—but maybe, since I'm here, would he allow me to come visit?"

It was my turn to dodge. "I'm hungry. Let's eat."

I took him to Chinatown for fresh greens and tender dumplings and watched his chopsticks dive in and out of his bowl with his familiar precision. This was Father, his capable hands as swift as swallows, not the chatty fellow sitting across from me, layered, loafered, louche. He prattled on nervously about some of my Gejiu pals. Two of my classmates made it to college, including a girl who'd gotten a scholarship to Honghe University in Mengzi. Others were working in manufacturing plants or driving trucks or selling goods. Had I heard about Yu? She'd had some fellow's baby, and her heartless father had disowned her.

"She's here in San Francisco. Living with Uncle and Auntie."

His eyes bulged in disbelief. "Your uncle is so generous! Supporting not only my son but also Yu and her baby. I must thank them in person. When can I see them?"

"Uncle and Auntie work long hours. If you present yourself, they'll feel duty bound to host you and they don't have the time."

"Then what about your *ye ye*? He's retired. He must have time to see me."

"He's an old man," I said. "A shut-in. He keeps to himself all day." I felt bad yanking so hard on the Chinese groove, but I needed Father gone.

"I don't want to be any trouble," Father said doubtfully.

"You can buy them a box of chocolates," I offered. "I'll take it to them myself."

"A box of chocolates?" Father frowned. "They've been very good to you, bringing you into the business and housing you all this time. I'll ask Deng to loan me some money so I can take them out for dinner. Pick a nice restaurant. Someplace special."

I promised to do as he asked. I was still stalling.

After lunch, I brought him to meet Eddie's mother and Grandma

Low. Perhaps I could persuade him to leave if I showed him that even here, a long way from Gejiu, I had a couple of Chinese aunties on my case. "They keep track of everything I do," I said, stretching the truth a little.

I rang the bell. The window flew open and Mrs. Low called down, "Come up! Come up! We would love to see you."

The room was as before: neat, simple, cheerful. Mrs. Low gave me a hug, and I introduced her to Father. Her pink hair was gone, restored to black and gray. After trying out a few phrases in this and that tongue, the three of them settled on speaking Cantonese, which Father, I was surprised to hear, spoke better than I expected. I had rarely heard him use it because he never left Gejiu.

At Mrs. Low's request, I brought the stool that was kept in the stairwell, and she invited Father to sit. He settled himself and drank a cup of tea and asked Grandma Low, resplendent today in lapis blue and leopard print, to tell him about the village where she was born. Then Bill Lee came upstairs and joined the little party, joking that Father looked so handsome and vigorous, he must be my older brother. He began to regale Father with his memories of Grandma Low, "the prettiest bride of them all," and Father listened in genuine delight. I might've been on our street in Gejiu listening to the elders unhurriedly enjoying a long and newsy chat. Looking out of the window, I saw the tourists, as before, but also the residents taking part in neighborhood life. A man pushed a handcart stacked with boxes of produce. There were kids playing and shop owners swapping jokes. A young woman in high heels ran lightly through a doorway, and I thought again of Mother, and how she and Father used to walk hand in hand down the blossom-scented paths through the park.

But Father wasn't dwelling on memories of the past. He was talking and laughing with the others as if in the company of friends. The single room reminded him of home, he said, as we regained the street. He didn't like the marble palace where Deng had brought him or going out night after night with Deng and his associates, as he'd done for many months in my absence. "They're looking for women; they drink till they're falling down." He shook his head in dismay. I remembered Deng's complaint that Father was a lousy drinking partner and realized I'd not seen him take a drink since he'd arrived.

"I'm very happy to see you," he said, "but I'm missing my simple life."

What's the expression? *Music to my ears.* "Then why don't you go home? Gejiu is where you belong."

"No," said Father forcefully. He caught himself and pulled a wide smile as fake as his hair lacquer. "Deng needs me. I don't want to let him down."

"He doesn't need you! He's using you as an errand boy like he used me. Please, Father. Go home. Then I won't have to worry. That would be best for us both."

Father shook his head. "Excuse me, I'm sorry. Forget what I said. I'm happy here. Happy to see you. It was just a passing moment." He patted my arm clumsily and scurried back to Deng.

27.
In the Clear

ON THE FIRST OF NOVEMBER, HENRY REAPPEARED. He showed up unannounced at the saltbox one afternoon, dropped at the curb by a taxi.

"You're home!" I cried joyfully before I noticed that he carried no suitcase, only a canvas carrier bag with "Beit Hayeladim" on one side and Hebrew words on the other. The logo was a tree with spreading branches that sheltered a circle of children.

"I came to see my lawyer. He wants to talk to me about those documents you found in Huntington's briefcase."

I'd found several pages and sent copies to Henry. The briefcase and suitcase I'd secured in Henry's closet.

"You can drive me tomorrow," Henry said. "That taxi driver just charged me an arm and a leg." He barreled into the house. His step was firmer, and his hair looked fine and white framing his nut-brown face.

"Where's your suitcase?" I asked.

"I've still got a few things here, haven't I? City clothes, of no use out on the land. Find my gray suit. I'll wear that." I trailed after him as he inspected every room. "You did well," he said. "It's nice and empty."

"But you're back now, right? You've come home?"

"Don't say anything next door about the lawyer in case it doesn't work out."

I went to tell them that Henry had returned. Aviva was in the kitchen; Ted was out with Yu and Baby.

"It's about time he showed up," Aviva said. "He's been gone for a month! I'll come over."

"Wait a while. He wants to rest. And tomorrow he's got appointments."

"Doctor appointments?"

I professed not to know.

"He won't come home for our sake but when he wants a doctor, he has no trouble jumping on a plane," Aviva said. "I guess we can be grateful he didn't drive."

He'd told me that he'd sold his car to the repair shop in L.A. because there was always someone at Beit Hayeladim to give him a lift when he wanted, which wasn't very often. He had everything he needed right there.

"God knows the house needed a thorough cleaning out, but it's time to get him resettled. I'll take him furniture shopping. It'll be a fun project for the two of us," Aviva said.

I reported her plan to Henry. She invited him to dinner, and he flatly turned her down.

The next morning, I borrowed the crapmobile and drove Henry

to his lawyer's office. He kept Huntington's briefcase in a bag on his lap the whole way there. When I returned an hour later, he was empty-handed. He said I'd done well in preserving what I'd found.

"My lawyer says it will seal the deal," Henry said.

I didn't know if he was speaking of Ted's fate or his.

I TOOK FATHER TO Chinatown again to visit Grandma Low and Eddie's mother, and again, their company put Father at ease, but it wasn't enough to convince him to return to Gejiu. He wanted to meet Henry to say his thanks. Seeing no way around it, I promised to arrange a visit.

"Of course he should come," Henry grumbled. "I don't know what took you so long to ask. But wait until this goddamned business is over. I'm on pins and needles, waiting to hear from the lawyers. You'd think I was asking them to clear my son of murder."

A phone call came. Then another. I ferried Henry to a second meeting at the lawyer's office. In the evening, I cooked our supper and washed his clothes and showed him my lessons from Professor Luo's class, but he didn't pepper me with questions as he used to do or tell me to practice harder. I described for him the steady progress that Eddie, Paloma, and I were making on the app, but he didn't listen. Instead he turned on the radio to bark at the local news. In the morning over breakfast, he wondered aloud what Kate and company were up to.

Aviva came, bringing a casserole. "I'm glad you're back; we missed you. Ted says hello. I'm sorry he's not here. He had someplace to be."

"I'll talk to him later," Henry said, steering her to the door.

At the end of the week, the phone rang again, and Henry fumbled to pick it up. He called to me at once, "Put on the TV!"

I hurried to the living room and switched on the ancient box. Henry stood to listen like a man before a judge. A government official wearing a drab suit and a bureaucrat's stern expression came into view. She said that criminal charges were being filed against Huntington Wong for multiple acts of an egregious illegal nature. Not only had he falsified public records about his legal place of residence, but he had also solicited bribes in an ongoing, systematic scheme that betrayed the public's trust. Documents had turned up in his personal papers, including a long list of businesses located in District Four. Next to the names, former Supervisor Wong had written numbers—payments, the official said, that Mr. Wong had received in exchange for his promise of political favors.

"A thorough investigation has produced no other suspects at this time," she said. "Henry Cheng, the owner of the residence where Mr. Wong claimed to be living, wrongfully and knowingly provided Mr. Wong with a false address, but Mr. Cheng was not involved with the payments scheme, and he will not be criminally charged."

I took hold of Henry, his face ashen as if powdered by factory dust. "Did they have to use my name?" he said. I tottered him to a chair. He asked me to turn up the volume.

"Here we go," he said. "My lawyer."

"Mr. Cheng is very sorry that he allowed his cherished memories of Supervisor Wong's parents to cloud his better judgment," Henry's lawyer said. "He's paid a high price for his mistake: a stain on his long-standing reputation as a beloved public high school teacher who's taught generations of San Franciscans, not to mention the pain he caused his son, who had nothing at all to do with Supervisor Wong's misdeeds, as the investigators have clearly concluded. Given his advanced age and his full cooperation, Mr. Cheng now intends to return to his quiet life."

Henry passed a hand over his face. "You can switch it off now," he said.

"So it's over?" I asked. "Ted is in the clear?"

He gave a slow, grave nod.

"Because of you," I said in relief. "You figured out how to do it."

"You were the smart one," Henry said. "Smart enough to know what was in that briefcase. You gave me solid evidence. I used it to make a deal. I wish they hadn't said my name. But they made no promise about that. They're lawmen. They couldn't pass up the chance to name me."

"I'm sorry," I said. I offered to bring him a cup of tea, or would he like a drink?

Henry straightened, forceful again. "Go get him please. I'm ready."

I knocked on the door to the saltbox stretch, my heart climbing high in my chest. I asked Ted, would he please come? His father had something to say. Without uttering a word, Ted pushed past me and strode out the door. In that moment, I wished I could've spared Henry the pain of facing Ted.

Henry stood with his back to the picture window. His hair was disordered and his ears looked too big for his head, as though his skull had somehow shrunk. He fumbled a hand near his throat, checking to see if his tie was properly knotted though he wasn't wearing one. The two remained standing, Henry using all his strength. I placed myself in the doorway.

"Were you watching?" he asked Ted.

"Yes."

"You saw they got Huntington?"

"I saw," Ted said. "So what?"

"And didn't charge you or me?"

"What's your point?" Ted said.

"My lawyer made a deal. I gave them information, and they left you and me alone."

"You let Huntington use your address and you lied to me about it."

"I didn't," Henry said. "I told them I did but I didn't. Who would believe that anyone would be as blind as I was? I thought he wanted my company, my friendship. My *wise counsel*, as he called it. I didn't know Huntington was using me for cover. If I'd tried to persuade them otherwise, my credibility would've been shot. Nobody's that big of a fool. So I told them that I let him stay here and that I kept it a secret from you. The important thing was to make sure that they left you out of it."

Ted folded his arms across his chest. "Go on."

"I gave them Huntington's papers. My lawyer turned all of it over and said I'd cooperate."

Ted didn't budge. He didn't look my way. "They would've gotten that stuff on their own. You saw them on the news carrying boxes out of Delilah's parents' house. They could've served you with a search warrant."

Henry shook his head. "They wouldn't have found it. I didn't know it was there. It was Shelley who found the briefcase. But I've left him out of it. I don't want them making trouble for Shelley, so I told them it was me. The expert can prove that Huntington wrote the list. If it comes to a trial, I'll testify that it was among Huntington's personal papers, which I found in my garage."

HSW. Stamped in gold. The greatest stroke of luck I've ever had in my life produced good fortune for someone other than me, an irony I've never forgotten though I've lived very happily in that rueful state.

"And you expect me to be grateful for this, when I didn't do anything wrong?" Ted said.

Henry spoke quietly, humble before his son. "I don't expect anything. I just wanted you to know."

I walked Ted back to his house. We stood together in the autumn air. The streetlamps had just come on, and the evening was cool and dark.

"It didn't cost him anything to make that deal," Ted said, and for the first time in a long time, he sounded uncertain. "Though I grant you he was clever."

"It didn't cost him much. Only his reputation," I said.

Ted fell silent.

"My cousin Deng has gotten hold of my father," I said. "He's somehow tricked him into doing what Deng wants. I didn't know what was going on between them. Now it's too late. I let it happen. I didn't pay attention. I was glad to let Deng take over. It was a relief to not have to look after Father myself." Guilt flared at that last confession, a burn on my conscience that I'd fended off for months.

"Ah," Ted said.

"I didn't want the job, so I left it for Deng."

"Like I left it for Huntington," Ted said. We looked at each other in dismay.

"We let it happen," Ted said.

"We outsourced our fathers—"

"They had to look elsewhere, and it didn't turn out so well."

I nodded glumly, for what could be done about it?

At least I knew this: it was time to come clean to Father as Henry had done with Ted. I borrowed the car to bring Father to meet Henry, and as we drove, I told Father all that I'd been hiding—that I wasn't rich and wasn't successful and wasn't looking for a wife. I'd been employed by Henry as cook and nurse and housekeeper, and Henry, in his kindness, was paying my school bills. Ted and Aviva didn't own a store; they were ordinary people with ordinary problems not so different from anyone else's.

"But you wrote to me—"

"All lies, I'm sorry. I didn't want you to worry. You were so sad when Mother died. I know how much you miss her. I thought it would make you happy to hear that the big success she dreamed for me had come true."

He turned away coldly. "Mother raised you to be brave, not dishonest." The sternness of his profile carved a wide ribbon through my gut, leaving me with a heated shame deeper and wider than I thought I would have to admit. When I started to say more, he put up a hand for silence. Only days ago, there'd been comfort between us, a shared enjoyment as we walked through Chinatown. He might never trust me again.

We arrived at Henry's house. Henry came to the top of the stairs and greeted Father warmly. Once inside, he offered Father his chair. Father protested—he wouldn't displace his host—and they went back and forth, chasing the Chinese groove. They spoke in Kunming dialect, Henry embarrassed at how haltingly it came, while Father assured him that should Henry ever return, the language of his birth would resurrect. The similarities I'd conjured between them the first time I'd laid eyes on Henry looked less convincing now that I saw them together, though they shared the low forehead and the mole like a licorice button. I went to make them tea and snacks, and when I returned, they were deep in conversation about the war years right before Henry and his sister, Grace, left home. I'd never heard Henry say her name before.

"Your father knows his history," Henry said with approval.

"And then you went to New York City?" Father asked. "What was it like to live there? Were you already a teacher by then?" He drew out Henry's story, same as he'd done with Mr. Bill Lee and Grandma Low. In Gejiu, in the lasting shade of Mother's death, Father had seemed old and broken, but seeing him now after a long absence and in the company of white-haired Henry, I saw that Father was still a vital man. Henry was smiling, buoyed to be talking to someone new and younger whose attention reassured him that he had interesting things to say. In all the stories Father once conceived, and the folktales and legends that Mother used to tell me, miraculous transformations took place. People changed into animals, animals into people; gods alighted on the earth, then zoomed up to the heavens again. Father was a changed man, or maybe not. Maybe he'd always been like this but hidden away by grief. He laughed at something Henry said, and I had the sudden, strange sensation that I was seven years old again, and that Father was about to lift me up, put me on his bicycle, and pedal me to school, making sure I was perfectly balanced.

"Thank you for looking after Xue Li," Father said to Henry.

"It's not charity," Henry growled. "I'm getting my money's worth."

They shook hands when we left, and in the welter of the night as I watched him bid farewell to Henry, I found that I was proud of my father.

28.
Millennium Deng

WHAT DID THE OLD MAN HAVE TO PAY TO MAKE HIS problem go away?" Deng said. We were at a bar late at night and the shots were flowing.

"He told the truth, and they believed him."

"You have shit for brains," Deng said. "I know a deal when I smell one. I'd like to meet him. Sounds like he's got connections that could be useful to me down the road. You've got a good deal going too, right?" he added shrewdly. "With the old man? He's giving you money?"

I nodded. "He wants me to stay in school."

Deng shifted his bulk on the barstool. The hair on his upper lip no longer looked thin and reddish but black and glossy, another false note. "You talk about him like he's your long-lost grandpa," he said.

"He's been very good to me. Same with Uncle Ted."

"You think I could get in on that?"

"Not with Ted," I said. "Yu and the baby are living with him and his wife."

Deng's eyes flickered, but no fresh bead of sweat popped on his shiny face. "She suckered them into it like she tried to sucker me."

"Something like that," I said. "She's doing great, by the way, more beautiful than ever. She and her daughter have got a family now who really cares." The household had been bustling for days. With the investigation over and Ted back to work, Aviva was planning a party for Yu and Baby, "a baby-naming ceremony," Aviva had called it. She'd invited all their friends, *the whole multi culti mishpocheh*. I asked Yu what name she'd chosen. She hadn't decided yet, but *Shelley* was still a contender. Aviva objected. One didn't name a baby after someone living, she said, but I asked, couldn't Yu make an exception? After all, it was Ted and me who'd rescued her from the bitches.

"I could," Yu had smiled. "I could do anything I want." A wild look had come into her eyes at the thought of the freedom she had. I didn't share any of that with Deng, though I chuckled to myself to see him flush when I mentioned Yu's beauty.

"Thanks for keeping an eye on my father," I said, ordering Deng a fresh drink. "For looking after him at home and bringing him here to see me. I've been worried about him since I left—"

Deng snorted. "What about your business partners? You going to introduce me to them?"

"You're planning to stay for a while, right?" I asked.

He downed his drink. "I'm never going back to Gejiu. There's nothing for me there." He sounded like I had way back in January.

"What about my father? When can he go home?"

"Oh, I don't know. Could be days, weeks. Might be months the way things are going. I look after him better than you ever did."

"You're the better man," I agreed. He was sweating profusely, the perfect time to switch things up. I got him into a Lyft and took him for karaoke, promising him women and tequila. The pair of us crooned our way through Sinatra—in Mandarin, you understand, which sounds even better—then I brought up Father again.

"How about sending my father back? He's homesick."

Eyes glassy. Spit sucking at the corners of his mouth like Baby's bubbles. "I'm not through with him yet."

"Let him go home next week, will you?" I tapped my finger on the table. "I can take his place. I know a lot of useful people. I've got good contacts. Henry believes in me. He could be helpful."

His speech had slowed, but he made himself understood. "Your father's worth more to me than you are. You were always asking questions: *Why this? Why that? I have a better idea; do it my way.* Your father does as he's told. When people see him jump at my command, they know that I'm important."

"He wants to go home! Please. He only stays because he thinks you need him, but you don't."

Deng laughed. "You dumbfuck. He's here because he owes me money." He laughed again. "Look at your shit face. You don't know a thing about it."

"You're the dumbfuck. You're the fucking liar."

"Ask him," Deng said. "He owed so much interest on what he borrowed for you to come that he couldn't pay the debt. I paid it for him. Now I'm the one he owes. I don't see what the problem is. You're here because of me."

The floor tilted under my feet; the music rocked harder. I slammed my fist on the bar as hard as the jackhammer beat, screaming at Deng for lying, but I knew from my vertiginous state that he was telling the truth. Deng just laughed and smacked me fondly upside my head.

"You're just jealous that I've got your father," he said.

THE NEXT DAY, I tried to talk to Deng again at the Millennium Tower. He smirked when he saw me waiting. Father was with him; I wished he wasn't—I didn't want Father to hear me begging Deng for his release—but I didn't get the chance because Deng strode right past me and straight to the elevator bank as Father limped to catch up. The doors opened, and Deng marched in. I got in and held the door for Father.

"*Kuai, kuai, kuai!*" Deng yelled at Father. Hurry, hurry, hurry! Exactly the way that he used to summon me. Father winced and shuffled faster, every step a stab. "Hurry up, bastard," Deng yelled again.

Enraged, I threw a punch at Deng, but he was quicker and stronger. He caught me in a headlock and pummeled me with his fist. Then he threw me out of the car as the doors slid closed.

"Xue Li," Father exclaimed as he tried to lift me. I got to my feet and dusted off and told him it was nothing, a minor misunderstanding. "We were joking around," I said. My sockets felt so out of whack that I thought for a horrible second that my eyes had rearranged themselves to be like everybody else's. I brought Father over to a seat by the window.

"I'm sorry, Father," I said. "I'm sorry I lied to you, sorry for this mess. Please forgive me for leaving you with Deng."

He sat slumped and hardly breathing; I feared he couldn't speak.

"We have to get you home," I said. "Cousin Deng says you owe him money, the money that you paid for me to come."

His hands flew up. "No, no, no. It's nothing like that. I don't want you to worry."

"But is it true? Because I can help you pay Deng back."

He hesitated. "I'm sorry," he said. "You aren't the only one who lied. I lied too, about where I got the money. I was afraid to tell you."

"It doesn't matter," I said.

He shook his head, ashamed. The light I'd seen revived in him, that little flame, was out.

"How much? Do you know?" I asked.

He whispered to me: "Thirty-three thousand yuan."

Thirty-three thousand! Five thousand U.S. dollars. What trick had Deng played to get Father stuck on that hook? My ready reassurances turned up their toes in my throat. Seeing my shock, Father sagged even lower.

"I didn't borrow that much to begin with. I don't know what happened."

That shithead Deng happened, I thought, *with his fat, shiny, fecal-stuffed cabeza.* My gorge rose, reinflating me on the spot. Deng wasn't there to punch again, so I pounded the bench between us. "Believe me, Father, we're going to get you home!"

Father straightened, eyes full of hope. I didn't know how I'd free him, but I knew I had to try.

29.
Barter

A LL NIGHT, I COGITATED. I CONSULTED MY INNER silkworm and searched the garage of my thoughts. My mattress stash of three hundred bucks was a drop in the Deng-slung bucket. I couldn't ask Ted and Aviva. Their concern now was for Yu and Baby, and though I couldn't do much for Yu myself, at least I could stand aside. At last, as the sun rose, I hit upon the solution. I'd follow stranger Ron's advice, and what Henry had done too: when you can't pay with money, you barter.

I sent Deng a message: *Meet me at the karaoke bar tonight. I'll make it worth your while.* I waited there impatiently, rehearsing. My blood surged as I recalled how Deng had shouted at Father, *kuai, kuai, kuai.* No way would I ever let that happen again.

Deng swaggered in. He cackled when he saw my bruised and swollen face. "You were already a dumbfuck. Now you're ugly too."

I didn't waste any time. "I want you to wipe clean everything we owe you."

Deng sighed. "We've already been through this."

"I have something to give you in return."

"You have that kind of money?"

"Something better than money."

He had enough respect for me that his eyes narrowed in interest. "This better be good," he said.

The black fish in my tummy gave me a violent bump. It knew how much I didn't want to hand over my golden treasure. I plunged ahead, smooth with confidence, silky with temptation, laying out my brilliant plan for TinRoad's success. I described every detail we'd organized so far and promised him my full share of rights. I pledged to introduce him to Eddie and Paloma—Paloma, I knew, could keep control of slippery Cousin Deng while leveraging his skill as a fearless entrepreneur with great connections. I'd give my friends a full and honest picture of Deng, and then I'd bow out of the game. All this I promised Deng. I even gave him my origin story: how I had hit upon the idea when the laptop I sent to Father never reached him but the lucky key chain did.

"You dumbfuck. I took the laptop," Deng said.

"I know," I told him. I'd already guessed it. "But it's still a great idea that's going to make you a fortune."

We haggled for a bit, though I knew the deal was mine. We added a rider to our terms that restored the full amount of the debt at 5 percent fixed annual interest should the venture fall short of certain key metrics. Deng grumbled that he was taking all the risk. I put five hundred dollars on the bar next to his meaty hand, three hundred of mine and two hundred more I'd gotten from that emperor among men, Eddie. Deng licked his lips at the sight. It was a tiny down payment, I said, on the windfall he'd be making.

"He's a drag on me anyway," he said, pocketing the money.

We shook on it and raised a glass. After all, we were family. In return for my Third Achievable, I got my father back.

30.
Ruth

IN THE MORNING, I WENT OVER TO THE SALTBOX stretch to do one last job for Aviva. She, more than anyone, had seen at the start how useful I could be—to her and to myself.

"Ted!" Aviva called. "Upstairs. Bring it upstairs! Put it all in the kitchen."

Ted squeezed his way through the crowd of their friends, toting laden trays that Aviva had over-ordered. I set out the food, poured the drinks, cleared the plates, and unstuck the bathroom door for kid after jiggling kid. The house was full of the multi culti come to celebrate the naming. They greeted me with kisses and hugs, the whole mixed-up crew thumping me on the back, *congratulations*, because there was a baby in the house. Yu had chosen the name Ruth after Aviva's departed mother. She'd had the idea and then

asked Ted, and they'd kept it a secret from Aviva until the day before the ceremony when the rabbi called them on the speakerphone
to settle the final arrangements for the *simchat bat.* "Her name is
Ruth," Yu said. Aviva held on to Ted and cried.

I made space on the counter for more food their friends brought.
"It doesn't matter to the rabbi that Yu isn't Jewish?" I was still at-
tempting to nail down the rules, perplexing though they were.

Aviva paused and looked toward Yu and Baby. "Close enough.
We do the best we can . . ."

". . . with who we are," Ted said.

We crowded into the living room with half the guests spilling
into the hallway. The rabbi, a tall, ample, gray-haired woman whose
give no quarter rectitude reminded me of Miss Chips, stood at the
center of the circle. She wore a stitched cap and layer upon layer of
colorful garb that looked more like tablecloths than clothing. Ted,
Aviva, and Yu with Baby waited just outside the room. I stood in
the doorway looking at the collection of faces, each unique, no
multiples among them, and thinking of the missing. Aviva met
my gaze and smiled wistfully, her brief, sad expression speaking to
me of her son, Eli, and of Leo, growing up and apart in the shelter
of the Children's House, and his parents, Kate and Orit, who had
found a new family to join.

"Brucha haba'ah," the rabbi said, blessed is she who comes, and
Yu handed Aviva the baby, who was wrapped in a shawl that Aviva
told me had been used at her parents' wedding. Then the three of
them with Baby proceeded into the room to where the rabbi stood.
She pointed to a chair, "Elijah's chair," she called it, and Aviva
placed Baby momentarily on the chair, then picked her up again,
smoothed the shawl, and handed her back to Yu.

"Wait," Ted said.

The rabbi stopped.

"Wait, please. I'll be just a minute." Ted worked his way through the crowded room, down the stairs, and out the front door. Guests peered through the windows to watch his progress. I didn't have to; I guessed where he was going. Baby fussed, Yu cooed, Aviva stayed quiet. She looked different than I had ever seen her. Not victorious, but calm.

Ted returned with Henry. I'd been so preoccupied that I hadn't attended him well that morning. He was unshaven, his shirt was wrongly buttoned, and his belt was cinched too tightly, which made his pant legs flare. But he was there on two firm feet, his eyes as bright as Leo's when a story was being told. People stretched out their hands to Henry, saying hello. He looked with care at every person, and I could see that he was hoping that one of them would be Kate.

"Okay?" the rabbi asked.

Ted and Aviva nodded. Yu placed Baby into Ted's arms and he lifted her to the circle.

I LEFT BEFORE THE party ended and walked toward the park. The uniform avenues that had looked so bleak to me upon my arrival now seemed like village streets. There was the telephone pole that Leo and I raced to; there was Crouder's favorite hydrant. Here was the crack in the sidewalk that made Leo shout with joy when we flew over it on the bike, Leo riding bareback and wearing no shoes or helmet. On either side of the street were all the homes whose occupants had annoyed Henry in one way or another, a sure sign that they were neighbors.

Low clouds covered the sun, and the park was damp and muted, its tall trees somber in the late-November light. I thought of the sparkling waters of Gejiu's Golden Lake and the deep red color of the pomegranates in the fall and the bright pink flowers of the Yunnan crab apple trees. They would be a happy sight after my months of living in the fog, and the smells and sounds of the noodle shops and night markets and tin factories and teahouses would welcome a countryman home.

For I'd decided, you see, to go back. My adventure had come to a close. I knew that Father wouldn't leave if I wasn't going with him because there was a groove between us, father to son to father, and it was telling me to go home. Not just for Father's sake but for mine. Whatever happened next, I wanted to share it with Father and to see the flame in him leap back to life. Flame-lit Father might still have chapters ahead, a turn I wanted to witness. As for me, who could know when and where my next escapade would begin? What tasks would be required of me and what strangers in the woods would stop and help me along the way? Peach Blossom Land wasn't anything like I had expected. Given my substantial, protuberant, talented Zheng nose for adventure, the same was probably true of whatever home awaited me, the one I would make for myself.

The sky changed, the mist thickened, then drops began to fall, the first of the season. I walked to the bison pasture and stood a long time outside the fence, watching them run in the rain.

HENRY PROTESTED—what about my studies? What about the house? There was still work to be done. But he knew that I was leaving even before I told him, having lately humbled himself, father to son to father.

"Promise me you'll keep going with your studies," Henry said.

I shook my head. Promises were a tricky business—Father's

to Mother, mine with Lisbet, the ones I'd made to Father that I'd never intended to keep. Any pledge I might make would be only to myself.

"But I'm grateful for everything you did for me," I said. "Will you please come to lunch with Father and me so Father can thank you properly?"

"For what?" Henry said. "He owes me nothing."

"For being my *ye ye*," I said.

I drove Henry to Taraval Street, where Father was waiting. He'd made arrangements with our waiter friend, and the table was set with special red napkins and a vase of carnations from Father. We introduced Henry to our waiter friend, who declared that he'd instantly seen that Henry had the face of a Yunnanese. He brought us three steaming bowls of Crossing the Bridge Noodles.

"This is good!" Henry said. "Our cook used to make this dish. My father could eat three helpings."

"Like Xue Li," Father said. "Growing up, he had a bottomless stomach."

"Still true," Henry said.

"Like a bull," Father said.

"A very big bull with four stomachs," Henry said, and the two enjoyed the joke while I called for a second helping.

For the rest of the hour, Father and Henry spoke of the local foods and strong tobacco and rugged beauty of Yunnan. Henry described places he remembered from his youth, like the karst formations of Shilin outside of Kunming, where he was born. He asked about Dianchi Lake, where he used to row as a boy. It was still very beautiful, Father told him. Despite all the changes, Kunming was still the City of Eternal Spring.

Henry called for the check, but our waiter friend, beaming, told him that it had already been paid. At Henry's mock outrage,

Father shyly smiled. He wasn't accustomed to being host, and his cheeks were pink with pleasure.

"Thank you," Henry said. "And thank you for our talk today. You're the only family member I'll have the chance now to meet. I'm too old to make the journey home even if I wanted."

FATHER SLEPT DOWNSTAIRS THAT night while Henry and I sat talking. "You're not the only one leaving," Henry said. "I've decided to return to Beit Hayeladim. I like it there. I'm signing up for good."

"Because I won't be here?" I said, dismayed. I had planned to ask Eddie's mother to help find a Chinatown lady who could take care of Henry.

"No. I spoke with the folks there before I came. I'm joining the collective."

"What about the house?" I said.

"I'll keep it for a while longer," Henry said. "Then I'm going to sell it. I'll need the money to pay my way at Beit Hayeladim."

"Have you told Aviva and Ted?"

"I told them yesterday. Ted was surprised but not Aviva. She knew I was ready for a change."

"You'll be with Kate. And Leo."

"That's right," Henry said. "In fact, Kate's coming to get me. She's driving up tomorrow. There are a few things I'd like to have with me. The hallway chest. Some pictures of Diana."

I went to the kitchen and poured us the last of the bourbon, thinking of the day I first met Henry and proposed that I move in. "I think it's brilliant," I said, bringing him his drink. "A brilliant solution." Same as Aviva had said to me all those months ago. Old as he was, Henry had learned to bounce.

TED AND KATE PACKED her car with the last of Henry's things. Aviva and I waited on the sidewalk. Henry was inside unplugging the toaster and lamps, so he didn't have to pay for a kilowatt hour more than required.

"Are you sure this is okay?" Ted asked Kate.

"Of course it is," Kate said. "It's a pleasure for us, not a burden. There are lots of people to help."

"You have to promise to call me whenever you need a break," Aviva said. "I'll come spell you. I want to check the place out—maybe I'll retire there."

"But you're sure?" Ted asked again.

"Please, Ted," Aviva said. "Listen to Kate. Take them at their word. Come inside for a minute, Kate. I've got some things for Leo."

The women went into Ted and Aviva's house and I went to fetch Henry. He walked down his front steps without once glancing back.

"I left my rod and reel," he told Ted.

"There's room for it," Ted said.

"Try that lighter-weight line," Henry said. "You'll get the hang of it."

Ted smiled briefly. "All right, I will."

Kate came outside and settled Henry into the car and checked his seat belt and made sure the sun wasn't shining in his eyes. Seeing her tender care for his father, Ted finally relaxed.

"He'll be happy there," he said to Aviva as Kate and Henry drove away.

"I've been trying to tell you," Aviva said, linking her arm in his.

After that, Ted and I went out for a last patty melt and a beer. I thanked him for all he had done for me, and he thanked me in return. "Before you came, we never spoke of Eli. Now we talk about him freely." He slipped me an envelope, no cash in it. He'd written me a poem:

> *I rose early this morning*
> *To walk in the Honghe River valley.*
> *I had only the birds for company*
> *And the smell of woodsmoke.*
> *History calls me home*
> *And I turn and approach it.*

It was Henry who paid the way home for Father and me. Bonus wages, he gruffly said, for labors above and beyond.

31.
The Old Family Home

IGUESS YOU KNOW THE PUBLIC PART OF THE STORY. My app became a grand success, making millions for Eddie, Paloma, and Deng. But even they couldn't have predicted the effect of TinRoad on the worldwide matchmaking business. It happened purely by accident; it wasn't part of the plan. People all over the world began finding their mates when a traveler delivered a package to their door, which made the business grow even faster. According to data analytics, my app is the number one driver of mixed marriages worldwide, pairing people across borders, continents, nations, and tribes. Across class, race, ethnicity, religion, and foot-paring, tale-spinning, food-scrounging expertise. All those happy endings make perfect sense to me. Why wouldn't one open the door with hope in one's heart to a package sent with love?

Ted and Aviva helped Yu go to college. They decided they wanted to travel more and study a foreign language, so they took night classes at City College to try to learn Mandarin. Aviva gave up but Ted stuck with it, though his accent is really bad. They've been to every country in Western Europe plus Israel, Peru, and Japan. Every few years, Ted and I reunite in Kunming and I take him to the lake where his father rowed as a boy.

Henry settled at Beit Hayeladim, where he still lives. He needs extra help these days and hired one Chinese lady caregiver after another until, finally, a relative of Yu's from a village west of here signed up for the job. She's working on Henry to bring her whole family over. She'd better hurry up; he's almost a hundred.

Henry held on to the house for several years. He couldn't bring himself to sell it to a stranger, so he rented it out instead. A few years after the app started making a profit, Eddie and Paloma insisted over Deng's objection that I be paid a starter's fee. With the money I received, I helped Ted and Aviva buy the saltbox from Henry, and so I became, like countless of my countrymen, a holder of real estate too expensive for most Americans to own. Yu and her daughter, Ruth, live in the house at present. They have a dog, a little black-and-white mutt with a mark on his right ear who showed up one day on their doorstep. I like to think he's Crouder's bastard sponging at the old family home.

My wife, Sarafina, and I live in Mengzi, and we have a beautiful six-year-old daughter. Sarafina is teaching her to speak Swahili, and I'm teaching her English. We're both on the faculty at Honghe University, where I went to college. My subject is history—the Boxer Rebellion to the present, with a unit in Miss Chips's honor on western interventions, good and bad. My country's past and present also has its good and bad, for better and for worse, which is a barter made by everyone who calls a country "home."

Sarafina teaches mechanical engineering. We met when she hand-delivered a package to me that Lisbet sent from Nairobi, a guitar she bought as a present for me at the Maasai Market. So I guess you could say that Lisbet found me love.

The aunties disapprove of us. The feeling is mutual.

My wife and daughter like to visit by laptop with Aviva, Yu, and Ruth. They chat about school and work and the films they've seen, and how Henry is doing. Aviva has decided that when the time comes, Sarafina and I must send our daughter to the U.S. for college. "We have a whole house waiting for her," Aviva says. "There's room for her parents too."

And what, you ask, of Father? Did he have chapters left in him yet? He went home and found a job and a new café where he likes to sit and visit with friends, and though I see him take delight in watching the scene around him and hear him frequently remark on a grandmother hurrying with a child on her back, or a lad proudly walking on legs too short to strut, or a bus driver's colorful cursing, he's never put those notes together to tell a whole story again. Eventually, he took an interest in various neighborhood ladies. He lives with one now, a loud-mouthed woman, nothing like Mother was, but Father is happy enough.

Sometimes, when he's alone, I visit him in Gejiu, and he sits on the bed, eyes closed, his back to the wall, and asks me to tell him a story. I do this for him as Mother once did for me. I've learned a lot of the old folktales from books I found in the library. He likes to cheer for improbable heroes and laugh at high officials outwitted by clever old men. But when he's in a melancholy mood, he asks for the story of the fisherman in the Peach Blossom Forest.

"Not that one," I say. "It has a sad ending. The fisherman never finds his way back to the forest."

"Your mother liked the ending," Father tells me, "because the fisherman went home."

And I go home after that and see my daughter into bed, and after she's arranged her pillows and had her drink of water, I stretch out on the floor to tell her a story about a girl on an adventure, an adventure always changing, in a land across the sea. It's not easy to please her, and that pleases me, for she never wants the same story twice.

Zheng Xue Li
Mengzi, Yunnan Province

With translation ("The Story of the Peach Blossom Forest") by
Leo Choy Hazan
Los Angeles, California

Acknowledgments

THANK YOU TO MY dear brothers, Philip Y. Ma and the late Christopher Y. Ma, who reached out across years of silence to seek the family lost to us. You brought our father comfort.

Thank you to Sanford, Eliza, Hannah, Emily, and Zachary, who sustained me throughout. Wei Wei time is the best time.

I'm deeply grateful to my agent, Stacy Testa, for the utmost care and commitment. Thanks and best wishes to Geri Thoma and the Writers House team.

I bounced high with happiness on the day this book found a home at Counterpoint Press, whose contributions to literature I've long admired. I've stayed aloft ever since, thanks to the expert guidance of Dan Smetanka and Dan López; the work of Laura Berry, Barrett Briske, Nicole Caputo, Wah-Ming Chang, Rachel Fershleiser, Megan Fishmann, and colleagues; and the wonderful cover art by Na Kim.

Thanks also to:

Bora Lee Reed, Peter Fish, Natalie Baszile, and Allison Hoover Bartlett for your generosity and friendship.

Margaret Carter, Diane Cash, Elisa Clowes, John Gutierrez, Tony Stayner, Kyra Subbotin, and Misha Weidman for books, love, and more books.

Liz Nichols, storyteller.

Robert Eu, Mrs. Norma Halteh, Catherine Hartman of City College of San Francisco, Karen Levi, Teresa Pantaleo, Mark Subbotin, Chanan Tigay, and David Yang for supplying facts. The quote from Assemblyman Hector De La Torre was reported in the *Los Angeles Times*, July 27, 2008.

The fabulous Lynn Freed.

The Chinese Historical Society of America and their helpful exhibit "Chinese in the Sunset."

Andria Lo and Valerie Luu for "Chinatown Pretty."

Bill Rauch, Stan Lai, and the Oregon Shakespeare Festival for introducing me to the legend of the Peach Blossom Forest. When I asked my mother if she ever heard of it, my ignorance amused her. We had great fun finding different retellings of the tale.

The Corporation of Yaddo.

The City of San Francisco, my ever-changing home.

© Andria Lo

KATHRYN MA is the author of the widely praised novel *The Year She Left Us*, which was named a *New York Times Book Review* Editors' Choice and an NPR Great Read of the year. Her short story collection, *All That Work and Still No Boys*, won the Iowa Short Fiction Award and was named a *San Francisco Chronicle* Notable Book and a *Los Angeles Times* Discoveries Book. She is also a recipient of the David Nathan Meyerson Prize for Fiction and has twice been named a San Francisco Public Library Laureate. Find out more at kathrynma.com.